A Divine Bride Series Novel

The Rose and Her Warrior

Demi Clorissa

WHISPER
IN THE
WOOD
PRESS

To my Henry.
For if I know what love is, it is because of you.

Pronunciation Guide

Gods:

Deus - DAY-us
Oryah - Or-YAH
Diabolus - Dia-BOL-ous

Countries:

Zeroth - ZER-oth
Moonmire -Moon-MYre

Cities:

Alderdeen - AL-der-dean
Vespera - ves-pe-RA
Goulrich - GOO-rick

Locations in Alderdeen:

The Medicus Tower - MED-uh-kuhss Tower
The Palisade (the Pali) - Pa-luh-sayd
Valliss Castle - Val-LISS Castle
Silva Forest - Sil-VAH Forest
Moonshyne Market - MOON-shine

Fae Words

Ciùin - calm
Teine - fire
Mo chridhe - my heart
Pòg mo thòin - kiss my arse
Slanaigher - healer

Kindly Translated by
Henry Ashmore

Content Warning

The Rose and Her Warrior is not intended for
those under the age of 18.
The following are the content warnings:

Consensual sexual acts

Misogyny

Discussion of previous sexual assault (not by MMC)

Xenophobia (not by FMC)

*Mental Health including PTSD (which includes
flashbacks, panic attacks) and Anxiety*

Infidelity

Animal injury

Broken bones

Your mental health is important. Please reach
out, and seek support.

Please remember you are *loved*.

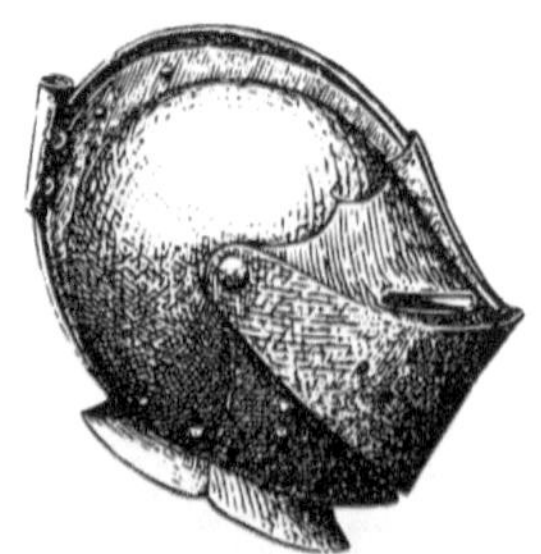

PROLOGUE

A loud, excited cheer reverberated around Valliss Castle's makeshift throne room as Hartwinn swept Anne up. She let out a squeak, her arms wrapping around his neck. Their eyes met. His gaze was all-encompassing, all-embracing. Love poured from him like an upturned bucket. He beamed it at her, eyes glittering with unshed tears.

Anne leant down as he pushed up, and their lips met. Sparks had fired the first time they kissed. Now, it was a slow burn, bubbling under her skin until she ached for his embrace. His hand tightened on her waist—a promise of what was to come.

This was how it was always supposed to be: his ring on her finger, her sweet perfume lingering in his sheets and his firm hold on her.

Their future may have been born from a promised handshake when she had turned eight and a hefty trunk of gold—an orphaned daughter of a powerful duke needing a place in society, matched with the quiet, kind son of a warmongering lord with his eyes set on her lands—yet, something unexpected bloomed from the arrangement. Lingering stares turned into whispered words, only to transform into stolen kisses in the maid's closets. More than romantic love had formed, but a deep friendship, withstanding even the test of angry adolescence.

Rose petals rained down on them, catching in the soft blonde curls around her face. Deus' priest was droning a sermon into the air. Anne couldn't hear a word, all but lost in those warm, inviting grey eyes. Hartwinn's lips were pressed to the shell of her ear—low murmurs of things he wished to do to her once she was out of all those frills.

Yet Death was an unexpected guest at their engagement. No room had been made for him. Nevertheless, he pushed his way in, demanding an audience with the lord of Alderdeen. A frightened scream echoed from the crowd as a body hit the floor with a loud thud.

Hartwinn's cruel, uncaring father, the great Lord Novak, clutched at his chest as he died.

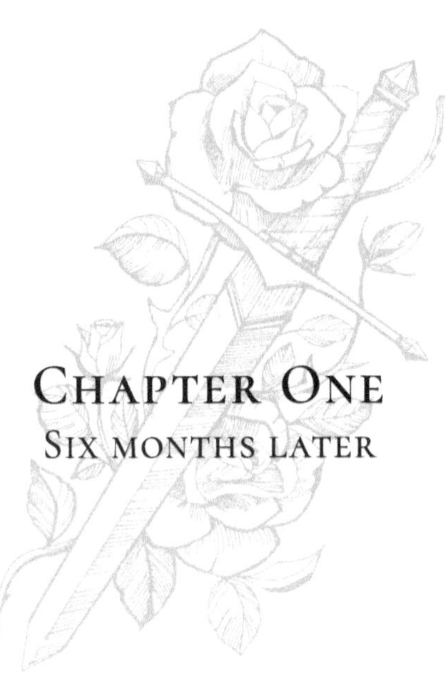

Chapter One
Six months later

With her heart in her throat, Anne raced through Valliss Castle, skirts in hands and slippers thumping rhythmically on the cold stone. She bumped into coal-hauling maids, spilling black crumbs across plush rugs, only to tangle the houndmaster's leads as he was walking the castle's hunting dogs in the cool evening air. Throwing a quick apology over her shoulder, she continued on, rushing towards the heavy front doors, hounds nipping at her heels.

Hartwinn was coming home.

Anne had received word that he would return to Valliss by nightfall. Yet the sun had set, the lanterns were lit and he still wasn't there.

A nervous, fizzing energy filled her.

They hadn't spent more than a few weeks apart for years. Now, over six months had passed. Not to mention, his letters had been few and far between. Rushed and brief. Worry had eaten away at the disappointment of his words. Anne's thoughts tangled in her mind, full to the brim of sticky, unsettling what-ifs.

What if he's changed his mind about the wedding?

What if he met another woman on the road?

What if he has changed?

She shook her head, attempting to rid herself of the thoughts, yet one stuck.

What if his feelings for me have changed?

Anne paused in front of a pane of crystal-clear glass, meeting her reflected gaze. A tight-lipped smile stared back at her instead of a beaming, excited one. Blowing out her cheeks, she exhaled. In and out. Until that ball of worry slid down her throat.

"You have no reason to doubt his feelings," she whispered to herself as a bubble of excitement formed in her. "He loves you, and you him. Nothing has changed. Nothing will change."

While battling the pins that dislodged during her sprint across the vastness of the castle, the large diamond on her ring finger caught the flickering candlelight scattered over the walls.

It was Hartwinn's mother's ring.

Worn by all the wives of the lords of Alderdeen.

It was weighed not simply by the sheer size of the gemstone but also the expectations that came with it. Anne must be a beaming, perfect wife and an even more perfect lady who pushed out son after son.

And I will be, she whispered silently. But even in her mind, her voice was wobbly. That anxious buzzing had returned to her skull as if a fly were drowning in honey.

Anne yanked the door open a crack and slid through it. She hurried down the stairs, parting the crowd with a hand, apologies falling from her. A tangle of curly black hair and icy blue eyes appeared from behind one of the lord's guards, an unimpressed look spreading across her heart-shaped face. Seanna Berac—Anne's oldest, most trusted friend, and her unofficial wedding planner—stared indignantly at her. In her slim arms, she held what was affectionately called *The Wedding Tome*. A journal of neatly written notes and reminders with scrap pieces of golden material, lace and pressed flowers. Seanna had started it the day after Hartwinn left, demanding Anne take her wedding much more seriously when in actual fact, Anne simply didn't wish to organise a wedding without a groom.

What if he prefers roses over marigolds? Or pheasant over chicken? Or a lute player over a singer?

Those spiralling questions swirled in her mind until the sharp point of her nail ripped at the soft lace of her sleeve. Anne exhaled once, demanding her nerves to calm.

She didn't need the tremble in her fingers to give her away.

He is the same gangly adolescent who stole kisses from you on the way to his tutor, and he will be the same man who went down on a knee and asked you to be his bride, Anne reassured herself. *Time won't have changed him ... But this world could have.*

A clink of armour settled in on her right, forcing all her muscles to clench. But as soon as she glanced over her shoulder, her body relaxed. The newly minted commander of the Silver stood behind her. Dayvis was a greying knight who walked with a slight limp but had a handsome, sun-weathered face. He may have been Alderdeen's most eligible bachelor, but Anne saw him as more than that—a friend, a quiet listener when she needed one. He was a vault, and her secrets were locked away with him.

He leant in and whispered, "You seem jumpy. Nervous?"

Anne pinned him with an annoyed look before surveying the crowd. "There is an awfully large number of people welcoming Hartwinn home."

"Far too many," Seanna said from behind her hand. Her own eyes skimmed the crowd, narrowing when she saw the court's biggest gossip, Edda. Their gazes clashed, but the buxom brunette narrowed hers and yanked her shawl around her shoulders tighter. "There are people here who just talk all day, and say very little."

"Shall I send them away, my lady?" Dayvis asked as Anne ripped another hole in the lace.

She nodded, clasping her hands together, stopping herself from battering the lace more. "Please. Keep those close to Hartwinn and his council. We need no gawkers."

Dayvis cleared his throat and trotted up the steps of Valliss. "I don't believe Hart—I mean, Lord Novak would want the whole cavalry out waiting for him. The ride from the fae is long and arduous. He will want a long soak and his woman."

The crowd grumbled, and soon, only a handful of people stood on the steps. The nervousness lurking in Anne's bones vanished as soon as those words left Dayvis' mouth. Her mind sharpened to a cutting blade, with one thought slicing through the rest. *He simply didn't just go to the fae. He searched out one specific fae warrior.* And she knew who.

The word "*Why?*" oozed from the cut.

Anne played with the frayed edge of the lace, a smirk curling her lips. "Shall we be expecting *the* Henry Ashmore to finally grace our court's presence?"

"I cannot—"

"So we *do* finally get to meet the man who Hartwinn speaks of more than his own betrothed?"

"Henry this, Henry that," Seanna added dramatically. "If I have to hear about his summers in Orynile once more, I may take a knitting needle to the ear. It is utterly unfair that neither of us were allowed to accompany him there."

"I, for one, would like to lay eyes on this mythical man. Just once," Anne added in.

"I bet he is handsome—"

"No, I bet he is old and wrinkled. Hartwinn did say he is over 200 years old," Anne cut in. "Is that why he is coming to court? For his age-old wisdom?"

An unconvinced pursing appeared on Dayvis' face. "I'm sure I don't have the faintest clue what you are both speaking of."

"Please, Dayvis. If I knew any better, I would think he would be rid—"

"Good thing you're not here for thinking, girl," said an overused, croaky voice behind her.

Sir Albert.

Anne held in a groan and plastered a smile on her face. She turned and said, "A bit late for you, sir? You may need the most beauty sleep of us all."

The elderly man with a wisp of white hair and keen, clear eyes hobbled down the stairs. His walking stick held most of his weight. The wicked thought of kicking it out from underneath him and seeing him toppling down the stairs almost overcame Anne.

He was a relic from the old Lord Novak—one Hartwinn should have been ridding himself of.

Albert waved an aged, speckled hand through the air, dismissing her. The simple movement boiled Anne's blood. "Now, shouldn't you be pouring over a wedding plan or discussing with your ladies how best to ensure Lord Hartwinn's son grows in your belly? Not out here discussing things you know nothing about."

The words slipped from her lips before she could stop them, "Shouldn't you be preparing to meet Deus or at least getting measurements for your funeral shroud?"

"Anne Davoy, that is quite enough from you," Dayvis warned, shaking his head. "*Apologise.*"

Anne dipped into a short curtsy. "I beg your pardon. I misspoke. It would be an honour to meet Deus so soon."

Sir Albert whirled around, raising his cane, but thundering hooves made him hiss a curse at her and scramble back.

Dayvis saddled up beside her and whispered, "Do not anger him, Anne. He holds more power than you think."

"He is a walking skeleton. Someone needs to lure him back to the necropolis. He needs to rest," she murmured back.

A snort came from Seanna, making Albert glare at them over his shoulder. They all waited with bated breath as the lord of Alderdeen rode high on his stallion, Boot, with only his two guards in tow.

Only two men.

And no mythical fae warrior.

Disappointment was evident in how hard Hartwinn rode up the gravel road.

He yanked Boot a to stop in a flurry of whinnies and stamped hooves. Shoving back his hood, he revealed his now-longer hair and a scruffy, overgrown beard. Sitting astride his stallion with his broad shoulders pulled back and jaw set, he looked lordly—like one of the many paintings that lined Valliss' walls.

Hartwinn smiled at Anne, but it didn't meet his eyes.

Something is *wrong.*

He swung from the saddle, landing nimbly on his feet. Anne launched herself off the steps towards him. Hartwinn opened his arms for her, and she slammed into him. His embrace was warm, welcoming and quieted every rambling, buzzing thought in her mind.

"Welcome home, Hartwinn," Anne murmured into his chest.

He pressed a kiss to her crown and whispered back, "I'm so very glad to be home."

Anne reluctantly let him go, only to slide her hand down to meet his.

"You're up far too late, and I know that's all I will hear about in the morning at breakfast."

She frowned and elbowed him. "You will not—"

"'Oh, by Deus, when will the sun decide not to rise so early? My head throbs. Someone, please, put me out of my misery'," he said, mocking her in a sing-song voice, elbowing her back.

Anne sputtered, faking outrage. "I do not sound like that."

Hartwinn simply arched a brow, the light reemerging in his eyes. "You do, and now I have to brief my council—"

Anne latched on to his arm, dragging him closer. "No. You can brief them in the morning. As Commander Dayvis rightly said, you need a bath and"—Anne breathed the words—"your woman."

Hartwinn's eyes rose over her head, fixing Dayvis with a cool look. "*My woman?* Is that what you are, Anne?"

"Am I not?" she asked, batting her eyelashes at him.

His gaze dipped to hers. Instead of clashing, they danced. His lip curled upwards, and he let out a huff of laughter. "Please, Anne. *My woman?* Here, I thought you hated the way men claim women as if they are property. Has time apart changed your tune?"

Anne dropped his arm and the charade she was playing. "No, you proposing to me did, you buffoon."

"There she is," he murmured, lips curling even higher. "There is my Anne."

Those words slid over her skin like silk, sending waves of pleasure down her spine. A part of her liked Hartwinn claiming her. Soon, he would be calling her his *wife*. That sent a thrill through her.

"Anne, my woman or not, is right. I need a bath and time to *think*. Things have changed."

"My lord, the fae—"

"Will be the top of tomorrow morning's discussions," Hartwinn cut in, waving Sir Albert away.

The old man narrowed his eyes, and those wrinkles around his mouth deepened. He was not a man dismissed so flippantly. Even Anne knew that.

"Come then, Annie. I need you out of those layers to scrub my back."

Chapter Two

The lord's chambers were expansive and took up an entire wing of the castle, a long corridor leading to lifeless, cool rooms. At the end, two wide, wooden doors laced with wrought iron stared back at Anne—tempting her yet filling her with a touch of uneasiness.

The lord's bedchamber.

She followed Hartwinn, eyes roaming the walls of paintings of hunting dogs and tapestries of roaring dragons. She had barely been in this wing, never needing to walk the halls. Until she grew bored one day. After that, she spent more time there than in her own rooms.

Hartwinn shoved open the doors to the bedroom and let out a soft curse. All his belongings had been meticulously placed around the room as if he had moved them himself.

Anne bit down on her lip to stifle the grin forming. "Nothing had been moved to your new chambers, and I thought I would surprise you. Do you like it?"

"Bloody Heylla," he murmured, turning in small circles. "Like it? I love it. You did this?"

Anne nodded and strode to the nearest shelf, plucking up the small clay statue of Hartwinn's childhood dog, lovingly called Flopsy. She held it to her chest, her thumb dragging over the long snout. "I even moved Flopsy over. It's official—you are the lord of Alderdeen."

"I think the whole ceremony made it official, Anne—or the *funeral*," he replied flatly, slumping on his bed. The mattress creaked under his weight.

"It was definitely the parade through the Lower, I think," she quipped back.

He was quiet for a moment, then said, "Thank you, Anne. This was very kind of you."

She delicately placed Flopsy back on the shelf and grinned at Hartwinn. Slinking over to the desk, she opened drawers and pawed through. Letters of rushed, slanted words stared back at her as if they were rudely awakened. Anne hadn't moved his documents; a member of his council had. The secrecy had her curious.

A flying pillow struck her in the back.

"Stop looking through my things like you are searching for secrets."

She smirked over her shoulder. "You've got no interesting secrets, Harty. Unless you call going to see King Sundryl a *secret*."

Hartwinn pulled off his boot, pointing it at her. "How do you know that?"

"Dayvis."

"That man can't keep anything from you."

Anne shrugged, closing the drawer. "Do you want to speak about it? You seem ... *disappointed*."

Hartwinn exhaled and yanked off his shirt. His body was not rippling with muscles but not soft from a life of luxury. She didn't baulk at his nakedness—she had seen him strip to his underthings more times than she could count.

Hartwinn bundled his shirt up and frowned at it. "He said *no*."

"And what did our famed warrior refuse?"

His eyes rose to hers. "If I tell you, you must keep it a secret. No gossiping about it with Seanna—with *anyone*."

Anne crossed her heart with her forefinger. "I promise."

"I went to Henry Ashmore to see if he would be the fae's emissary for my plans to expand the city."

"What do you mean '*expand*'?"

Hartwinn exhaled and dropped the shirt to his bare feet. He came over to the table, yanking a piece of parchment and a stick of lead from the same drawer Anne had been rooting around in. He drew a rudimentary shape of the city.

Anne gasped and exclaimed, "Fire all the official cartographers—"

"Now, I couldn't do that to Amelia," Hartwinn said with a laugh. He pointed to the bare space of land that led to the Sliva Forest. "Now, this is viable farming land, and we'd have even more if we cleared a few trees."

"I see."

"And, the fae ... Well, they are starving. That's what our reports are telling us. The great and gracious King Ewan and my father burnt all their lands during the war, and their crops never grew back. Their supplies are dwindling, let alone their population. Only a handful of children are born a year. Now I'm rambling ..." He paused, gaze tracing over the lines he'd made. "I wish to form a treaty with the fae, allowing the hurt from the past to be healed."

Anne's eyes roamed over the paper, mind working. An overwhelming sense of pride in Hartwinn filled her. He was already a much better man than his father, and he hadn't even sat in his makeshift throne yet.

"You want to offer the fae land, but what do we ask for in return?"

"I want nothing but to share the crops, and maybe tax the people. But—"

"Ewan wants their men, doesn't he?"

Hartwinn sighed, throwing the lead pencil down. "Unfortunately, yes. Their warriors are famed for a reason, Anne. They are glorious fighters."

"Why would he need an army?"

He was silent.

Anne's eyes glazed, and her words came out bitter and hard. "He wishes to cripple them so they never rise against him again, doesn't he?"

Hartwinn raised a brow. "I wouldn't call the five-year spat Sundryl and Ewan had over land an insurgency against the Crown, Anne."

"He *burnt* their forest, their lands and displaced and killed innocent people with your father at the helm. I don't think your brave, valiant Henry Ashmore would think it is simply a spat over land."

Hartwinn hissed between his teeth, pushing off the table and away from her.

Anne had struck him in a sore spot, and she didn't pull her punch.

"I will never forget what my father did, Anne. *Never.* All I can do is try to mend the hurt. Not that it matters now. I need Henry, and he said no."

Anne exhaled, fighting the urge to keep pressing until she got the answers she wanted. She pushed past Hartwinn and threw herself on the mattress. It was lumpy and sunk in the centre. *No wonder the old Lord Novak was a crankous bastard. He never had a good night's sleep.*

"But why Henry Ashmore?"

Hartwinn walked over to her, a looming presence in the fading lantern light. His gaze trailed over her lounging body. Anne's curves were obvious through the thin cotton of her nightgown. Reaching out, he swirled tentative fingers over the soft material of the skirt. His chest rose and fell as his hand slid down her thigh, right over her bare skin.

A tingling awoke between Anne's legs.

It had been months since they'd fallen into bed. In the days after his father's death, lost to his grief, Hartwinn had sought comfort in her arms. They had only stepped over that sticky, complicated line *once*— never again. That was only days before he had left, and they hadn't truly spoken about it. Not that Anne wished to right now. She wriggled, only inflaming the situation; the material gathered under her weight, straining across her hardened nipples.

"He is simply the right man. I wouldn't ask another," Hartwinn murmured, distracted. His fingers traced circles over the curve of her hip, causing her skin to prickle.

Anne reached down, smoothing his hand against her. "So no treaty unless it is with Henry?"

Hartwinn slid his fingers through hers. His hand was always a fraction too wide, too bulky to hold hands properly.

"No Henry. No land. No treaty."

With a squeal from Anne, Hartwinn yanked her upward until she was sitting right on the edge of the bed. He leant down until his face was merely inches from hers. The stink of horses and hay permeated her nose. His gaze searched hers—hope and something akin to adoration flared in those grey eyes, making her grin at him.

"I need to bathe, but be here when I come back?" he whispered, his lips a feather touch on hers.

A silent request to do more than kissing, touching and tasting.

With two fingers, he reached and yanked on the bow that held the neckline of her nightdress together. The material fell away, leaving only a sliver of cloth covering her taut nipples. A lick of heat caught flame in her core.

Anne's eyes flicked to Hartwinn as she dragged her hands up his chest right to the lacings of his shirt, curling her fingers through them. "You better scrub the stables off you. I've rolled with a stablehand once, and I will *not* do it again."

He gave her a fleeting kiss, then disappeared into his bathing chamber with a pure masculine smirk. A creaking twist of a knob, soft rainfall and a sigh came from beyond the door.

Anne flopped back, heart thundering in her ears. Her fingers tracked trails over the small curve of her breasts, a smile playing on her lips. He was home, back in her arms, and those thoughts that had sent her rushing around, barking orders at maids were soothed. But that worry lingered as if she had strained a muscle, aching every time she rose.

The door to the bathing chamber creaked open. A wet Hartwinn stood at the end of the bed, linen towel slung low on his hips, allowing that tempting trail of blond hair to lead where Anne's eyes lingered on a hardness pressing against the material.

She propped herself on her elbows, her eyes drinking him in. He was more sun-kissed than ever after spending days in the blistering heat. Even the press of his muscles were more defined. He had hardly dried himself, drops of water rolling down over his body.

A singular throb awoke between Anne's legs at the sight of him.

Her chin rose to meet his hungry gaze.

He wanted her.

She gripped the straps of her nightgown, shimmying it off over her hips. With a shake of her long hair, Anne was naked, leaving only her lace undergarment on. Laying back on her elbows, she smirked as his eyes roved over her nakedness. A flash of self-consciousness arose under his intense scrutiny. *Has my body changed since he's been gone?*

Instead of covering herself, Anne held out a hand. "Come to bed, Hartwinn."

He pulled off the towel, allowing the material to pool at his feet. Within a breath, he was on top of her, peppering kisses over her mouth, her jaw. His knee bumped hers to the side as he settled in between, rolling his hips against her. Anne's hands slid over his nape, tangling in his hair.

This is right. This feels right, she reminded herself.

Without hesitation, his fingers traced the swell of her breast, over her hip to delve between her thighs, skimming over her pubic hair to slip down her centre. He rolled his finger around that sensitive bundle of nerves, making her groan and writhe, building that gasping release.

"Good gods, you are *soaked*—"

Hartwinn paused, lifting himself off her. His lips left hers to glance down between their connected bodies.

"Wait, Anne—I think something is wrong."

She pushed onto her elbows, frowning. "What do you mean? You're doing fine—"

He pulled his hand from between her legs, holding it between them. Bright red blood coated his fingers. Anne's jaw unhinged as she stared at the blood. Spluttered noises came from her as her face turned as red as the bright crimson now staining her undergarments.

"I think you started your menses," Hartwinn said gently.

Anne didn't know what to do but ogle at the blood.

Crawl out from under him and flee to her room, never to be seen again?

Continue without worry of a seed planting?

Or simply die, right there in his bed?

Die. That is the only option, she decided.

Her brain couldn't form words as that hot, stomach-turning embarrassment overcame her. Instead, she flopped backwards and buried her face in a pillow.

"Anne, it's fine—"

"No, it is not. I wanted this to be *perfect* for you, for us—"

"It's natural—"

"It is ruined, Hartwinn." She pressed her face into the pillow.

"It's not—"

"I shall now simply pass away from embarrassment. Please ensure Carrots is well taken care of."

The mattress shifted as Hartwinn left the room, only to return a moment later after presumingly washing his hands. That sent Anne groaning, rolling over, now hugging the pillow. He slid behind her, his arm stretching across her hip to drag her closer.

"Carrots needs her mama," he said, pressing his lips to the side of her neck. "She bites every groomhand who even comes at her with a brush."

"They pull on her tail. That's why she bites," Anne said, muffled by the pillow. "That or she is simply a rotten horse."

Hartwinn nuzzled in, his warm chest moulding into her back. "All I need is you in my arms, Annie. Yet I wish ..."

"What do you wish for?" she mumbled, shifting to allow his arms to encapsulate her. Her eyes drifted closed.

His hand spread over the softness of her belly. "I wish that maybe it hadn't come.That it would be late. That our son would be growing here."

Her fingers tangled with his, dragging them up her chest. Anne didn't have the heart to tell him she had taken a contraceptive tonic after he had left her to journey to the fae. She hadn't even realised what she was doing until she had drunk half of it.

Instead, Anne yanked the blanket over their naked bodies, burrowing into Hartwinn's chest. Her finger traced over his curling body hair. "One day, we will fill this old castle with so much life it will make the stones creak. Oryah will bless us, I'm sure of it."

"I like that. The screaming giggles of children running up and down these halls may breathe life into the old bones," he said, voice thick with sleep. "Are you going to stay tonight?"

"Yes."

"Truly?"

Anne brought his fingers to her lips and kissed them. "Truly."

"You haven't slept in my bed for years."

"I may never leave it."

Hartwinn pressed a kiss to her crown. "I've been lonely without you, Anne."

"I missed you too, Hartwinn," she whispered.

Anne closed her eyes, listening to the soft snore of his sleep. Her face was still burning, but her heart felt full to the brim. However, a small voice, so quiet she could barely hear it over her other rambling thoughts, said, *Why did you take that contraceptive tonic if you love Hartwinn so?*

Chapter Three

Anne straightened a plate of crispy bacon once more as she fluttered around the dining table. Breakfast was always a meal they shared ever since she was a child. The sharp snap of a cane across their palms was waiting for them if they missed it.

Abigail stood behind her, reaching out every time Anne touched a plate or a spoon. Seanna slumped in a chair, watching her with bleary eyes. She had spent the night celebrating Hartwinn's return with the masses.

Anne caught them sharing a worried glance over her shoulder. "Eyes to yourselves, ladies!" she demanded as she turned a teacup around.

"What on Deus' green earth are you doing, Anne? He's had breakfast before," Seanna groaned as Anne sat right on the edge of her chair.

"I'm just making sure everything is—"

The door swung open, and Hartwinn sauntered through, grinning. He rushed up to the table to press a kiss to her forehead. She beamed up at him, her hands spreading out on the table.

He had shaved, exposing the remnants of a soft, boyish face.

"Good morning, Anne," he said as he leant over to snag a strip of bacon, crunching down on it. "Seanna."

"Hartwinn," Seanna grunted before guzzling her black koffee down.

He was already halfway out the door when Anne stood, motioning to the table. "Breakfast?"

"Not today. Actually, do we need to keep doing this?"

She leant on the table, blinking. "I don't know about you, but I can still feel that snap of his belt across my hands, Hartwinn Novak. What do you mean?"

"Maybe, we eat in bed, or in the gardens. Try something *new*. Things are changing, Annie!" he called out excitedly as he disappeared into Valliss.

Seanna glanced up at her as Anne's brows bunched and her eyes fell to the laden table. A feeling churned in her stomach—one she couldn't name. She sat heavily on the chair, her fingers fiddling with the silver, exhaling softly, fighting to spread that smile on her face.

Disappointment. That's what she felt.

Seanna reached for her, but her hand fell short. "Anne—"

"I guess no more breakfasts then," Anne said softly, not looking at her friend.

Seanna stood, her chair scraping. She collected her half-eaten toast and cutlery and moved right next to Anne—into Hartwinn's usual seat.

"We shall have breakfast every day," she said, crunching into her toast. "We do not need him."

The corners of Anne's lips lifted, and she repeated, "We do not need him."

THE CANDLELIGHT FLICKERED AS ANNE POURED OVER *THE Wedding Tome*, her finger tracing the soft lace. Her excited, rushed voice was flicked by the crackling fire raging before them. So much time had passed since Hartwinn had left, and she had much to talk to him about. He sat opposite her, brandy in his hand, eyes skimming over her bare legs, which were tucked under her. "Then, we shall be able to honey-moon to—"

"Yes, yes. Wherever you wish to go," Hartwinn cut in. "Come here."

"Was I speaking too much? There is much to go over, to discuss—"

"Come here, Anne."

She snapped the journal shut and extracted herself from her chair. Slowly, she walked over to him, her fingers trailing over wood, then swirling on the soft velvet arm. He uncrossed his legs, spreading them slightly.

"Are you still—"

"Bleeding?"

He nodded, taking another sip.

"Hartwinn. Not tonight. I want to *talk*. We haven't really spoken about anything since you've been—"

"Do you not want me, Annie?" he asked playfully. He knew she hated being called Annie.

Anne crossed her arms. "Not right now."

Hartwinn's eyes dropped away from her, and he scoffed softly before taking a mouthful of his brandy. "Now, what is it you wished to speak about? Roses or—"

"Is that all you wish to do now? Roll in my sheets?"

"I wish to be with my wife. I thought that's what you'd want," he snapped, taking another sip. Brandy always made him short and snappy.

"I'm not your wife just yet," Anne said, snatching his glass and finishing it with a wince. "And what has gotten into you?"

Hartwinn sighed, scrubbing his face. He was quiet for a moment as his eyes glazed over. "I'm sorry, Anne. I don't mean to be so terse. I just talk all day, every day. I have for the last two weeks. I'm getting sick of my own voice."

She took a step closer. "Council meetings?"

"That, and the nobles of court clamouring for my attention. And the master of the house demands I discuss what ale and wine we will have for the night of Diabolus' comet."

"Hartwinn—"

"Don't think I don't wish for your company. I *do*," he cut in, unable to stop. "I just don't wish to think for a moment about grain harvest or what battalion Ewan is sending to scare a village for daring to question him."

"That seems very—"

"Boring?" he cut in.

Anne snorted. "I was going to say *important*."

"I miss having *fun* with you, Anne."

She glanced down at him, her heart aching. He'd had only a handful of years to watch his father rule Alderdeen, and a few months that later passed to decide what kind of lord he wished to be, only to have his grief further complicate his mess of feelings. But a selfish part of Anne missed the hours of talking, of wondering that led to the early morning and that had locked away overflowing emotions. Nights where they didn't touch each other. That's when she felt the closest to him. Now, silence stretched out, and her own voice filled the spaces that were left.

She reached out her hand, the orange glow dancing over her skin. "Then let us go to bed."

His eyes warmed as his lips parted.

"To *sleep*. I'm not bedding you tonight—"

"Pray tell, why not?"

"You've drunk half a bottle of brandy. It would be improper of me to take advantage of you while you are intoxicated."

Hartwinn laughed, his cheeks bunching. "How proper of you. I do seem to remember a certain someone drinking a whole bottle of Father's good red, and then riding my fingers until I had to cover her—"

Anne flicked her hand at him, cutting him off. "That woman seemed to have more sense than you right now. Mine or yours, Hartwinn? Decide."

His hand slipped into hers, and she heaved him up, his body flush against her. He leant down and pressed a kiss to each of her cheeks, then her lips.

"*Ours.*"

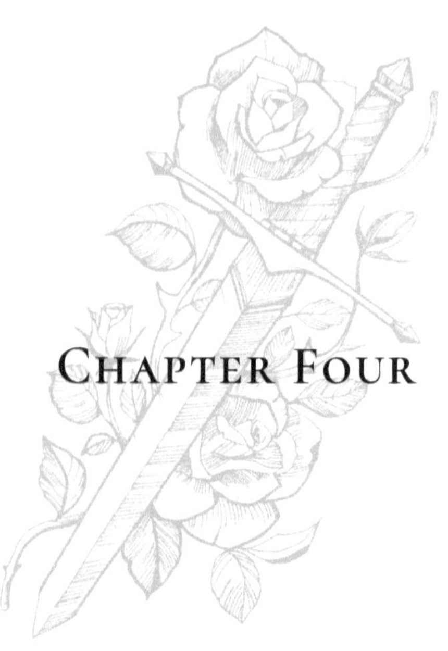

Chapter Four

Three weeks passed in a flash of golden, silky fabric and a pensive Seanna, muttering about flowers and their seasons. Late-night dinners were had around a candlelit table with whispers and skirmishes between the witches and humans, causing Hartwinn a throbbing headache and Anne a sharp tongue.

Albert leant forward. "My lord, these women need to be shown—"

"*Enough!*" Anne demanded, slamming a hand on the wood, rattling the silver. She took a steadying breath and continued, "I believe you've discussed this enough for today. Lord Hartwinn, Seanna and I will be retiring for the evening."

Albert groaned, shifting in his chair. "Hartwinn, control your woman—"

"Yes, my lord. *Control* me," Anne cut in, turning to an amused-looking Hartwinn.

He leant back, shaking his head. "I'd rather keep my bollocks where they are, Albert."

Anne smirked, scrunching her nose at him as Hartwinn winked at her.

Each set of eyes watched as she pushed back from the table, striding around to where the bottles of wine were kept. She grabbed two bottles by the necks and said, "Both of you. Garden. *Now.* We are celebrating."

ANNE'S OUTBURST LED TO HER SWIGGING WINE FROM A SEA-green bottle between Hartwinn and Seanna, lost in the manicured hedges of Valliss' gardens under the glittering, starry sky.

They all needed to have some *fun*.

Hours had passed, and they had nearly finished the second bottle she had swiped. Seanna, the most animated she had been in weeks, provided all the necessary details of all the gossip Hartwinn had missed out on while he was away, with Anne throwing in the especially juicy parts. He listened with wide-eyed interest, a smile playing on his lips, adding quips that made Anne giggle. Seanna clambered from the grass, staggering to her feet. "And that is why you lock the maid's closet door!"

"Or you remain *loyal*," Hartwinn murmured, nuzzling Anne's ear.

A squeaked giggle erupted from Anne, causing Hartwinn to nip at her earlobe. As she tried to push him away, her laughter filling the air, he pressed kisses over her jaw, right to her lips. Conquering her at last. Gags came from Seanna—body-convulsing exaggerated gags.

"All right, all right, we get it. Love disgusts you," Hartwinn said.

"No, *men* disgust me," Seanna quipped before raising her arms to the night sky, laughing as she danced through the silver moonlight.

Anne couldn't help but grin at her. Seanna was truly free. An heiress to a massive fortune who had her pick of suitors. None yet had passed the gruelling tests she made them endure. Some made it to her bedchamber, rolling in her sheets. But never to the foot of Deus' altar.

"None will ever bridle me," she had said once. *"None will ever get close to my heart, for it's too precious. More precious than gold or jewels."*

"Be careful, Seanna. Someone might think you're a heretic if you dance under the moon for too long," Hartwinn joked, tipping the half-filled bottle at her.

She cast him a wicked grin and began to curve her body, her bejew-elled fingers sliding over the tight velvet. Anne pulled Hartwinn to her, breaking the trance of temptation that had bubbled between Seanna and Hartwinn for years. Neither ever gave in to it, and she truly believed that neither noticed what bubbled and spat between them. Only ever-watching Anne had. It had been that way ever since Seanna had stepped foot in the court when Anne was twelve, and they all fused at the hips.

The "*Trio of Terrors*", a governess had once called them.

Seanna would lament and claim she was banished to Alderdeen from Goulrich, but in actual fact, she had been sent to teach Anne how to be a correct lady. To stamp out the wildness that was growing in her. But, little did old Lord Novak know, Seanna fed it, watered it and allowed it to bloom.

Anne knew the three of them would never part, nor ever wish to.

Seanna stumbled forward, cheeks flushed. She bent at the hip, poking Hartwinn in the chest. "Now, my lord, what would our king think of you accusing his favourite cousin of being a witch?"

"I would think he ..." His words faded off, and he cleared his throat. "I think he would say it's time for you to go to bed."

Seanna pouted at him, crossing her arms. "Why doesn't Anne have to go to bed?"

Anne lounged back and said, "As I am not the king's favourite cousin, I don't have a bedtime."

"You wicked-tongued girl. But, alas, you may be correct. I'd rather not have a thumping headache tomorrow when we begin on the seating arrangements—"

Anne groaned. "Can't people simply sit where they wish?"

"They simply cannot. This is a power play, my sweet Anne. You must consider each place carefully and thoughtfully. That is why you have me to do it, and not you."

Hartwinn's hand went to his chest as he solemnly nodded. "We would be lost without you, oh, gracious goddess of the tome."

A chorus of laughter peppered the air.

"The tome is a brilliant idea, thank you. And I know you, Anne Davoy. You couldn't organise a lay in a brothel," Seanna said with a sloppy grin and a hiccup.

Anne's lips popped open, fake outrage spluttering from her. "I can so—"

"You hate upsetting people, and I'm not above putting people I hate in places they will loathe. Like that old bat, Hicka. She will be as close to the door as possible ..."

Anne giggled into Hartwinn's shoulder. She could see the flop of grey hair and the ever-present fan waving furiously already.

Seanna bowed and whirled towards the garden exit. "Farewell, my loves. I shall find a bed to retire to—"

"Your *own* bed, Seanna!" Anne called out.

The pair watched their friend wobble a fraction, but she righted herself with a straightening of her bodice and strode from them.

Hartwinn elbowed Anne, snapping her attention away from where Seanna just stood. "Do you think any man will ever be able to tame her?"

Anne pushed off Hartwinn, scowling at him. "Why does she need *taming*? Seanna should find someone who wishes to see her run free, not catch her and break her."

"I've heard whispers—"

"About Seanna?"

"About the lovers she takes. All manner of men. Not all of them are nobles ... and not all of them are men."

Anne rolled on to her knees, face flushed and a fraction dishevelled. She poked him in the chest. "And what about the lovers you have taken?"

"What about them?"

"You've had a handful, at least from what I know."

Hartwinn shook his head, capturing both her hands. "Anne, there is no one else for me. Maybe when I was younger, I wanted you so much that I searched for you in other beds."

His confession didn't surprise her, nor the words leaving his mouth. They had done this dance before—when Anne found the first woman in his bed, and anger had her seething, hissing her words. But time had mellowed and softened those feelings. Until all she felt for Hartwinn was the lingering regret that she should have given herself to him earlier. But her own whispering, anxious mind had held her back.

"I don't care that you've taken lovers, Hartwinn, for I know no one has warmed your sheets in years," Anne said with a soft exhale. "And I know there was only one woman who has ever held your heart."

"Who?"

A smirk spread on her face. "*Me.*"

He returned the smirk and began to prattle on about what the council was whispering about—war and wheat crops.

Anne stared at him as he laughed, her head cocking. Had he really no clue that what he did was the same as Seanna? She had taken lovers, and so had he. Yet one made her used and tarnished, and the other was what was *expected*. If a respectable nobleman hadn't gone to his marital bed without laying with another woman—or women—they were seen as wasting their prime years of virility. If a woman even considered it, her value in the world decreased. Anne shuddered to think of what that gossiping gaggle of women would say if she ever spoke those thoughts out loud—or to Hartwinn, for it would ruin their night of fun.

"Well, do *you* need taming then?"

The excitement melted into something more daring, more wicked. "You offering?"

A laugh escaped Anne as she slapped him on the chest. She pressed her face against his shoulder, her hand sliding under his surcoat—a sad attempt to steal his warmth. His arms wrapped around her, and a comfortable silence settled. In a drunken, rambling thought, she realised that even though life was different to what she had expected, she was *happy*. The emotion came all at once, filling her veins as if the tide rushed the shore, making her grin against his shirt. Anne was sure it was seeping from her fingertips, soaking into Hartwinn's skin.

"Wine always made you a thinker, Annie, and by Heylla, you're doing a lot of it right now."

Anne's eyes flicked to his, pouting. She couldn't tell him, or could she?

Truth, she decided. She would tell him the truth.

"You make me a very happy woman. You know that right?"

Hartwinn searched her face, a soft look spreading across his features. "I'm very glad to hear that. Look, I'm sorry for the long days and even shorter nights. This is not how I wished to spend our months before we got married."

"You know, this night reminds me of my seventeenth name day. You stole Seanna and me that awful bottle of cooking brandy—"

"And you threw up in every potted plant you could find?" Hartwinn cut in with a cringe. "Let us not repeat that. Dayvis made us clean each one, remember?"

"How could I forget? I had to throw out the dress old Lord Novak got me for my birthday. But you are now the lord. You could simply command someone else to."

"Who should I decree that honour to?"

Anne's smirk turned impish, mischievous. "I have a few people in mind."

"You are wicked, Anne Devoy, truly wicked."

She laughed and held her hand out for the bottle. "At least I can hold my liquor better than someone I know—"

Hartwinn raised his arm up. "Who, pray tell, are you speaking of? Not your lord, your future husband?"

With a wobble, Anne rolled onto her knees, hands swiping for the bottle. "My lord, more like your wet nurse. I've put you to bed more times than I can count—and I can count quite high. Now, give me that."

A teasing spark lit in Hartwinn's eyes as he stretched to hold the wine bottle even higher. "Come and get it."

Anne grinned and launched herself at him, only to miss and fall flat in his lap. She stared up at him as those molten pools of grey bubbling with desire. Neither moved for what felt like an age, their eyes locked. Heat sank deep into Anne's body, awakening that throbbing, needy arousal.

Hartwinn broke the silence first. "The morning after I came back, you left before sunrise."

"I did."

"I need you to move into my chambers. Sleep with me every night, wrapped in my arms."

"Then command it. Demand me to."

"Move—"

"Yes, Hartwinn. I thought you'd never ask."

"Good gods, I want you right now. I want you so bad it hurts."

"Let me ease your pain then."

The bottle hit the ground with a thud, spilling whatever dregs were left across the cool grass. Then, Hartwinn's lips were on Anne's, hands encircling her rib cage, dragging her deeper into his lap. Her fingers threaded in his hair as his arms wrapped around her waist. Tongues swirled, hips rolled.

Their eyes met, clashing with need.

They had been apart for so long that desire was fogging their minds, clouding their better judgement. Gone were logic and safety; they clawed at each other like animals in heat. Fingers yanked on pants strings, and undergarments were shoved aside. Yet, even in their feral need, their bodies stilled. Waiting.

"Out here?" Anne murmured between kisses. "Shouldn't we go inside? Shouldn't we wait?"

"Right here. For I cannot wait another moment."

"What if we are caught?"

He dragged his smirking lips down her throat, sucking and biting. "Isn't that half the fun?"

Anne grinned back, her hand wrapping around his manhood without losing eye contact. His brows met, lips popping open. A soft sigh left him.

"You need to move—"

"Like this?" Her wrist undulated, stroking back and forth. "Do you like this?"

He buried his face in her breasts, moaning against her. A groaned *"yes"* came from the smother of material. Something awoke in Anne as Hartwinn muttered curses against her skin.

Anne grinned, realising she liked it—men moaning, whimpering, cursing just from being with her, and not even between her legs. With her belly full of wine and courage, she threaded her fingers through his hair. She pulled his face back, angling it towards her. "I want to hear you."

"Shouldn't I be saying that?"

Anne leant in, lips skimming his cheek to press a kiss against his temple. "You know what I sound like ..."

A soft moan left her lips, swirling in the shell of his ear.

That ache of need was building, making her slippery and warm at her centre.

"Gods, how I missed you," Hartwinn said, his fingers fumbling to slide between her thighs.

He circled her—once, twice—pleasure building. Anne threw her head back, her nails digging into his shoulders. Another soft moan left her parted lips, peppering the air.

"Anne—"

With a deep groan reverberating over her skin and a shudder of hips, Hartwinn spilt a warmth on her inner thighs. Neither moved, both panting, staring at each other.

Then, it was over.

That tension had snapped and dissipated. Leaving her sticky, sweaty and throbbing in places she shouldn't be.

"I lo—"

A shout rang out through the garden, and then scurried, hurried footfalls. Both Hartwinn and Anne cursed, fighting to untangle themselves and rearrange their clothing, only to sit side by side awkwardly as if they were blushing adolescents caught in the act.

Anne held in a giggle as Hartwinn raised a hand. "Over here."

A cloaked man appeared from behind a shrub, letter in hand. His eyes darted between them, confusion then understanding flashing across his face.

Hartwinn stood, clearing his throat. "What do you have for me?"

He held an envelope out. "All the way from the fae, my lord."

Hartwinn snatched the letter, tearing into it as if it were a love letter from the battlefront. His eyes scanned the parchment and glanced at the moon. A gleeful grin spread on his face as he choked out a laugh.

Blurry, rudimentary letters were all Anne could see.

Hartwinn gripped the messenger by the cloak, drawing him into a thumping hug. "Thank you. Thank you! This is wonderful news."

The man froze in his embrace, blinking at him. "You're ... welcome?"

Hartwinn pushed him out and whirled back to her. "He's coming, Anne. He is coming!"

"Who is coming?" she asked, rising to her feet. *Certainly not me tonight,* she added silently.

Hartwinn gripped her by the arms, crumpling the letter between them. He let out another loud laugh and dragged her into a spinning embrace, making her dance under the moonlight.

Anne stumbled back, head whirling. "Hartwinn Novak, if you don't answer me—"

"Henry Ashmore."

"What does that mean?"

"He said *yes.*"

Chapter Five

The midday bell droned in the air as Anne exhaled, hovering at the door to Carrots' stall. Sweat wicked at her brow, and a whiff of horse manure and hay filled her nose. She leant out of the stall, pushing onto her toes, hoping to see Hartwinn striding in. But there wasn't a sign of him. Anne exhaled, screwing her face up. "I'm sure he said just after the midday bell."

A snap of teeth in her ear had her whirling around to face her palomino mare affectionately known as Carrots—or Rotten when she was in a mood. And she was.

"No, none of that. You hear, Rotten? Be nice, or you will not get a run."

Anne, pushing past Carrots, strode to the opposite wall and slid down. Wood and stone surrounded her as hay cushioned her rear. Her back ached, and her pants and shirt were covered in muck. Yet, Carrots gleamed and glistened, her blonde mane and tail braided tightly, ready for a gallop down an overgrown path, nipping at Boot. The mare bucked her head at her, sniffing the air as if she was ready to leave the spacious stall to sink her hooves in mud. Anne held her hand out, allowing the horse to butt her prickly nose against her palm.

"He will be here soon, I promise,' Anne said, shoving a searching

Carrots away from her pockets. "I know. It's been too long since we've gone on a trot, hasn't it, girl? I've been busy."

Carrots snorted, unconvinced. A gleam in her dark eyes had Anne holding up a hand, giving her a stern look.

"I have!" Anne exclaimed, giving her a scratch between her eyes. Right where she liked it. "And so has Hartwinn. He has left me alone at dinner for three nights. Locked up in the council room. I knew things would change when he became the lord—"

But I didn't expect our relationship to change. Instead of talking through the night, we just explore each other's bodies, Anne added on silently.

Time dragged on and on. An annoyed energy filled the space, making her rip up hay, and Carrots pawed at the door of her stall with her hoof. The mare looked back at her, and Anne swore she saw the horse narrow her eyes in blame.

"Oi, Rotten, it is not my fault."

A pair of rushed steps clapped against the stone, making Anne stiffly scramble from the hay and rush to the door.

"About time—"

A young, flushed guard, Dilon, stood at the door, a note in his hand. "I beg your pardon, my lady. I have this for you."

"He is not coming, is he?" Anne asked, disappointment lacing her tone.

Dilon shifted, eyes averting. "I cannot say."

Anne held her hand out and said, "Whatever they are talking about in that room must be important."

He deposited the note in her hand. "As you say, my lady. I simply stand outside."

"Well, make sure you take your time going back."

He nodded, flashing her a grin before it faded away as Carrots stepped closer. Her large head lifted over the door, snorting at the young guard. Her reputation for being a biter was known far and wide.

"Good day," Dilon said, backing up before scrambling away.

Anne was too engrossed in Hartwinn's letter to even look up. A scoff left her as useless tears rushed to her eyes, blurring the words.

Cannot come riding today. I will make it up to you tonight. I promise.
Love, Hartwinn

Anne screwed up the note, shoving it in her pocket. "He promised, Carrots, that we would have time together today."

The horse butted her head against her as if to say, *"you promised me"*.

With a long exhale, Anne launched into tacking up Carrots, each movement sharp with frustration. Anger had not formed in the way she expected. It was shaped with a wallowing, icy sadness that had her bottom lip wobbling. She leant in and pressed her forehead to the soft, worked leather, her fingers tracing over the brand pressed in her mare's coat.

"This is fine, Carrots. I'm fine," Anne murmured, lips barely parting. "This is how it will be now that Hartwinn is lord, and I must get used to it."

Carrots throw her head, puffs of air leaving the mare, her excitement contagious.

Anne pushed off her, giving her a firm pat on her side. "That's right, Carrots. Just me and you, girl. That's all I need."

Anne swung up on the saddle and slammed her heels into the horse's sides, sending her sprinting from the stables and out of Valliss.

Anne rode Carrots hard and fast. The emotions she had choked down flowed from her and right into the whipping wind. The emerald green trees of the Sliva Forest blurred around her as Carrots' hooves slammed into the undergrowth. Strands of hair slashed across her cheeks in stinging lashes as the branches of the looming pines swayed in the gusty winds. Ominous, grey clouds rolled in across the sky, all but demanding the cool, biting drops to rain down on her. Yet, Anne rode forward still, not knowing where the path led her, allowing

Carrots to dart and weave. A fallen log arose in the distance, yet the mare never slowed, facing the block in her path head on.

"Carrots!" Anne yelled. "Jump, girl, jump!"

The mare's hooves left the earth as Anne clenched with all her might to stay saddled. Flecks of dirt shot up her legs as they landed.

Anne pulled Carrots to a heaving stop in a small clearing of trees as she fought to catch her breath.

She was deeper in the Sliva Forest than she had ever been.

A looming darkness edged around them, making Anne's head snap around at any shift of leaves in the breeze. An unseen pair of eyes fell on her—not human, but animal. Carrots snorted, turning in sharp circles, yanking on the bit on her mouth, smelling something in the air.

Anne leant down and patted her on the shoulder. "Easy, Carrots. There is nothing—"

A deep, rumbling growl came from behind her.

Anne's eyes widened as her knuckles whitened. Frozen.

Carrots—who had a better sense of survival than her—bucked and kicked, throwing Anne right from the saddle into the upturned dirt. She landed hard on her wrist with a crack and a hiss of pain. Anne didn't have time to wonder what had broken in her fall as she scurried onto her knees. Through Carrots' legs, she saw a pair of glowing eyes, surrounded by scruffy grey fur.

A wolf. She knew they didn't travel alone, but in packs.

"Go, Carrots! Run!" Anne screamed, clutching her wrist. "They are frightened of humans! Go!"

The horse raised back on her two back legs, front hooves shining and darting through the air as if to say, "*I will not leave you alone to these beasts*". Her shrill whinnies were loud in the swirling, stormy air.

Tears rushed down Anne's cheeks as more glowing eyes illuminated in the darkness. She scrambled to her feet, turning with the mare and slapping her on the rear, trying anything for her to gallop off to safety. Her horse was faster than any wolf—they would never catch her.

"Carrots, go!"

A flash of grey came from the corner of Anne's eye as a furry body slammed into her. In a flurry of sharp nails and fur, she was toppled to the dirt. The sharp teeth didn't puncture her flesh, but Carrots'. The wolf had sprung off her, only to latch on to the horse's hind leg.

Blood splattered Anne as the wolf shook its massive head, tearing into flesh.

A scream filled the air. Not a pained, frightened wail, but a battle roar. Anne fought to her feet and, without thought, threw herself at the wolf. Her narrow arms locked around its throat, squeezing. Nothing. She was too weak, but she wouldn't stop.

Carrots kicked out, fighting, her scared whinnies driving Anne on.

She threw her forehead down, slamming it against the top of the wolf's. Pain ricocheted around her skull, and her vision darkened for a moment. But the beast still didn't let go—Carrots was too tasty of a meal.

"Release her, you beast!" Anne screamed, clawing at the wolf's thick fur.

With a buck of Carrots' back legs, Anne went flying, slamming into the ground. But she wouldn't stop. Not while her beloved mare was still fighting.

A swish and shimmer of silver flew through the air. A knife had buried itself in the wolf's side. The beast let go with a squealing yelp and launched into the darkness of the forest.

Two men charged from the scrub, swords drawn. Carrots, scared and bleeding, saw the flash of iron and let out a sharp neigh, her feet kicking.

Anne pushed up on an elbow, wincing. "Carrots, stop—"

One of the men approached the frightened horse, hands out. His long, dark braid swayed with each cautious step. He turned his head, and a strong nose set above a pair of plump lips caught the fading light.

"Find the wolf and give her a better death," he ordered, his voice clipped with an accent Anne couldn't place. "She doesn't deserve to suffer."

"And leave you here with this man-killer?"

"Go, Cidran."

With a grumble, he darted into the forest, leaving them alone. Terrifyingly alone.

Anne watched as the man slowly approached the snorting Carrots, his arms stretched out in front of him, his steps light, nimble.

"Get away from her!" Anne demanded, rolling to her knees. "Leave Carrots alone. Don't you hurt her!"

"What a strange name for such a beautiful horse. I would never dream of it," the man said softly.

Carrots eyed him suspiciously. Every muscle in her body twitched as blood poured down her leg. The man darted out and grabbed the loose reins, causing her to throw her head around, whinnying in fear. He pulled her tight to him, his hand clutching at the strands of her mane that had loosened during the fight.

"*Ciùin*, sweet Carrots," he said into her neck. "*Ciùin*."

Carrots slowed and then stilled, dropping her head as if she was too exhausted to hold it up. Her breath came in heaving gasps as her nostrils flared. The rush of the battle had taken the bite out of her.

"What did you just say to her? No one has been able to soothe her like that," Anne asked.

He glanced over his shoulder at her, and their eyes met, drawing her in. A gentle smile spread on his lips. "Calm."

Anne exhaled, either from the sharp sting of pain in her wrist or from a smile that snatched her breath away.

Most definitely my wrist, Anne thought. *Or when I hit my head. Definitely that.*

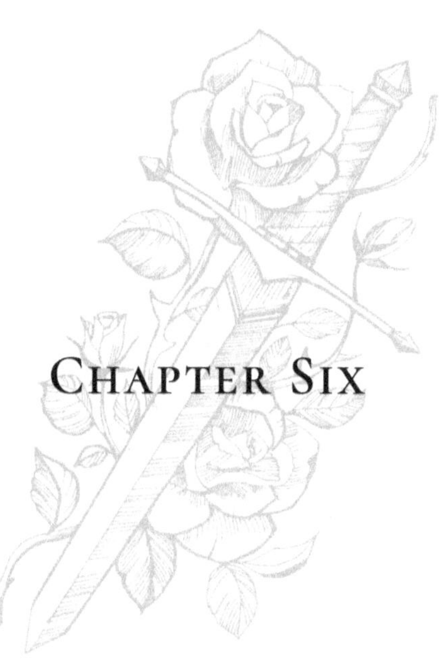

Chapter Six

Within a handful of moments, the handsome stranger had Carrots tied to a tree, a scrap of linen tied to the horse's oozing hind leg. Lowering himself with sigh, he crouched in front of Anne. Her stomach churning, she slowly raised her eyes from her purple, mottled, swelling wrist to sweep over the loose shirt he wore, hiding away a body of muscle, to dance over the golden pendant slung around his neck. A woman—Oryah, she presumed—was stamped on it. Her eyes finally found his high-cheekbone, sharp-jawline face. But what truly drew her gaze was the woody brown eyes staring right at her. Warm, inviting and utterly concerned for her. The simple look made her furrow her brow in apprehension at the sinful-looking man.

"Let me see your wrist," he said softly, holding a hand out.

An absurdly male hand.

One that knew its way around a sword—or a skirt.

Anne could hardly draw her gaze away from the scars that crossed his tanned skin. Her own twitched, wanting to turn his hand over and inspect it.

A life lived across those knuckles.

"It's merely strained—"

"Let me see it," the man urged, a fraction more demanding. "You may need a split or at least a bandage. It looks fucking awful."

Against her better judgement, Anne let her fingertips trail up his palm, flattening against his warm skin, hers small in comparison to his. From the edge of her vision, she saw his brows twitch together for a moment, but they smoothed even quicker. With no hesitation, he inspected her wrist, turning and twisting, making her hiss and wince.

"That is definitely broken," he explained. "You will need it reset."

"We are wasting time on me. Carrots is the one who needs a healer. She's going to get an infection—or worse, bleed out."

Anne launched to her feet quickly. Far too quickly. All the blood rushed from her head, sending her world spinning. The man rose just in time to catch her in his arms before she fell into the mud again.

"No, girl, *you* need a healer. Too bad Alderdeen is at least a half day's walk—"

Anne shoved away the man. "A half a day's *walk*? I rode for maybe a couple of hours ..."

"Your mare is a halfbreed, isn't she? Half *Luath* and half thorough-bred. That means she's *fast*. You may have had no idea how far you are from Alderdeen."

"Carrots is—"

The horse snorted, raising her head a fraction as if to agree with the man.

Anne narrowed her eyes at the setting sun. Darkness would be on them soon, and only Diabolus knew what lurked in the Sliva Forest at night. Anne pushed past the man, grimacing, straight to Carrots. "Thank you for your assistance. We will be heading off now."

"The sun—"

"Is about to set," Anne cut in, her free hand clawing at the tight knot of Carrots' reins. "Yes, I, too, have eyes."

"And can those eyes see in the dark?"

Anne's fingers flattened against the leather. He was right. She'd be turned around in the darkness of the forest. But she had no clue who the man was, nor his intentions. The hairs on her neck rose at the simple thought. He had done nothing to make that tight coil of fear knot in her guts *yet*. However, the night may set another beast free.

"She cannot die, sir. I cannot let her die."

"Nor can you. I presume your life is much more precious than that of a horse named Carrots. Rest here for the night. I will find something for a fire—"

"With you? *Alone?*" Anne asked, not turning to him. Her words were heavy with unspoken meaning—doubt and distrust.

A chain around a box of memories rattled quietly in her mind.

The man was silent, but he shifted on his feet. Then, all his words came out as a splutter. "I did not mean—I do not mean to rest *with* me. This isn't—I ... am not—I do not ..." He cleared his throat. "I vow not to even come near you. You can stay with your mount on that side of the clearing, and I on this side. And we will not be alone. My companion, Cidran, will be returning soon."

A buzzing, anxious thought arose, forcing Anne's hand to clench around the leather. *How will I fight off two of them?*

"I need to get back—"

"I see my words are getting all muddled up as they usually do," he said with an exhale. "Let me speak plainly. I do not wish to harm you in *any* way, nor do I wish to frighten you. I only wish to pass through this godsforsaken forest without any further issues. I only came to your rescue because I could hear you screaming. I thought a wolf had you in its jaws."

His rushed confession made that edge of suspicion blunt.

Carrots nudged Anne softly, her dark eyes half open. They all needed rest if they were to get back to Alderdeen in one piece.

"Only because it is getting dark. And if you dare raise a hand at me, I will get Carrots to crush your bollocks. She doesn't particularly like *men*."

The man nodded solemnly. "Not a finger."

Anne slid down the tree, her legs aching. "And whoever said you could *rescue* me? I was doing a fine job myself."

His eyes trailed over her face, lingering on her lips for half a second. "Fate, I believe."

Anne's eyes dropped away, right to her bare ring finger—she'd not worn her ring to ride in case she lost it. She was readying to warn the man that she was betrothed, but instead, she said, "What would fate have to do with this?"

He squatted in front of her, his hands falling between his knees. "It drew me here. Did it not for you?"

"I wouldn't call it fate that drew me here, sir. I'd call it a broken promise."

"You could tell me more about this promise while we collect firewood, Fate."

"Fate?"

"Would you rather simply tell me your actual name?"

Anne raised her chin. If he found out she was Hartwinn's fiancée, he could decide not to take her back, and fill out his purse with gold instead. Leave her with her throat slit. Yet, a tiny part of her wanted to be nameless, unknown—as if *she* could decide who she was.

"Fate it is. And what do you wish for me to call you?"

The man pursed his lips, eyes narrowing. "Gordyn."

"That's definitely not fake."

He shot her an impassive look, raising his brows.

"Anyway, where would we even get firewood from? There are no woodchoppers here."

He frowned at her. "We gather it from the forest floor. Sticks and logs will do."

Anne's cheeks heated with embarrassment. "I knew that."

"Of course you did."

She scrambled up, shoving past him. "I will go collect—"

"With a broken wrist?"

As if summoned, her wrist—which hadn't moved from where it was planted to her chest—throbbed.

"I have another hand, don't I?"

Gordyn didn't answer her, instead untucking his shirt from his pants. The strip of linen wrapped around Carrots' leg had been torn from the bottom of his shirt. Anne had been too busy staring at the mottled, swollen joint to even realise it.

He gripped the shirt in his hands, poised to rip it again.

"Stop." Anne's hand shot out, sliding over his knuckles. "*Stop.*"

Both their eyes dropped to where their skin met. Anne tore her hand away as if he had burnt her.

"You're not going to have any shirt left if you keep ripping it," she said with an exhale. Then, she added softly, "Rip mine."

"Fate—"

"I can't rip it myself, so you will have to help me."

Gordyn took a step closer, his gaze not leaving hers. His woody brown eyes searched each inch of her face, connecting the freckles. Warmth bloomed between them, spreading into Anne's skin. Her eyes dropped away, clutching her wrist to her chest. Gordyn's fingers brushed over the curve of her hips. An exhale left her when he yanked her blouse from her pants.

He smoothed the material between his fingers. "This is too fine for a stablehand."

"I'm not a stablehand."

"I know that much, Fate."

Her eyes rose upward, only to be caught in his gaze. "Who do you think I am?"

"Someone I should probably stay away from."

"Why?"

"Because I have this sneaking suspicion you'd have me praying at Diabolus' feet to meet again."

Anne's gaze fell away, but her cheeks warmed at his words. She resisted the urge to add those words into the tangled mess in her head. *He could be charming me, lulling me into a false sense of safety. All in an attempt to lower my guard.*

Her eyes shifted to Carrots, who was more interested in chewing the sprouting grass. Not at all alert—worse, she appeared *relaxed* as if nothing untoward was happening.

"You don't know me at all. You don't even know my name. I could be anyone."

Gordyn hummed in response as he yanked a blade from his hip. "It's just that I would like to know any woman who would throw herself to the wolves to save a horse."

With a flick of his wrist, he tore a strip of linen clean from her shirt. His fingers ever so slightly brushed over her bare skin, leaving a trail of heat in their wake. Anne stepped back, breaking the pull that drew them together.

"I ..."

The words "*I am engaged*" died on her tongue.

"Yes, Fate?"

With a swallow and averted eye, she said, "I should stay with Carrots. What if those wolves come back, or her wound opens again? Someone needs to be here with her."

All Gordyn did was hum a response. He reached down and plucked a stick from the fallen tree—for a splint, she presumed. Using gentle hands, he pressed the snapped stick against her swelling skin, and then wrapped the short strip around her wrist, looping over her thumb. The bandage was tight, and the stick rubbed, but it soothed the aching for the moment. Yet Anne knew nothing would stop the constant throb that radiated up her arm. Not until she could have the women of the Medicus Tower lay their healing hands on her. Gordyn's touch lingered for a fraction, making a churning, bitter taste coat her tongue.

"Now, firewood, wasn't it? Perhaps you should retrieve it before the sun fully sets unless *you* can see in the dark," Anne said, a fraction rushed, stepping back from him right to the solid tree trunk, her free hand snapping out and gripping Carrots' bridle, pulling her closer.

Gordyn simply stared at her, his eyes softening. "You do not need to be so frightened of me."

Anne shook her head, unable to raise her gaze any higher than his chest. "You're one of the many things I should be frightened of. But, for whatever idiotic reason, I'm not. You make me uneasy, suspicious, but not fearful." She tilted her chin upwards, right to the first of the stars twinkling in the night sky. "And I don't know what that says about me."

Gordyn's brows met, lips parting as if he wished to say something more. Yet, all he did was nod and disappear into the tree line.

Anne exhaled and slid down the tree. *That was stupid, Anne. You have more brains than to confess something like that to a complete stranger in the middle of the forest,* she thought, berating herself. *You should have at least pretended, fawned at him. That would have stilled his hand. Now, what will happen?*

The night began to stretch across the clearing, darkening the shadows and making Anne jumpy and nervous. Gordyn hadn't returned. She quickly glanced up at Carrots, who was now sniffing at her broken wrist. "You did this."

She snorted as if to say, "*you should have simply fallen better*".

Anne pressed her head to Carrots' prickly nose. "Just because a man, albeit a very handsome one, flutters his lashes at me doesn't mean I go all gooey. He could be a smirking, virginity-stealing rouge for all you know."

A soft laugh came from behind her. "If they were given willingly, were they ever truly stolen?"

"Good thing I have nothing left to steal," Anne said quickly, without realising her words.

Gordyn cocked his head, his brows pushing together, but a shocked laugh left him. "You human women are often more softly spoken."

Heat just didn't travel over Anne's face but down her neck, leaving red splotches of skin in its wake. She spluttered out, "Forget I said that. I don't know what's gotten into me."

Gordyn dumped the firewood at her feet, brushing the stray bark off his dirty shirt. "Good to see a night in the forest loosens one's tongue."

Anne stared at the logs and sticks, resisting the urge to chew her nails.

"Believe it or not, I have never built a fire," she confessed, pulling her throbbing wrist to her chest.

"I believe it," Gordyn said drily. "Those hands have never seen a hard day's work in their life."

"They have too!" Anne said sharply, watching him assemble the twigs in a small triangle. "It's just something I wasn't taught. I can play a mean lute though—well, a handful of chords. Oh, and I can fold a napkin into a swan."

"You can add being a wolf fighter to the list," Gordyn added. A crooked smile spread across his face, but his chin dropped a fraction, allowing a lock of dark hair to fall over his eyes. He reached up and tucked it behind his ear. His fingers ran along a sharp point instead of soft roundness.

"Fae," Anne breathed into the space they shared.

That smirk fell, as did his eyes. "I see."

"I have no qualms with—"

He pinned her with a dark, hungry look, making her heart pick up pace. He leant forward, that sling of gold shining in the moonlight. "The fae? We are brutes. Wild things, after all. Or is that just what your king says? I may devour you whole and spit out the bones."

Anne huffed a nervous laugh and flicked the swinging pendant around his neck. The gold hit his skin with a thwack. "A girl could only wish."

It was a sad attempt to quell the rising tension.

Gordyn searched her face, something akin to confusion muddying that hot look. That crooked smile lingered on the corners of his lips. "You are ... something else, aren't you, Fate?"

"What do you mean?"

"Not many would simply agree to stay in the forest with a complete stranger. Alone *and* at night. Let alone a fae male."

"First, I had little choice in the matter. And second, Carrots trusts you, so I do," Anne explained with a shrug.

Gordyn sat back with an exhale. "What?"

She turned her head to the horse above her, now nibbling on a leaf. The linen was soaked but no blood ran down her pale leg, much to Anne's relief.

"You see, Carrots came to me from a place not many horses make it out of—the King's Cavalry. She was strong-willed, headstrong. They ..."

Gordyn's hand clenched around a twig as a flare of something like anger crossed his features. "Try to beat it out of her?"

"Worse. They were going to put her down. End her life because she refused to bow to a man's orders. I couldn't stand it, wasting a perfectly good horse because she cannot stand in line without nipping the others or bucking at the sight of iron. So, I bought her and spent weeks with her, trying to gain her trust. Failing at every point. I soon discovered it was me who needed to trust *her*."

Anne scratched the soft underside of Carrots' chest, flicking off the mud on her coat.

"Since then, we have been inseparable. I'm the only one she doesn't bite—well, hard, at least. So if Carrots trusts you to come near her when she is frightened and bleeding out, I can trust you."

"Now I understand why you tried to fight off a wolf for her."

Anne exhaled a soft laugh. "I admit that wasn't one of my smarter moments, but I'd face a pack of wild beasts for her."

Her gaze lifted to find Gordyn staring at her, something brewing in those brown eyes. Shifting, uncomfortable with the intensity of his stare, she quickly added on, "I don't know why I told you that. Now, how do we light—"

Gordyn dug his fingers in the earth and whispered, "*Teine.*"

Fire sparked at the top of the small bundle of sticks. Gordyn leant closer to breathe life into the small flame.

Anne exhaled, eyes widening. "I have never seen—"

"Fire?"

Anne rolled her eyes. "*Magic.*"

Gordyn sat back on his hands, glancing to the darkened sky. "Magic is all around us, Fate. You just need to know how to look."

Silence settled between them as the night stretched out. Cidran didn't return in the hours after the fire was lit, and the forest darkened to an eerie pitch-black. The night air chilled Anne through her thin linen blouse, even with a fire burning. She stood, yanking on the girdle with one hand. Gordyn watched with a grimace as she shoved the saddle off Carrots' back. It fell with a loud thump.

"That is expensive—"

"Better face the stable master's wrath than freeze," Anne cut in, pulling the blanket under it off. "Fae don't normally linger this close to human cities. You must be travelling to the coast to board a boat for Moonmire. Where are all your supplies, horses?"

Gordyn's lips flattened as if that was a source of frustration. "We lost them, as well as our horses ..."

Anne paused halfway down, turning her head. "You *lost* them?"

"Yes, they galloped off," Gordyn replied, poking a stick into the fire, causing embers to scatter into the sky.

Anne settled into one of the tree roots, dragging the warm, musky blanket over her lap. "Pray tell, how did they gallop off?"

"My companion forgot to tie them up, and those wolves spooked them."

A laugh escaped her, then another until she was bent over, clutching her sides. "That was—"

"Stupid," Gordyn said with a teeth-clattering shiver. "I am very much aware, and so are my sore legs."

Anne flicked the blanket over and patted the ground. "Join me. I will need your help getting Carrots home tomorrow, and you cannot do that if you're frozen solid."

Gordyn's eyes darted away, narrowing. He exhaled, his breath swirling in the darkness. "I do not think—"

"Good gods. I can hear your teeth chattering from here. Now, come."

Gordyn nodded and crawled around the fire, saddling up next to her. His arm brushed hers as he settled in. Anne reached over and threw the blanket over his lap. She glanced up at him as he looked down. A ghost of a hand pressed between her shoulder blades, yet she cleared her throat and looked away, her fingertips brushing over the indent left by her engagement ring. From the corner of her eye, she could see Gordyn's warm gaze lingering on her as a slight flush coloured his cheeks.

"You should get some rest," he whispered, his hand slowly clenching by his side.

"Don't tell me what to do," she snapped back, but her tone had no bite.

A smirk played on his lips as he leant down, and Anne's breath shallowed out. "Or we could stay awake and—"

"Oi, Henry! You should have seen the size of this mutt. She nearly took my arm."

Anne all but launched herself from Gordyn, nearly tripping into the fire.

Cidran, his redhead companion, sauntered from the darkness. His eyes darted between them, a feline smirk curling. "Did I interrupt something?"

"No—"

"Your real name is Henry?"

He straightened before bending at the hip, bowing low to her. "Pleasure to meet you. I am Henry Ashmore, son of King Sundryl, Ruler of Orynile and the forest beyond. And you are ...?"

Fucked. Absolutely fucked, Anne answered silently.

"Tired. And going to try to get some sleep," she snapped instead, reaching down, snatching up the blanket and striding over to her mare.

"Fate—"

"Remember my warning. Carrots is very *accurate,*" Anne cut in, sitting heavily right under her horse's snorting head.

She rolled over right into the root, dragging the blanket over her, and closed her eyes. Sleep would be evasive, with her throbbing wrist and her tangled thoughts. The men were whispering, but she captured a word or two.

"Cidran—"

"She ... a witch, Hen ... witch."

"Marriage ... not ... death."

A scoff. "Might ... as well."

Anne shifted slightly so she could still see both. The orange glow shadowed Henry's cheekbones, darkening his eyes. He wasn't what she thought he'd be like—not a greying, scarred warrior. He was *worse.* He was beautiful, warm and kind.

He is the *Henry Ashmore, and I almost let him kiss me.*

But the call of sleep was too strong, dragging Anne to a dark abyss, another thought added to the mess between her ears.

And I wanted him to.

# Chapter Seven

The morning was icy and frigid, and it was not from the frosty layer of dew that covered the grass or the fog that lingered.

It was Anne.

Sleep *was* evasive, making that irritable edge form—one she hated. The swelling on her wrist had spread up her arm, stretching her skin uncomfortably. The whole left side of her forehead thudded, and from Cidran's gagging reaction, it was *nasty*.

"I presume you'd be quite pretty if it wasn't for the—"

Carrots snapped out, her teeth clattering together, making the redheaded fae leap back, letting out a squeal.

"Bravest, deadliest warriors, my arse," Anne muttered, yanking at Carrots' bridle.

Henry never baulked at her, simply casting her that soft smile, making her heart clench. He held out the water he had collected before the sun rose so she could drink, he rewrapped her wrist with gentle hands and even offered to take her to a stream to wash the dry blood off her body. Yet Anne could hardly look at him, making Henry clear his throat and shift on his feet. Confused words collected on his tongue.

The night had passed—but her feelings hadn't.

He was beautiful, coated in the orange glow of the fire, but in the soft pink, misting light of sunrise, he was breathtaking. Born to be gazed upon in the soft hours of morning before the world woke. She glanced at him far more than she should have.

He looked towards the west, or was it the east? Anne didn't know.

"We have maybe half a day—"

"We have to get back to Alderdeen. For Carrots' sake," she said, dumping the blanket over the deep curve of the mare's back. Blood had dried on her pale coat, as had the linen strip.

She needed a healer, and fast.

"I presume you will be missed, too, girl," Cidran said with a stretch.

Anne glanced at the forest, less terrifying in the daylight. "I don't normally venture out to the woods for the night."

"That is obvious," Henry muttered under his breath.

Anne narrowed her eyes at him, but instead of lashing him, raised her chin and pulled on Carrots. She walked with only a slight limp, making Anne exhale.

A lame horse was a dead horse. And Carrots seemed to have nine lives.

"Good girl, Carrots. Such a good girl." Anne's hand smoothed her coat with a newfound joy. She cast a toothy grin over her shoulder at Henry. "Do you see that? Just a little limp."

His eyes had never left her face as that gentle grin spread. "Just a little limp," he repeated.

Her lips parted as she met his gaze. Something had happened the night before—a reaching of hands between two strangers. Yet, her hand never should have lifted, let alone brushed fingertips.

"Shall we?" Cidran asked, turning and walking backwards. "Or do you both wish to stare at each other some more?"

Both Anne and Henry's eyes dropped, and spluttered words left them. Wordlessly, Cidran raised his brows at Henry as he stormed past, leaving Anne alone with Carrots.

"Come, girl. Let's go home."

Anne had never walked for so long in her entire life. Her boots rubbed raw on her little toes as she swayed down the path they had finally come across. The men had set a brutal pace—one she was not used to. Her body was accustomed to leisurely walks through the gardens or down each side of the Moonshyne Markets, only to pull herself into a carriage if her legs grew weary. Yet, she said nothing. Not a single complaint left her.

Her injured hand had slipped between the buttons of her blouse as a makeshift sling. The other was wrapped around Carrots' reins, as close to the mare as she could be. The men walked in front, still having quiet, whispered conversations.

"What in Heylla are you two old maids whispering about?"

Cidran turned to look at her, his pace never slowing. "Ah, she speaks."

"Leave her be, Cid," Henry ordered in a low grumble.

"If you must know—"

Anne nodded with a fake excitement. "I must."

"I have been betrothed," Cidran confessed as if he were a man about to be executed.

Anne's shoulders tensed. "Is that so? To whom?"

Cidran pulled a crumpled letter from his pocket and cleared his throat. "'You are to be wed to Maeve Magntai—'"

"The witch queen?"

Henry turned to her, surprise working across his face. "You know witches?"

"No, of course not," Anne said sharply. Too sharply. "King Ewan would not allow that."

Both men turned to her, confusion flashing across their features.

Anne allowed the reins to unravel, slackening the leather. The men didn't deserve an explanation for her sharp tone, yet she gave one. "To be associated with the witches meant more than death—it meant King Ewan's eyes turning to me. And I've had enough of his eyes on me. Enough for a lifetime."

The men shared a look, but Anne quickened her steps enough to break through the two, leaving them in her and Carrots' dust. She had cracked open a box of memories that should have remained closed. Better yet, it should have been encased in iron and dumped at the bottom of the Tishyalla Sea. If she allowed a singular one out, she wouldn't simply walk to Alderdeen—she would sprint, running away from the ghoul that haunted that painful winter in the capital.

Her eyes glazed as that box rattled, demanding to be felt, and a ghost of an unwanted touch skimmed over her dirty body. A warm, calloused hand fell on her arm, making her leap out of her skin. Anne, without realising, had frozen right in the middle of the path.

"Fate," Henry said softly. "You need not bleed for a wound that is closed."

"And what do you know about bleeding?"

He glanced down, his lips pursing. "I bleed because my wounds are still open and oozing."

"This is awfully deep conversation for someone you just met," Anne said, allowing her shoulders to relax with an exhale.

"I see someone in need of advice—"

"Yet you give me none!" Cidran said, slinging his arm over Henry's shoulder.

"I do. You simply *ignore* it."

Cidran leant over Anne. "You are a very *peculiar* stablehand."

"I'm not a stablehand," she snapped, glaring at him. "Not that there's anything wrong with that."

"I'm gathering you are much more than that," Henry murmured, those searching brown eyes skimming over her face again. "Much more."

Anne's eyes flashed to him, her cheeks heating. Without another word, she turned and stomped down the path, Carrots' teeth snapping in the air at Cidran as they passed him. With a snort, the mare picked up her pace to a prancing trot, pulling Anne along.

She wasn't the only one desperate to get home.

I haven't thought of Ewan or that winter for a very long time. I must be tired.

No one spoke—at least, not to her. Henry had settled next to Carrots' lowering head. His hand absent-mindedly stroked along her neck. Anne swore she saw the mare bat her lashes at him, all but preening at his touch.

The traitor.

Soon, the thick groves of the Sliva Forest tapered out, and they walked through sparse fields. The beginnings of Valliss could be seen in the distance.

Anne's heart thundered in her chest.

"We are close!" she called out, yanking a tired and grumpy Carrots along. She bucked her head but followed. Yet, Henry and Cidran had slowed, an anxious anticipation in each step. Anne knew why: the deal Hartwinn had struck. A place of peace for their people, yet still a bitter pill to swallow. It would be as if *she* were crawling to Ewan, asking for a scrap of bread when all he had ever given her was a winter full of nightmares and a lifetime of hurt.

Impossible, she thought. *I could never.*

Anne resisted the urge to turn and look at him. To peer at the man who marched to the gates of Heylla and demanded a place at Diabolus' table, even at the cost of his soul. Instead, she set her eyes on the wide road that led right to Valliss.

The King's Road.

The compact dirt was solid under her feet. She exhaled with such relief that tears welled in her closed eyes. Her legs shook, but she demanded that they take her all the way to Valliss. All the way back to her room, where she could shove all she had experienced into another box.

Shouts and thundering hooves had her eyes snapping open.

Hartwinn rode high on Boot, Dayvis close behind him, along with at least half of the lord's guards, all on their own galloping mounts.

"Anne!" he shouted. "Thank the gods. Anne, you're alive!"

A hiss of breath had her turning to find Henry standing right behind her. The stream of horses flowed past them, going far too fast to slow, yet Anne was trapped in Henry's gaze. The flash of confusion was muddled by something akin to hurt.

"You are *his* Anne?" he asked as a line formed between his brows.

Her eyes never left his as she said, "And you're *his* Henry."

Horses surrounded them, whinnying and stamping hooves, yet neither moved, nor flinched. A sapling had been planted. A singular root had grown, and it could not be yanked from the dirt. Not by her, or him, or the world they had found themselves in.

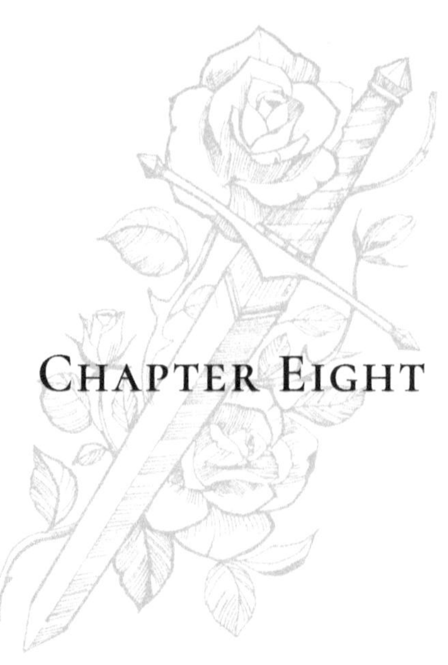

CHAPTER EIGHT

HARTWINN'S TIGHT EMBRACE ENCASED ANNE, DRAWING HER close to his chest. Her eyes fluttered closed, breathing in his warm, clean linen smell. All those turbulent emotions settled in her chest. She rested her sore forehead on his shoulder.

Hartwinn feels safe. He always has.

His hands cupped her cheek, angling it up to him, wincing as he took her in. "You made me sick with worry, Annie. When I came to bed and you weren't—"

"You have the infamous Henry Ashmore to thank for Carrots' and my safe return, Hartwinn."

His eyes flicked over her shoulder as a wide, toothy smile spread on his face. His hands left her, only to stride over to Henry. He threw his hand out for him to clap, and dragged him into an embrace.

"And what luck you crossed paths!" Hartwinn exclaimed, pushing him out.

"Not, luck. *Fate*, Hartwinn," Henry said, a tight smile spread on his face.

"Whatever it was, I'm glad you're here."

Hartwinn led Henry through the crowd of men and horses towards a carriage with a familiar hand on his back. They spoke with bright eyes and soft laughs, leaving Anne alone with Carrots butting at her elbow.

Dayvis dismounted, landing in front of her. He took her in, casting an inspecting eye. "You look like shit."

"Have I turned into a mirror?" she murmured, shooting him with a cool glare.

He nodded to Carrots, who was snapping her teeth at Boot. "She threw you, didn't she? I said if she threw you—"

"She would be dog meat. Yes, *yes*. Understood," Anne snapped, raising her broken wrist to him. "Can I see a healer before you interrogate me and threaten my horse?"

All the exhilaration of the past day had finally worn off, leaving her weak and woozy. She swayed, vision forming blackened dots. Her uninjured hand fell to Carrots' side, steadying herself. But her legs gave way, collapsing into another horse. Dayvis cursed, already shouting at the men. Hartwinn turned, but Henry was quicker, shoving through the men and horses. He caught her just before her broken wrist took another fall.

"I've got you, Anne," he muttered, laying her on the ground.

"You said my name."

"I did—"

"You shouldn't be so familiar," she whispered so softly she wasn't sure she even spoke.

Henry's eyes widened, lips parting, but before he could speak, Hartwinn was in the dirt, shouldering him out of the way. He appeared above her, concern creasing his blurring face. Anne's hand rose once, reaching for Hartwinn. He captured it and pressed a kiss to her palm.

"Hartwinn ..."

"I'm here, Anne. We need a healer! *Now!*"

Her eyelids were growing heavy, falling in fluttering lashes. She was fighting the unconsciousness looming over her, but she was losing. The world grew faded, the swaying branches above her now nothing more than green splotches.

The men were talking above her.

"Let me—"

"I've got her, Hartwinn. Just open the door to the carriage. I will bring her in."

"Right, right …"

Her limp body was lifted, held to a warm, solid chest. But what surrounded her as she fell into oblivion wasn't the familiar smell of Hartwinn, but the smell of a long-forgotten forest. Dark and woody but fresh as if the sky had opened and rained down on her.

It was Henry.

THE BONE SNAPPED BACK INTO PLACE WITH A STOMACH-turning crack. A scream slid through Anne's gritted teeth. Then, as soon as the healer's hands left her, a lungful of curses spewed from her as she exhaled. Freya, the tight-lipped healer who had treated her for all manner of things in the years since the woman had come to Alderdeen, slipped off her bed.

"You're full of poppy milk, Anne. No need to be so dramatic, " she quipped before reaching into the sloppy mess of plaster and strips of bandages. The mixture was layered over a tightly wrapped bandage, cooling her thudding, hot skin. Freya worked fast, dripping over the plush rug in her haste to set the bone.

Anne turned her tear-stained face to Hartwinn, her bottom lip quivering. "Make sure they see Carrots. Her leg is nasty—"

"I don't care about your bloody horse right now, Anne," he cut in, brow furrowing. "Listen, I was thinkin—"

"That's a dangerous habit."

"We should get married sooner," he finished.

That sobered her up. "What? *Why?*"

"I thought …" He paused, his fingers threading through hers. "Because I thought you had *died* in those bloody woods, Anne."

Guilt churned heavy in her guts. "Well, I'm alive. And you didn't seem too worried about me when you found me."

Hartwinn blinked at her, confused. "I—what?"

"You walked away from me right into Henry Ashmore's arms."

An emotion flashed across Hartwinn's face so quickly she missed it. "Way to change the subject, Anne."

"I'm not—"

"I think we should do away with *The Wedding Tome*. Keep it simple. Me, you and Deus."

She chewed her lip. "Seanna will not be pleased. She is single-handedly organising this."

"And am I marrying Seanna?"

Anne exhaled and glanced towards Freya, whose hands were covered in a mix of sloppy white muck and crusty, drying flecks as she wrestled to cast her wrist.

"No, you aren't."

Their wedding had always been a dream of golden silk, laughter and raining petals. Not a cold, quiet affair with a balding, age-spotted priest.

"No."

"Anne, this is supposed to be—"

She turned to him, eyes searching. "What, more *romantic*? We aren't two lovestruck adolescents running away, defying our families' wishes, Hartwinn. I—*we*—have been told this day, this joining of our families is the most important day of our lives. We cannot simply stroll to the temple and be handfast. It's not right, and it's not what's been *planned*."

Hartwinn frowned at her. "If you aren't lovestruck, you've fooled this entire court. Worse, you've fooled *me*."

Anne groaned, laying back. "That's not what I meant. You're muddling up my words."

"I suggest you find the right words then, Anne."

Freya cleared her throat and excused herself, muttering about washing her hands. Neither spoke, nor did they look at each other. They hadn't meant their lashings, yet hurt still simmered in the air from misplaced words and worried feelings. Slowly, Hartwinn pushed off the chair and stood over her as if poised to leave, and Anne readied herself to beg he stay. She didn't wish to be apart from him, not after the night before. Fear of the woods and those wolves still lurked in her heart. Suddenly, he kicked off his boots and crawled onto the bed.

"And what do you think you are doing?" she asked softly, angling her chin up at him.

"Joining you, Anne. I want to be near you."

She shot him a soft grin and shimmied over, careful not to move her arm. He curled up next to her, his fingers linking with hers. Drawing her hand to his lips, he pressed a kiss on each of her knuckles.

"We shouldn't be fighting right now," he whispered against her skin. "Not after I was so close to losing you."

Anne's shoulders loosened. "I don't wish to fight. Not at all. You must know that this isn't simply a wedding for me, Hartwinn. This is much more …"

"Then what is it? Explain it to me. I could be convinced to stay my hand."

"Two powerful houses joining," Anne said seriously.

Hartwinn scratched his chin, eyes narrowing as the cogs of his mind turned.

"You know that *right*?" she asked quickly, needing to know the answer.

"Of course," he assured her, bringing his hand to her chest.

"Our feelings aside—Heylla, even if we didn't have feelings for each other—this would still be happening."

"But I proposed—"

"After old Lord Novak told you to right? I bet he said something awful like I'm finally ripe for the plucking …"

Hartwinn pressed another kiss to the dip of her wrist, leaning forward until their noses touched. His eyes searched hers, adoration lighting the grey to a sparkling silver. "I've wanted to marry you ever since I was nineteen, Anne Devoy. My father had nothing to do with it—"

"He initially did. Well, both our fathers did—"

"Anne, I love you. That is why I proposed to you. Not a handshake deal made decades ago. Not because of a promise made by two dead men. Because I don't want to—no, I cannot—do all this without you."

She inhaled, her eyes growing wider as Hartwinn leant down to seal his words with a kiss—a desperate kiss. Her free hand captured his cheek, pulling back with a grin. "I love you too, Hartwinn. I have ever since I kissed you in that bloody closet when I was seventeen. There is no one for me but *you*."

Anne's words rang through the air as if she had struck a chord on a lute, resounding around the stone of her bedroom. She had whispered them late at night when the entire world was asleep, murmured it to him the night they had laid together for the first time, even saying so to the glass as she watched him learn how to swing a sword. Yet, now that she had said those words, it all felt too real, and something akin to panic clawed at her throat.

"You kissed me? If I recall—"

"You kept nervously rambling, and I knew why you had taken me there."

"You were always the bravest of us."

"Or the stupidest," she murmured, wincing.

The door to her bedroom swung open. Freya was flanked by Seanna, whose cheeks were wet.

"Anne!" she called out, rushing past the healer to throw herself at the end of the bed.

"Seanna, I'm—"

"In need of peace and quiet. Now, that cast will dry in an hour. Do not move between now and then," Freya ordered, collecting her healer's bag. "I've left your handmaiden with some pain relief. Take it before the pain gets too much, or it won't work. You do not win a prize for being in the most pain. Now, out," Freya ushered Seanna and Hartwinn like naughty chickens who had gotten into her garden. "Out. Both of you."

"Can Seanna stay?" Anne asked in a small voice.

Hartwinn's brows twitched together, yet he allowed Freya to yank him off the bed and push him out of the room. With the door closed, Seanna crawled into the space Hartwinn left, lying next to her, hands tucked under her cheek.

"You had us seriously frightened—"

"Hartwinn just told me he loves me."

They spoke in unison.

Seanna's lips smoothed a fraction. "And what did you say back?"

"That I love him, obviously."

"*Obviously.*" She reached over and pressed her finger between Anne's brows, smoothing the line that formed there. "Then why do you look so pensive?"

"I don't know."

Seanna searched her face. "What happened out in the forest, Anne?"

She turned to face her oldest friend, tears finally welling. Her voice was wobbly when she replied, "I do not *know*."

Seanna's face tensed in confusion before drawing her in, careful of her setting wrist. Anne cried, soaking Seanna's blouse. Not tears of happiness or pure joy as she had expected when Hartwinn had finally said those words. But because of the strange ache that rose with every breath, that pressed against her rib cage as if wanting to be free of its fleshy prison.

CHAPTER NINE

ANNE SPRINTED DOWN HALLWAYS, SKIRTS BUNCHED IN HER uninjured hand, cutting through the bright beams of midmorning light. Stray curls fell from the elaborate bun Abigail had spent an hour pinning, brushing her cheeks. Sweat collected deep in her armpits. The heat of Valliss was suffocating, sweltering since the change of winds blew in chill nights and frosty mornings, causing every fireplace to be burning.

Yet, Anne had another reason to sweat.

She was late.

Anne stumbled to a stop at the ornate doors of Hartwinn's throne room, as she called it. It housed the seat of Alderdeen, and the Novaks had sat on it for eons as if they ruled the land.

"They haven't started yet, have they?" she asked the guards, wincing at the sharp edge of the bodice cutting into her.

"You haven't missed much," one answered.

"If anything, you've missed the boring bits, my lady."

"The fae haven't arrived yet?"

"Nah, not yet."

Great, she thought. *I can at least contain myself before I see Henry again—or find an excuse as to why I never told him who I am.*

Anne fluffed her skirts and tucked a curl behind a jewelled ear. With a long exhale, she nodded to the knights. The doors opened with a groan, cutting Hartwinn off mid-sentence. But he didn't miss a beat, launching back into his speech.

"... I believe it is in our best interest for our people to join. Not only to labour in our fields or fill my coffers with coin." He paused for the rumble of laughter. "But to allow the mixing of culture, of people once facing off on the battlefield. I wish to bring a handful of fae to Alderdeen, and I hope the man I spent time with as a ward will assist in leading Alderdeen into a future ..."

Anne crept around the edge of the room, past whispering women and dashing gentlemen, transfixed by Hartwinn. He was an excellent orator, warm, charming and funny, and it was hard not to be swept up. He had to be, or his tutor took a cane to his knuckles. The worst punishment of all was when old Lord Novak would simply cast that singular disappointed look at him. It had him spiralling for days.

Anne pushed her way to the front, waiting for Hartwinn to finish. He spotted her, and she gave him a little wave. With a raised brow and a strained smile, he finished his speech and lowered himself into the chair. A thunderous applause surrounded her as she rushed to his side, her hand falling on his forearm—a silent apology.

"Anne, lovely for you to join us," he whispered behind his hand.

"You see, Abigail wanted to try a new hair—never mind that, I'm here now."

The doors of the throne room swung open, revealing Henry and his redheaded companion, Cidran. Henry was clean, shaved and dressed in a lush emerald, making his bronzed skin glow. Yet, Anne could barely look away from the tight stretch of material across his biceps. Henry yanked on his tunic once as a strain emerged in the muscles of his neck. It was as if he was uncomfortable with the soft slink of velvet on his skin. Like he had only known rough cotton or the tight grip of leather.

Henry surveyed the room with a cold warrior's assessment. Then, he stepped into the parting crowd as eyes devoured him, readying for him to be served for the next feast. Whispers spread through the masses, and Anne resisted the urge to slink behind the chair. Hartwinn rose from his seat, smile spreading. Rushing down the steps, he pushed his way through nobles and courtiers until he met the fae males.

The whole court seemed to hold its breath as the men faced each other.

Hartwinn smiled, throwing his hand out for Henry to clap, and dragged him into an embrace.

Everyone breathed out—except for Anne.

"It is my immense honour to welcome Henry Ashmore and Cidran Villarreal to court," Hartwinn said, an overwhelming joy evident in his tone. "Henry is acting as King Sundryl's emissary and will be assisting in leading the expansion of our great city. I do hope you all will make him and his men feel welcomed."

The air was sucked out of the room as Henry's eyes rose over Hartwinn's shoulder to find Anne standing straight-backed next to Hartwinn's wooden throne. The world seemed to fade away as their gazes met. Something sparked between them—something forbidden. Her bodice pressed against her skin as her breaths deepened. She slowly descended the stairs. Right to him. Hartwinn was speaking excitedly, yet Anne could hear none of it as her heartbeat was pounding through her skull.

"I believe you'd have me praying at Diabolus' feet to meet again." Henry's words harmonised with that heady thudding, creating an unsettling, warm feeling deep inside of her.

A brush of warm, calloused fingers over her elbow had her blinking, returning to the world. Anne blinked up at Henry, who stared down at her, his gaze a muddied mix of confusion and concern.

"Pardon?"

"He asked if you're healing well, Anne," Hartwinn answered. "Your face seems to be more—"

"I believe these things get worse before they get better," she cut in, casting Hartwinn a wide-eyed look.

Henry cleared his throat and nodded. "How is Carrots?"

A grin stretched on her face as she nodded excitedly. "Well, Carrots is getting the finest treatment. The best in all of Alderdeen."

"Anne demanded the grandmaster healer to see her."

She rolled her eyes and laughed. Her joy must have been infectious as Henry's lips twitched upwards. Hartwinn motioned for them to move through the room, introducing Henry to all those who they would have to convince to allow the displaced fae into the court.

"She felt obliged to. None may suffer in Alderdeen—and that includes horses," Anne whispered.

"I'm very glad to hear that."

Her hand went out and gripped Henry by the sleeve, stopping him. Hartwinn walked on, nodding to the bag of bones, Albert. "I'm seeing her this afternoon if you wish to com—"

"I have other engagements. Council meetings and such," Henry cut in, a fraction sharply.

Anne dropped her hand from him as if he had scolded her. "I see."

"It would also be improper to be alone with Hartwinn's betrothed."

She scrambled as if that warmth that had grown in her was desperate. "I don't know what you mean, sir. We wouldn't be alone. There are stablehands, and the stable master ... and Carrots will be there."

His gaze clashed with hers as he leant down a fraction, his voice lowering to barely a whisper. "You know *exactly* what I mean, Fate."

Her cheeks warmed as a soft breath left her.

"Henry! Over here," Hartwinn said, waving him over.

Both their eyes snapped away as Anne took a step back, not having realised she had drifted towards him.

"If you will excuse—"

"You're being ridiculous, Henry Ashmore."

He smirked, light playing in his eyes as he bowed. "Be that as it may, I'd rather not risk my bollocks."

Anne watched him disappear into the crowd before turning right into Seanna. Her face pinched, and her hand snapped out and gripped Anne's elbow, dragging her from the overfilled throne room. Right into the gardens surrounding Valliss. Right into the sharp sunshine.

"If you would be so kind as to explain to me why the man Hartwinn has idolised since he was a child is looking at you like that."

Anne shifted from foot to foot, chewing the nail beds of her free hand. "I don't kn—"

"Liar. Anne Devoy, you filthy, rotten liar." Seanna sat down, yanking her skirts up, allowing the sun to shine down on her bare legs.

"Something has happened. You haven't chewed your nails since you were sixteen."

Anne's finger popped from her mouth. She could still feel the skin-prickling smack of the governess from when she was caught chewing her fingers bloody. *Old habits perish even harder, I guess,* Anne thought silently, before slumping down beside her friend.

"I may have committed a grave sin," she said in a hushed tone.

"Murder?"

"*Worse.*"

Seanna straightened. "Worse than *murder*?"

"Adultery," Anne replied seriously.

Seanna pressed her lips together, but laughter escaped in huffs and snorts. "*Adultery?* What has made you so worried that Diabolus is going to crack open this earth and eat your soul for adultery?"

Anne held her hand up, ring shining. "This."

Seanna stared at it, then, her gaze dropped. A fine muscle in her jaw flickered. "What you and Hartwinn do—"

"No, no, it's not that."

Her gaze rose to Anne's. Daring and disastrous hope flared in her eyes. "Oh, I don't understand—"

"I nearly kissed Henry Ashmore."

Seanna's jaw popped open, and spluttered noises left her. She regained some grace, then exhaled sharply, sitting back. "You work fast, Anne. He has only been in court for two days."

Anne's hands dropped in her lap. She began pulling at the lace of her sleeves. "It felt—I don't know, *right*? I have never been looked at like that before." Her hand went to her heart. "I've never felt anything like this before."

"And yet, it cannot be anything more, Anne. You will marry Hartwinn in the spring, and Henry will simply be a dream that lingers long after you wake up."

Anne slumped back. "But what if Henry tells Hartwinn what nearly happened? I will be shamed in court."

Seanna whistled and stood up, smoothing her bodice. "I never knew you to be so *heartless*, Anne Davoy. What is worse is that you sound like awful Edda, worrying for your own reputation over your oldest friends."

Anne groaned, her hand smoothing over her forehead. "Seanna, I didn't mean—"

"And what of Hartwinn? Cucked by his own childhood idol and his blushing bride. If I was you, I'd forget all about Henry and this error you've made."

"Seanna, that isn't fair."

"None of this *fair*. Not for anyone."

With that, Seanna strode from the garden, leaving Anne's mind in tangles.

She is right.

Anne knew she should forget Henry and how his smile drew the air from her lungs and never replaced it or that flicker of flame set ablaze within her from his fleeting touch. Fate was what drew them together, making their worlds collide, leaving destruction in its path. As Anne allowed the warm breeze to capture her stray curls, would she be the lone survivor, her world crumbling around her?

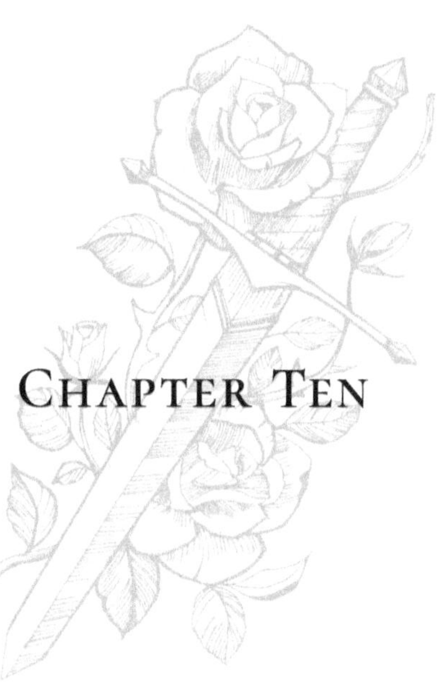

Chapter Ten

In between busy, overwhelming dinners with polite, stilted small talk between the Alderdeen nobles and two new fae inhabitants, Anne attempted to change Carrots' dressings while dodging the mare's sharp bites. However, she was eluding more than snapping teeth; she was hiding from Henry's burning gaze, which seemed to find her in every room, through every crowd. Still, he was trying to be polite to the point of it being painful, lingering on the edges of conversation, holding doors open for her with a mouthful of words he never said. Yet, she couldn't escape to her hidden sanctuary in the library with its leather bound books. Anne needed to be the blushing bride on the arm of her future husband—who had no idea that she had been dreaming of Henry and his warm touch since she had left the forest.

He was haunting her without even realising it.

Anne's casted hand tightened around Hartwinn's elbow. The wine in her other hand was bitter and too tart. They had been talking to yet another skeleton from his walking graveyard, Frederick, who was rambling about grain supplies and how to appropriately divide them amongst the new arrivals who would soon be flooding the city. Hartwinn—the perfect picture of interest—nodded and patted Anne's ever-tightening hand, placating her.

"Here we are talking of grain when we have bigger problems," Albert piped up, bringing the foaming ale to his moustached lip. "We must begin to train the men for battle. Ewan can call on you at any time. Our army has gotten lazy, boy, and now, the expectation to fold in these fae warriors will take time to ensure they know who their *true* masters are."

"Is there to be a battle?" Anne murmured to Hartwinn, staring up at him with wide-eyed worry.

He patted her hand again—an act she found a fraction condescending. "No need to worry, sweet love. We will not see any fighting this close to Alderdeen, but we will soon need to discuss your ancestral lands—"

"Hartwinn, not here. Listening ears are *everywhere*," Albert said in a hushed tone.

Anne cast her fake smile around the skeletons who saw her more as a breeding mare than a lady. She raised her chin and said, "Our king has already fought nearly all the nations in Zeroth, gaining so much power, yet he wishes to turn his war horses on to the last and smallest, weakest nation? The witches. What do they have that he wishes for? It's not lands or riches. He has plenty of those. Does he want magic?"

The men shifted from foot to foot, none wishing to answer.

Fredrick leant in and said, "He wants—"

"What our king wants and needs is none of your concern, girl," Albert cut in.

Anne allowed a sickly sweet smile—more akin to a grimace—to spread and, through clenched teeth, said, "You don't get to tell me what is or is not my concern, Albert. Especially when he has to march an army across my lands."

His eyes narrowed at her. "*Your* lands? You mean Lord Hartwinn's lands. As your guardian—"

"I haven't needed a guardian since I was eighteen—"

"But the law states if you marry before you turn twenty-five, all your lands, titles and riches go to your husband. And when is your wedding again?"

"Spring. A month before my birthday."

Albert took a swig of his ale, sucking on his teeth. "That's interesting. Now, how about you run along and let the men talk?"

Anne's eyes rose to Hartwinn, a demand in her gaze.

Defend me.

Yet all he did was that infuriating patting of her hand, nodding at Albert. He never once looked at her, nor pushed Albert back into his place. Anne yanked her arm back as if he had stung her. Her tongue rolled around her molars as a scoffed laugh left her. Ire rose so quickly in her it burnt away all sorry, guilty feelings she had for Hartwinn, leaving only that raging bitterness.

"Yes, Anne. I'm sure they are missing you on the dance floor."

She finished her warm wine in one gulp, then shoved the empty glass at Hartwinn's chest. That's when he finally glanced down at her, a nothingness swirling in his eyes. It shocked her that he was playing a game—and he was on the losing side. A spitting insult curled on her tongue, but that overwhelming need to be seen as the perfect, doting, meek wife squashed it. She whirled around, Hartwinn hot on her heels.

"Anne—"

She took a step back, shaking her head. "Don't you dare. You knew, didn't you?"

"Father told me, but it's such an archaic law that I never—"

"It was never your father, was it?" Anne exhaled sharply as tears edged her vision. "It was Ewan who pressured you?"

"No—well, yes," Hartwinn snapped. "He just asked for us to marry before spring."

"You know I despise—"

Those phantom fingers skimming over her skin stole her words right from her mouth.

"That's why I waited. I hesitated. I wished to know why the sudden interest in our pending wedding. You know I never wanted to control—"

"Yet you are," Anne cut in. "You even asked to marry me sooner. Does Ewan intend to march sooner?"

"This is a sensitive situation, Anne. This is more than—"

"I could ever *know*? Do you think I lost my intelligence when you slipped that ring on my finger? I had the same lessons and read the same books as you, if you don't recall."

Eyes fell on them as fans waved in front of whispering lips.

"This isn't the place to discuss this, Anne. Tonight—"

"I will be returning to my room tonight, Hartwinn. I don't think I'd sleep a wink next to you."

"Anne, *please*."

With a whirl of her skirt, she stormed away, shoving between people, in desperate need for some fresh air. People called her name, but she was too enraged to stop, too hurt that Hartwinn knew the whole time about a ridiculous, stupid law. Anne slid through the cracked door to the balcony, and cool air curled around her bare shoulders. But it wasn't her heaving breath she heard. It was Henry's.

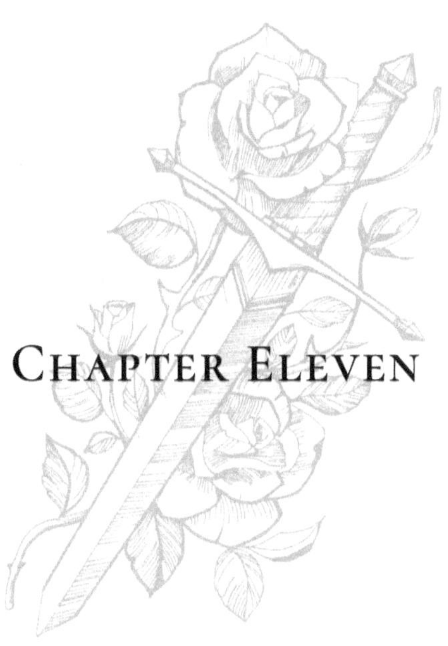

Chapter Eleven

Henry was squatting down, head hung. His hands above him gripped into the marble railing so tightly the whites of his knuckles pressed against his skin. He was rasping, wheezing as if he couldn't breathe. Anne rushed to him, her hands hovering over him, not knowing what to do. Her eyes took in his heaving chest, the sweat sticking strands of hair to his forehead and the squinting, pained look on his face.

He looked like he was battling something—and *losing*.

Anne spun around, taking a step. "I will fetch a healer, or Cidran—"

His hand snapped out, gripping her skirts, stopping her.

"No," he gritted out. "He cannot know. No one must know."

Anne shook her head, confused. "That you're ill—"

"That I am *terrified*."

She exhaled, glancing back at him. He was looking up at her, those brown eyes glassy, a silent plea in his gaze for her to not go.

He wasn't scared. He was haunted.

"I won't leave you, Henry. I won't," she said softly, untangling her skirts from his grip. His hand dropped between his knees. Anne clumsily lowered herself down next to him, then, as if by some habit, she patted the stone next to her. "I promise I'm not going anywhere."

Henry sat heavily as if the weight of what was frightening him was too heavy for his strong legs to hold up. Anne reached out, and with a grunt, undid the clasps of his tunic, allowing him more room to breathe. She sat back, her arm brushing his.

Neither spoke but allowed that comfortable silence to stretch out.

Henry leant his head back, glancing at her from hooded eyes. "I know this is not what you—"

"I know what it is like to be scared, Henry."

"You do?"

"Mine comes out in trembling hands and such a strong constriction of my ribs I fear they may shatter under the pressure."

"What terrified you?"

Anne pursed her lips, fingers picking. "A man."

Henry nodded, understanding seeping out in a single sigh.

"What about you?" she asked quickly, not waiting for that box of memories to rattle free.

"The heat of the ballroom. The laughing, the shouting, the merriment. All too close to the screams of the battlefield I walked off years ago."

"The wounds that bleed?"

"Yes, Fate. Now, I am all right. You should return inside," Henry said gently.

"Should I now?" she replied with a poke to his chest. "I wasn't aware you could presume to tell me what to do."

"I would never," he said, capturing her hand. "Yet, you should not be alone with a man who is not—"

"Yes, I understand. It is improper, uncouth and utterly scandalous," Anne said with a laugh.

Henry let out a soft huff, his thumb skimming over the valleys of her knuckles. His eyes followed the path of his touch, yet he never asked her to go again.

Anne smirked at him. "If—"

"A lot of dangerous questions begin with 'if'."

"If I wasn't Hartwinn's be—"

"Do not finish that sentence."

Anne let out a disappointed exhale. "Why?"

"You are playing with fire, Fate, and you are not the one who will be burnt."

Anne searched his eyes, only seeing flecks of golden brown burning in the darkness. A warmth brewed there—a devastating warmth.

"Would facing the flames be worth it?" she whispered before the words lingered too long on her tongue to ever be spoken.

Henry reached out, curling a stray lock around his finger. "I do not know you, *Anne*."

"And I don't know you, *Henry*. But would you like to?"

"Very much so," he whispered.

"I escape out here often. No one comes out here. Too cold, too dark. You're more than welcome to share it with me if the masses become too much."

His brows knitted. "That is very kind of you, Anne."

She cast him a soft smile. "You're welcome, Henry. We all need an escape every now and again."

A bellowing laugh came from the doorframe, making his attention snap over her shoulder. Anne turned to see Cidran stumbling out, his arm around Hartwinn's shoulders, his cheeks ruddy, eyes unfocused.

"*Henrrrry* ..." Cidran slurred, waving the half-drunk whisky bottle about. "Our new lord wishes to welcome us to his court ...*personally*."

Anne's spine straightened. Gone was that soft smile she wore, a strained grimace tightening her lips. Hartwinn clutched the neck of the bottle, pulling it from Cidran's hand, drinking deeply. Something dredged in hurt was brewing—and not from their earlier spat.

"But I see you are being welcomed by the rose of our court, Anne," Hartwinn said, offering her a deep bow. "She is quite furious at me."

"I am," Anne snapped, pushing to her feet with a grunt. "I don't wish to speak to you while you're—"

"Having fun?" Hartwinn asked, waving the bottle at her. "You wanted me to have more fun right?"

She rolled her eyes, batting his hand away. "You're drunk."

"It's my party, Anne. Of course I'm drunk!" he shouted. "I'm lord now. Deus rest my father's bones. I shall do whatever I want, you know." He took a wobbly step forward, his hand gripping her face. "And if I want you, I will have you."

That box rattled hard, making Anne's fingers tremble. A brush of warmth and velvet skimmed over her elbow as Henry stepped in behind her. She grumbled a curse under her breath, pulling her face from Hartwinn's hand. "Bed. *Now.*"

Henry stepped forward, hand hovering. "Shall I help his lordship to bed?"

Anne slipped her arm around Hartwinn's waist, stabilising him. "His lordship will be fine after a bit of bread and sleep. This is a dance we know well. Thank you though."

She guided Hartwinn closer to the door as the drunken idiot crooned words of pleasure and lust in her ear. Anne ignored him with a tight face. "I apologise for his behaviour. He can usually handle his liquor, but Hartwinn is still grieving, you see ..."

"Understandable," Henry replied, nodding. "You better get some bread and take him to bed."

"Annie, let us retire for the night. For I wish to crawl under your skirts and live there."

"Harty, I'm about to box you around the ears if you don't shut your mouth right now."

"Yes, ma'am!" the lord slurred, casting a sloppy salute to her.

Anne half dragged Hartwinn to the entrance, pausing before entering the raging, loud party. She cast the same soft smile over her shoulder and mouthed, "Until next time."

ANNE DUMPED THE SLURRING HARTWINN ONTO HIS BED with a heave and a grunt. "God gods, you're heavy," she groaned, resting her good hand on her hip.

He leant back, cocking his head at her. "What were you doing with Henry outside?"

"Talking," she replied curtly as she squatted to yank his boots off.

"About?"

"Nothing."

"Not about what happened in the forest?"

Caught unaware by his question, Anne's hand slipped from his boot, sending her sprawling backwards. She fell on her elbow lest she rebreak her wrist. She huffed, annoyed. "Whatever do you mean—"

"Henry told me."

A chill went down Anne's spine as her stomach flipped. Her eyes rose to his. Lips parting to spill out a lie or the truth, she couldn't decide. He leant forward, a sloppy smirk on his face. "He told me how you fought off a wolf. A *wolf*, Anne? You cannot even lift a sword."

"It would have killed Carrots—"

"Worse, It could have killed *you*, Anne. All over a stupid horse ..."

She exhaled sharply, narrowing her eyes. "I will not stay if you continue to speak of her that way. If she didn't risk her life for me, I would have been."

Hartwinn shook his head, leaning further down. "If Henry didn't wander past and put the beast down, you would be."

"You're speaking of him as if he is some sort of gallant knight riding in for the rescue. All he had was a blade. I didn't."

"Yet you leapt on a wolf—"

"And I would do it again."

Hartwinn threw his hands in the air, hissing out a breath. "Of course you would. You are brave, intelligent, but you can be so—"

"*Idiotic?*" Anne finished flatly.

"You said it, not me."

Anne rolled on to her knees, crawling to him. She rested her cheek against his knee. "I never meant to give you such a fright, you know. I was just angry. Things are changing, and I—"

He trailed fingers over her cheekbone. "I'm sorry, Annie. For all of it. I never wished for you to feel—"

"*Lonely?*"

Hartwinn seemed to sober up at her confession. She hadn't even realised that was the feeling until she said it. The months since their engagement had been full of long days and cold sheets, yet hope flickered in her like a single candle in the dark.

"You—Anne, I never—"

"We will not speak of this when you are full of more whisky than sense."

"Will you come to bed?"

Anne rose to linger between his legs. With one hand, she cupped his cheek, thumb tracing the lines already forming around his grey eyes. She leant down and pressed a kiss to his forehead.

"Not tonight. I still need some space, Hartwinn. This hurt me. More than I think I realise."

Without letting him convince her to stay, Anne rushed from the lord's wing, nearly running down the corridors, right to a door that was not her own. She slammed her hand against the wood. Time ticked slowly as she glanced up the corridor. The door cracked, and a bleary-eyed, dishevelled Seanna appeared from the darkness. A tear escaped from the welling as all Anne had been suppressing rose in a drowning tide.

"Can I sleep here tonight?"

Seanna watched the tear roll down her face, then pushed the door open. "As long as you don't steal all the blankets."

CHAPTER TWELVE

THE DINING ROOM WAS BUSTLING, EACH CHAIR AT THE LONG, rectangular table full. Ladies and men talked with animated waves of their hands, laughter filling the air. Anne leant back in her chair, her hand rubbing her full belly. Next to her, Hartwinn was talking in low murmurs to one of his advisors. His hand found hers, tangling fingers. Smooth skin pressed against the rough edge of the cast.

Neither had spoken about the law that hobbled her, nor her late-night confession.

Anne presumed he was too in his cups to remember. Still, she had avoided every opportunity. It wasn't Hartwinn's fault—none of it was. But the urge to spill her guts to him had been a difficult one to resist. Her thumb traced the groove between his forefinger and his thumb, making his gaze flick to her before returning to his conversation.

Am I lonely? No, I am surrounded by life and laughter. How could I be lonely here?

That small voice whispered, *But yet you confessed to it as if you are in Deus' temple.*

Anne's eyes trailed over the lively court full of smiles and life. Every night, Hartwinn seemed to host another noble or dignitary from the far corners of Zeroth. An endless loop of the same conversation: marriage, babies and ladyship. All topics she had prepared and tried answers to.

I am excited to marry Hartwinn.

Babies will come. Sons, Deus willing.

I am well-versed in how to run a household, let alone a castle.

All except him. Henry. Every chance he got, he asked her another question—innocent, simple questions, yet her heart thundered each time she got to speak with him.

"What do you prefer, carrots or parsnips?" had been the evening's question.

She answered, with an eye roll and a giggle, "Carrots, *obviously*."

He was swept up in a sputtering conversation with Dayvis and the masses around him before she could ask what his preference was. His shoulders were tense, and an almost bewildered look crossed his face. He said something Anne couldn't hear, but it made awful Edda—who also happened to be Sir Albert's fourth wife—stand abruptly, throwing her napkin at him and storming from the room. The sad sack of bones slowly trailed behind her, cane striking the stone. Henry hung his head, and Cidran clapped him on the back.

"He is truly *awful* at this," Anne whispered to Hartwinn, pulling her hand free of his.

"I'd expect as much, Anne. Henry was brought up in barracks and stables, not eating off fine porcelain at a king's dining table," Hartwinn explained, eyes lingering on his fingers. "All of this would be foreign, so unknown to him, considering he is well-loved by his soldiers."

"And yet, he cannot seem to warm up to anyone here."

Hartwinn groaned, pressing his fingers to his eyes. "Anne, you should have seen the mess in the war room. The yelling, threats, daggers being slammed into my priceless mahogany table. I thought I was going to have to cover up a murder."

"What happened?"

"Albert opened his mouth. That's what happened."

"Typical," Anne said with an eye roll, propping her chin on her hand. "It's almost like he needs a tutor or something. Goulrich would have such services, not here."

"Like someone who has come to Alderdeen as a stranger before?"

"Yes, exactly," Anne replied with an enthusiastic nod. "Someone who can show him how to *survive* in this Heylla den—"

"Or how to use a fork, at least," Hartwinn cut in with a laugh.

"He knows how to use a ..."

Her words faded away as Hartwinn elbowed her and nodded to the fae warrior shoving a wedge of potato in his mouth with his fingers. Anne bit down on her lip as she watched him drag his tongue over his palm, swirling around his forefinger, capturing the dripping butter. Warmth bloomed in a place that was not appropriate at the dinner table.

Hartwinn hummed beside her, making her drag her eyes away from Henry. He was smirking at her, that mischievous twinkle in his eyes. "If only we had someone in this court who had such tutelage."

"No."

"Annie," he crooned her name. "*Please.*"

"I simply cannot. I'm far too busy organising our wedding—"

"Seanna is all over it, much like an ant to honey. We even had a meeting about it today—one that went on far too long, I might add. You will not have to lift a finger, so you will have plenty of time to educate Henry. He needs to—*this* needs to work."

"For the fae warriors to fill out Ewan's army?"

"No, much to Albert's frustration." Hartwinn scratched his chin, exhaling. "Not a single fae warrior will fall into his ranks. Alderdeen's forces, yes, but not the king's. Those wishing to come to Alderdeen will be offered land, and a chance to farm it. I may call on them, I may not. I may let them live in peace, a place of safety, and never expect them to see another war."

Those churning emotions threatened to spill out in confessions best kept a secret. Anne reached up and dragged her fingers over his stubbled jaw. "You're a dreamer, Hartwinn Novak. Every day, you prove you're a better man than your father."

"It is the least I can do, for I bear the sins of his wickedness as his son. Anne, please?"

She met his hopeful gaze. Selfishly, she wanted to spend time with Henry, find out how each cog of his mind worked—and to find out more about him than if he preferred carrots or parsnips. But Hartwinn had no idea they had almost shared a kiss, let alone how much her mind wandered to him. He would be heartbroken if he ever found out. Yet, this was more important than affairs of her thundering heart. This was for Alderdeen—her home.

"I wouldn't ask this if I didn't think you would be the most helpful. I just want this to work so badly. I—"

Her thumb drew across his lips, silencing him. "Just let me ask Henry before we fall into a pit of despair. He may say no."

Hartwinn nodded against her hand, a smile spreading on his face. Anne couldn't help but smile back, her hand slipping from him. He launched into another animated conversation, hands waving.

A pair of eyes burnt into the exposed skin of her décolletage, slinking over her skin like the slip of silk. Slowly, Anne's gaze travelled over the half-eaten plates and spilt wine. Right to him. Their eyes met almost shyly. What she found had her sitting back, her finger trailing over the carved arm of the chair. A spark flared in those brown eyes, drawing her in. She swore she saw not desire or lust but a soft, demanding *need*.

The sun had forced its last rays across the soft grass of the gardens. Anne savoured the warmth in her bones before the crisp night air prickled her skin. She had pulled her skirts high, leaving the creamy skin of her legs exposed, sunning them. Her hair hung around her shoulders, a daisy tucked behind one ear. A discarded book and half-drunk bottle of red wine were beside her on the grass.

She was alone. Once again.

Seanna had left her to argue with the cook about how much dried fruit was to be in her wedding cake, and Hartwinn was nose-deep in the castle's ledgers and sums. Even he was trying to rope her in to help calculate costs. Mathematics had her running from his office.

Anne took a swig, allowing the dry alcohol to coat her tongue. The wine had relaxed her, releasing each of her tense muscles. Her head lolled back, eyes closed. A soft hum of a song she couldn't forget slipped from her lips.

"That is a pretty song, Fate," a voice crooned behind her.

Anne snapped her eyes open to find a smiling Henry standing over her. His dark hair was loose, cascading around his high cheekbones.

She scrambled to her knees, still looking up at him. "It's a song I heard one of the women sing. It's about a knight falling in love with a princess."

"I presumed it's a doomed romance."

"Very much so, yet he cannot help but wait for her every night in the hope she walks past her window so he can see her for just a moment."

"I can understand the urge to look."

Anne's cheeks warmed as she nodded to the grass. "You can join me if you wish."

He lingered for a moment, staring down at her. His hand reached down, ever so gently brushing over her cheekbone. Pulling the flower from her hair, he brought it to his nose, dragging the scent deep.

"I never imagined I would see a flower again," he said quietly. "My land has been burnt. Only ash remains from the remnants of the battles. Yet, the top layer of soil *needs* to burn, allowing the fresh shoots to force their way through the dirt. To regrow what your king has tried to strip away."

Anne sat heavily on her rear, eyes on the softly swaying garden beds and hedges. She struggled to imagine it aflame, burning to ash. All her mind would conjure was the sadness, the pain of watching one's home burn.

"I didn't know it was that bad ..."

His hardening gaze rose to the horizon, his lips pressing, opening. Lost for words. So, Anne spoke, filling the air with one simple command, "Join me, Henry."

"I do not think—"

"Stop thinking, then, and just *do*."

With a quick glance over his shoulder, he clambered down, then spread out next to her across the grass, so close she could feel his radiating body heat. Tension filled his shoulders, and he tightly clenched his hand around his shin.

He was uncomfortable.

Anne reached over and grasped the wine bottle, taking a mouthful.

With a roll of her tongue, she captured the stray drops. She offered it to him. His eyes were not on the sea-green glass, but on her lips. He cleared his throat and glanced away. "I fear if I have one drop, I may not stop ..."

Anne tilted her head, eyebrows meeting. An awkwardness flowed between them. She hadn't thought he would join her, and she recognised he did it on a whim. Instead of talking, she racked her mind for conversation—anything—aching to hear him speak with that deep, rough voice. It was not made to orate the finest poetry at court, but to bark commands across a battlefield.

"I have a proposition for you," Anne spluttered out.

"Now, I think that is most improper." Henry looked away, the tips of his pointed ears reddening. "You are *betrothed.*"

She blinked at him as the cogs of her mind slowed. Her hand slapped over her mouth as a laugh spilt from her. "I'm *not* propositioning you. I simply meant I have something I wish to speak to you about."

"I have a feeling I may need a drink to have this conversation," he said, yanking the bottle from her.

Anne watched with a strange fascination as he drank, the bob at the centre of his throat hypnotising her. His teeth dragged over his bottom lip, forcing her to bite down on her own. She had desired men before, ached for them, but this was different. She wanted to know *him*—more than what he felt like rolling in her sheets.

"You know, even in Orynile, staring is considered rude," he said, arching a brow at her, making her flick her gaze down.

"I noticed you are having a difficult time ... with *court.*"

"What do you mean?"

"For example, last night at dinner. Edda, Albert's wife. She was upset over something you said—"

"That I was surprised the old prick could even make her his wife without keeling over?"

Anne smothered a laugh by pressing her lips together.

He took a swig. "Now, that was stopping Cidran from saying much worse, mind you."

"Even if it is true, we shouldn't say it," she said, her eyes lowering to the tufts of green grass below them. "If you like, I can teach you a few things. Just enough for you to not make mortal enemies of Hartwinn's court."

"I bet you could teach me plenty, Fate," Henry whispered. "What do you want in return?"

Anne wet her lips and whispered back, "To get to know you."

"That is dangerous," he replied softly.

"Worse—it's *deadly*."

Warmth spread across her chest at her confession as she tried to yank the bottle from him. His fingers slid over hers. Rough, calloused. Both their eyes sank to their joined hands, then, as if timed, rose to each other's lips. Tension grew taut as something—or someone—caressed her nape. A soft touch, guiding her towards Henry. She did little to resist it. The space between them shrank smaller and smaller with each passing moment until his gaze shot over her shoulder, snapping the tension like a twig. His lips smoothed, and his grip loosened and dropped away.

"What would these lessons entail?" he asked absent-mindedly, his attention locked on something fast-approaching.

"Manners, rules of the court—what in Heylla are you looking at?" she asked, turning.

What she found was the gaze of Hartwinn, an angry frown slashed across his face, standing a few feet from them, a red rose in his hand. Anne jumped back from Henry, dropping the bottle, spilling the dregs of the wine over the blanket and his lap.

"*Shit*," she muttered, scrambling to her feet, leaving Henry sprawled across the grass, staring at his ruined pants. "Hartwinn!"

Without saying a word, Hartwinn spun on his heel and angrily threw the rose on the ground before storming away. Anne was left standing there, arm extended, cursing her awful luck. She should have known he'd be looking for her, but she had been so engrossed with Henry that she hadn't even noticed him. Groaning, she turned to see Henry had stood, holding her discarded book.

"The day after tomorrow. Noon. We begin," Anne said, distracted, launching herself over the grass, calling out over her shoulder, "Don't be late, for I am a strict teacher."

Chapter Thirteen

Anne let out a sharp exhale as she stood outside Hartwinn's chambers, working up the courage to knock.

He hadn't been at dinner.

According to Abigail, he preferred to take his meal in his room—and not with her. That annoying buzzing almost had her launching from the table to go to him, to smooth things over. Yet, her legs locked her to her chair, forcing her to marinate in the worry that she'd completely ruined things. An irritable edge formed, making her combat the sharp words growing on her tongue. What made it worse was that Henry had kept his distance at dinner, too, sitting further down the long, busy table than he ever had. Seanna had contained her just enough with distracting gossip, but that soon faded as the masses retired to bed and left her alone. Anne could hardly bear the tight feeling in her chest for a second longer, nearly sprinting across the castle to him.

A soft groan came from the other side of the door, and her stomach dropped. Her hand shook as she slammed on the wood.

"If that is you, Anne Davoy, I do not wish to speak to you."

She pursed her lips, crossing her arms. "Hartwinn Novak, you open this door right *now*."

Footsteps came from beyond. "What do you want?"

Anne swallowed and exhaled. "I think we need to speak about—"

The door swung open. A dishevelled and flushed Hartwinn appeared, a frown slashed across his face.

She had obviously interrupted something.

"About what I *saw*," he said bitterly. "Or that you left our bed after a fight that is yet to be resolved?'

"No. About what you're doing *now*," Anne retorted, pushing past him.

Her nerves sent her storming into his darkened room. Turning, she saw nothing. An empty bed with unkempt sheets. An uncorked vial of oil sat next to his bed, and his clothing littered the floor.

"I'm here alone, if that's why you are searching my sheets."

She spun back to him. "Then why are you all flushed? Why did I hear groaning?"

Hartwinn's eyes dipped as he wet his lips. "If you must know, I was ... pleasuring myself to thoughts of you."

Anne's whole body flushed as a warmness bloomed between her thighs. "I see."

He stepped towards her, pinning her against the bedpost. His hand gripped the wood just above her head. "And I haven't finished."

Her eyes rose to his, only lingering on his lips for a fraction. Her breath shallowed out as Hartwinn leant down. He brushed his lips over hers. Once, then twice.

Anne did something truly idiotic.

She kissed him.

As lips parted and tongues swirled, feelings twisted deep inside of her—one coated in that sticky, hot need, and another that tasted bitter, chilling the heat in her veins. Yet, her need for a release was stronger. Her body had been coiled tight for days.

Hartwinn's hands bunched her skirt, yanking the material up to disappear under. Anne exhaled, parting her legs a fraction, readying for a rush of pleasure. Yet, his hands went right to the round curve of her rear, squeezing.

Maybe he is taking his time, Anne thought, her hand twisting in his shirt.

She pressed more fervent kisses over his lips, his jaw, down his neck.

Hartwinn gripped tighter as a soft moan fell from him. Need was building slowly. Not in the way that just the promise of a brush of lips had ignited a fuse inside of her, but soon, it would fill her veins, singing for him.

Anne hooked her leg around his hip, his erect manhood flush against her thudding core. Their eyes met as she began to grind herself on him. She bit down on her lip, eyebrows meeting as if she could simply release from it. Yet, Hartwinn knew she needed *more*, but a distracting, selfish desire dripped from him, coating her in his own sticky need.

A need for his *own* release.

He was too far gone to worry about hers—or was it misplaced anger to withhold her pleasure? A twisted punishment for what he had seen earlier.

"Gods, you make me *insane*," he murmured, his hips thrusting against her. "You're all I've been thinking about."

"Tell me ..." Anne breathed. "What do you think about?"

"So many things. Spreading you wide to watch my cock—"

A deep, reverberating groan came from him, and a warm wet patch formed between them.

All that sensual tension snapped, and an awkward, strained one replaced it.

Hartwinn gasped for breath, resting his forehead against her shoulder. His hand was still squeezing her rear. Anne's leg dropped away from him, her core painfully thudding. The sweat slick on her skin turned cool and uncomfortable. A bitter taste of shame rose, coating her tongue with that poison, making her swallow it down until it filled her, churning and churning.

"I don't think we should have done that," she said softly.

Hartwinn's hands immediately left her body, and he stepped back. His face twisted. Anne pulled her skirts down, a line forming between her brows.

Neither looked at the other.

They had used each other—and not in a needy, sweaty way, but in a desperate need to prove something. *But what?* Anne couldn't even gather her thoughts enough to understand why her heart ached.

Before her mind could slow, Hartwinn exhaled and strode into his bathing chamber, slamming the door.

Anne jumped, unable to stop her fried nerves from twitching. She stood for what felt like hours, her hands screwed in her skirts, tears welling in her eyes. A rush of water came from beyond the wood. The door creaked open. Hartwinn stood, wet and in fresh clothing in the doorframe.

"I presumed you'd run again."

"I thought about it."

He strode into his bedroom and slumped on to the foot of the bed. "We need to talk, and not about that abysmal performance."

Anne sat down next to him, her hand slipping between her knees. "I think we need to slow down."

"Slower? Do you wish for me not to touch you?"

"No, I think we need to be friends—"

"We have been friends, Anne. For *years*," Hartwinn cut in, turning to her.

"But we haven't been engaged before. Deus, we'd never even had sex before you went to your knee." Anne raised her hand, the diamond shining in the lantern light. "This changes *everything*."

"Why?"

Her hand dropped. "Because it does, Hartwinn. Our friendship has changed, which means we must find our way on a different path. And I'm not sure I—"

"Have a companion?"

She nodded, picking at the skin around her nail beds. "I don't say this to hurt you."

"I know," he said with a sigh.

"You cannot expect me to jump into bed with you—"

"But you're willing to jump into bed with someone else."

"We aren't speaking about *that*, Hartwinn." A tear rolled down her cheek. "We are speaking about us, this wedd—"

"Not this again," he cut in with a groan.

Anne shook her head and exhaled. "None of this is coming out right. You love me, Hartwinn, I know you do ..."

"But?"

She took his hand, pulling it into her lap. "You were my best friend, and I miss him. I thought all this would be easier, but it's not."

"Isn't friendship what all great loves are built on?" he asked.

"Do you believe that?"

"With my whole heart," he answered earnestly. Hartwinn reached out and brushed away the tear that escaped. "And if you need *time*, tell me."

"We don't have time, Hartwinn. You must marry me before I'm twenty-five right?"

"That law—"

"Is archaic and barbaric." Anne's hand went to her chest. "They are my lands, my title, given to me by my father. You have no right to *take* them from me."

"Don't be dramatic, Anne. I'm not *taking* them from you. I just didn't tell you because I knew how you'd react." He waved a hand at her. "You're just proving me right."

"Then you know why I'm hurt that I had to learn it from that bag of bones who thinks that law is just and *fair* and not from you."

Hartwinn exhaled and sat back. "You've never cared about them until now. Father had been running them for you since you were orphaned—"

"And you never tried to take me with such ferocity until now," Anne snapped back, more annoyed at herself than him. He was right; she'd let others take control when she should have. "We've only been together *once*. Yes, we've messed around and kissed, but you've never been like this. That changed things. Now, things are different ... Maybe *I'm* different."

"But ..." Hartwinn's eyes dropped to their tangled fingers. "You came in here kissing me like you *needed* me, Anne, like you wanted to be *together*—"

"And look how that *ended*," she finished with a cock of her head and brow raised.

Hartwinn looked at her, then away. His brows twitched as a laugh erupted from him, and his hand slapped to his mouth as stomach-clenching laughter spilt between his fingers.

"Why are you laughing?" Anne asked, slamming her hand on the bed. "We are having a *serious* conversation."

"That was mortifying, Annie. I thought I'd have to climb out the window rather than face you."

She looked at him, then a giggle left her, loosening her tight shoulders. "It was just *unexpected*, that is all. I guess I can take it as a compliment."

Hartwinn let out a long sigh and flopped backwards, his hands covering his face. "Again, *mortifying*."

Anne curled next to him, pulling his hands from his face. "What are we going to do, Hartwinn?"

His arm fell behind his head, his eyes meeting hers. He looked so earnest it made her heart hurt. "We give ourselves time and grace. What we have is changing, but our love is *strong*, Anne. Stronger than the turbulent seas we have found ourselves in. I love you, and I know I can make you happy. That's enough for now, don't you think?"

What if those feelings change, mutate? Anne asked silently. *What if other feelings form? Anger—or, worse, bitterness from losing what we had. What then, Hartwinn? Do we simply sail into a storm and wreck on rocks just below the sea's surface?*

Instead, she replied quietly, not believing the words leaving her lips. "Of course."

He hadn't truly listened to a single word she had said.

"Then it's settled. We navigate these new waters, marry in the spring and let Deus handle the rest."

"Settled," Anne repeated as a crack formed in her heart—one so tiny she barely felt it. Yet, with each thudding heartbeat, it split her heart right down the middle.

Chapter Fourteen

It was Henry's first lesson, and Anne was hand-shaking, stomach-turning nervous. Her hands hovered over the table setting she'd had Abigail set up, straightening a wine glass. A set of crisp white, gold-rimmed plates were laid out, surrounded by a range of silver cutlery—much more than they had ever dined with. If Ewan ever stepped foot in the castle, the boxes of clinking silver would be dusted off.

Anne lifted a spoon, reflecting her pensive face. *He is late, or am I simply early?*

Her eyes flashed to the timepiece on the wall above the door. The long, slim metal arms hadn't fully struck twelve, yet it felt like she had waited hours for him.

Anne replaced the spoon with a soft clink and slumped into the chair. Her fingers went straight to her mouth, chewing on the already bloody skin. Apprehension had filled her to the brim so much that she spent her morning digging through and yanking dresses from her cupboard, only to discard them in a flurry of velvet and silk.

She had decided on a soft pink gown that was layered in hand-sewn flowers—one of her favourites. Anne had more silk dresses in her cupboard than there were in some dressmakers' stores, a rainbow of colour at her fingertips. She had always loved soft, pretty things, but more so, she loved the artistic eye of dressmaking. Each of her gowns had its own quirks. A too-short hem, a bodice ribbon that she had sown on or the back-aching, painstaking embroidery that ran down sleeves or up her bodice. Yet even with the simplest gown of cotton and lace, she felt as if she were wearing a piece of art, masterfully created.

A sharp rap came from the door, and Anne's fingers popped from her mouth. She scrambled to her feet, smoothing her skirts. Her heart thundered in her chest. It wasn't a stolen moment in the forest or a cold balcony—it was *more*.

"Enter."

Henry appeared from behind the door, smiling.

Anne pushed the seat back, her fingers tangling at her front. "At least you know you should knock."

He slipped through the crack, closing the door with a click. He paused for a moment, hand on the door before turning, a crooked smirk spreading on his face.

"I was raised in a castle, not a barnyard."

Anne's brows twitched a fraction at his hesitation, her stomach dropping.

"That is surprising, considering you don't know how to use a fork."

"Fork?" Henry asked innocently. "What is that?"

Anne rolled her eyes and rushed over to him. Her hand gripped his sleeve, yanking him closer. "Well, you're about to find out."

A soft whistle came from Henry, eyes dancing over the silver. "Good goddess, do you have Hartwinn's entire armoury laid out for lunch?"

She dropped his arm and crossed hers, the bulky cast making it difficult. "If you're not going to take this seriously, I will not teach you a single thing."

"Anne, I am teasing you," he cut in, turning that honeyed look on her. His hand lifted to hover over the small of her back. "This is—thank you. I have been feeling a little out of my depth. Especially after Hartwinn has just announced a ball in my—"

"A *ball*?" Anne asked, turning, eyes widening. "He said those exact words?"

Henry frowned at her and replied drily, "I can speak the common tongue."

She whirled to the table, plucking up select silverware and dumping it to the side in a clatter. Her thoughts rushed between her ears, a plan forming in her mind's eye.

"Anne—"

"This changes everything," she cut in, rearranging the cutlery.

Henry reached out and caught her elbow, stopping her. Her eyes dropped to the hand pressed against her bare skin, where warmth was bleeding into her.

"Anne, stop. I do not understand—"

"A ball is the perfect place to *debut* you."

His hand loosened, only to slide down her arm, fingers brushing the dip of her wrist. "Debut me?"

Anne's eyes flicked to him. "As a well-mannered courtly gentleman. It will be perfect."

Henry glanced at her, confused, his lips pursed, brows lowered over those woody eyes. "Am I not a gentleman now?"

"Not in this court's eyes," Anne explained hurriedly. She waved to the chair next to the one she had pushed out. Yet, Henry stood, looking at her.

"Is there—"

"Shouldn't I help you?"

Anne blinked. "With what?"

"Sitting ..."

She plopped herself down, frowning up at him. "I can sit—"

Henry took a step in. Anne fought not to follow him with her eyes when the tips of his fingers brushed over the sensitive skin of her shoulders as he gripped the chair. He leant down, his warm breath cascading over her skin, sending a thrill down her spine. A brewing panic arose in her from the battling feelings—one that was light like butterflies wings yet heavy as lead.

"Fate—"

Anne shoved the chair right back into Henry's stomach. A grunt came from behind her. She slipped out, taking a wobbly step back. "I am engaged to be wed," she announced.

Henry still held the chair, his eyes boring into her. "I know."

"I love him," Anne said, feeling awfully dumb for simply stating it.

"I presume you do."

"Then why—"

"Why are we drawn together?" he cut in.

"Yes," she breathed.

Henry's hands tightened on the chair as his gaze dropped away, not answering her.

"I think we should—"

"We haven't done anything, Fate."

His words rang out between them. They hadn't crossed that imaginary line—only danced close to it.

"Yet," Anne whispered. "We haven't done anything *yet*."

His eyes flashed to hers. "We cannot—"

"We most definitely cannot." Her uninjured hand reached over and straightened a fork. "Then what are we to do?"

"You wished to know me, isn't that right?"

She nodded.

"Then get to know me, Fate, as I get to know you."

"Is that not—"

"We do not have to touch to know each other."

She bit down on her bottom lip, thinking, considering it. It could be enough—it had to be enough.

"Deal. No touching."

Henry held his hands up and grinned. "As you wish."

Without another word, Anne lifted lids off serving dishes, revealing delicately cut sandwiches, tiny pastries filled with creams and a crumbling, pastry meat pie. She slid into the seat that was not held by Henry. Anne needed to fight the pull he had on her, and she needed space for that.

"We can work on table manners, how to dress and dance, all while I can tell you about the court and its inhabitants."

The chair squeaked on the stone as Henry slumped down, elbows on the table, to rest his cheek on his fist. A grimace tightened Anne's face as her eyes repeatedly dropped to his elbow, then back up to his face.

"I do not dance," he said, his arm slipping from the table.

Her lips smoothed. "But you fight?"

"That is completely different—"

"No. It's the *same*. This is simply another type of ... battlefield," Anne said, her forefinger trailing over the small butter knife. "Instead of swords and shields, we wield words and fans. Instead of battle plans, it's dance steps. And the victor is not always who emerges from that muddy battle."

"I see," Henry said with a scratch of his chin. "And are you the fearless general?"

She laughed, shaking her head. "I'm a grunt in a battalion, that is all. Hicka is the general. She would outrank Hartwinn if she was born a man."

"Hicka?"

"You haven't met her yet. She is elderly, and only comes to Valliss for important social occasions. Like the ball—"

"Or your wedding?"

Anne exhaled at his words—the sharp reminder of what could never happen. With a strained smile, she waved to the array of silverware and said, "Shall we start with how to use a fork?"

Chapter Fifteen

Days had dragged, and the sun rose and set. Their lessons were frequent if not brief, for Hartwinn had Henry holed up in his office discussing land. Anne knew more about Henry than ever. His favourite colour, where he was born, how many siblings he had. And yet, she wanted more until she was drowning in the knowledge of him. Even so, they never touched once—not even fleeting brushes.

Anne flung her arms over her head as she flopped back onto her bed, her loose curls pooling on the stone floor as she stretched out. Her body was full of nervous tension as if, with each passing moment they spent, she was poised to be caught again.

Seanna was sitting on her high-backed velvet chair, feet curled under her. The tome of neatly written notes, flower pressings and scraps of fabrics was open on her lap. "... and we cannot forget about the flower girl—"

"Yes, we *cannot* forget about the flower girls," Anne cut in, rolling over, pulling herself from the bed.

Her room was messy.

Dresses and underclothing were strewn across the floor, her bed unmade and rogues and perfumes scattered under her mirror on her vanity—a direct reflection of her mind. She needed to move. Dangerously, she needed to get into some sort of mischief. Childish as it may have been, she needed the rush of a thrill. And the night of the comet was still a week away.

Anne stomped across her bedroom, over plush rugs thrown across the cold stone floor, cutting through the rainbow of colours that her stained glass windows scattered through her room. Right to Seanna. She was still flicking through the pages, talking.

Anne closed *The Wedding Tome* with a snap.

"Anne, I was reading—"

"Their trunks arrived yesterday."

"Whose?"

Anne's finger traced over the leather, lips pouting. "You know *who*. Do you think they brought fae wine with them?"

Seanna arched a manicured brow. "Why?"

"Because I'm awfully thirsty."

"And it's not an excuse to rifle through Henry Ashmore's belongings."

Anne crossed her arms. Seanna was right.

"Why don't you just ask him for it?" her friend asked with a sigh.

"That is no *fun*."

Seanna gave her a narrow-eyed, pinched look. "How you of all people are about to marry a powerful lord and rule the most wanted strip of land in Zeroth is beyond me."

"That isn't a no."

Seanna smirked, dumping *The Wedding Tome* on the floor with a thud. "That isn't a no."

THE HALLWAY THEY CREPT DOWN IN THE EAST WING OF Valliss Castle—where most guests were housed—was eerily silent. Only the slip of a stray giggle echoed down the hall. Seanna and Anne were arm in arm, almost tripping on their feet.

"I cannot believe you convinced—"

"There was no arm twisting, Seanna," Anne cut in, grinning. "You're a *willing* accomplice."

"We mustn't be late. We have your wedding dress fitting this afternoon."

Anne waved her worries away, glancing up and down the corridor. She paused at his door. How did she know it was Henry's room? Something inside of her told her as if she knew she would have to find it one day. Her hand rose slowly—too slowly for Seanna, who snapped out and yanked on the handle. The door swung open with a soft creak.

Anne considered the open doorway with a soft hum. "They didn't lock it.'

"Most likely, I believe they thought no one was stupid enough to break into their rooms."

Anne glanced at Seanna. "I've never been praised for my intelligence—"

"Actually, you have. More than once," Seanna replied flatly.

Anne spun around, backing into the room. With a grin, she said, "What was that? I think someone is in this room. We must *investigate*."

Seanna groaned, rolling her eyes, but followed her in.

ANNE INITIALLY THOUGHT THE ROOM WAS BARE, SPARSE, unlived in. Yet as her eyes skimmed and her hand trailed over the tightly made bed, she found he had touched parts of the room. A pile of leather bound books, letters scattered across dressers, clothing thrown over a chair, vials of elixirs sitting next to a basin. She walked over to the books, opening the jackets, devouring the words. He was reading books on the history of Alderdeen and the surrounding Sliva Forest.

He was *trying*.

Next, she plucked up the elixirs, cracking the vials. His scent flooded her nose: wood, leather and spice. It was his soap she had smelt each time she lingered close. The urge to pocket it overcame her, wanting to smell him when he was not around.

Anne turned to find Seanna watching her with an oddly disgusted look on her face. "Do you wish to sniff his worn shirts next, or maybe his socks?"

She rolled her eyes, replacing the vial. "Do you want to stand there, gawking, or do you want to help rifle through his belongings?"

Seanna exhaled and strode to the large wooden chest under the window. Anne joined her, crouching. She dragged her fingers over the lid, feeling the sprawling vines carved into the wood—a touch of nature in that stone labyrinth. She shoved it open, and gently placed on a pile of shirts was a dark emerald green bottle, corked with a dripping, golden wax sealing it. Anne could see the fizzing wine bubbling against the glass. She reached in and lifted it. A laugh escaped her, already feeling the rush of elation in her veins.

"And what do we have here, ladies?" Cidran crooned behind her.

Anne shot up, hiding the wine behind her back. Henry and Cidran stood in the doorway, amused looks across their faces.

Seanna stepped forward, beaming a tight smile at the fae. "We were walking—"

"And we heard a noise in here," Anne added, rushing to meet her. "So we'd thought we would investigate."

"Yes, investigate," Seanna said, nodding. "Make sure your belongings are safe."

The fae males shared a look, lips twitching.

"Thieves are about, are they?" Henry asked, stepping closer. His eyes skimmed over Anne, flushed and fighting a smirk. He leant closer to her until his warm breath brushed over her skin, causing it to prickle. "Or, are they *here*?"

He reached behind her, snatching the bottle and holding it up high.

"Hey!" Anne exclaimed. "Give that back!"

"Give the wine you stole from my own chest back? The laws are strange here, Cidran."

"Very strange," he murmured in reply, a knowing, smug smirk spread on his freckled face.

Anne held her hand out. "As payment for my lessons."

"*Payment?* I think our deal is equal payment."

Cidran turned, eyes sparking. "Your *deal*? Pray tell the rest of us what that entails?"

Both Anne and Henry spluttered, denials falling from their lips. Neither looked convinced.

"Anyway, we should be going," Seanna said, giving Anne a shove towards the door. "Lady Anne has an appointment at the dressmakers. You know, for her *wedding* gown. She is to be wed to Hartwinn, if you have forgotten."

Henry's arm fell to his side, and he said, "I haven't forgotten."

"It seems like you have."

Henry and Cidran parted as Anne pushed her way through. Henry's hand brushed over hers—a small, fleeting touch that sent her heart thundering.

THE AIR IN THE CARRIAGE WAS TENSE. A DEATHLY, uncomfortable silence had settled between the women. Anne shifted in her plush, velvet seat, resisting the urge to chew on her fingernails. Seanna's eyes were locked on the ever-shifting view outside her window as the carriage wound down from Valliss to the upper city. Her plump lips twitched as she pressed them together. She was angry, fuming with Anne.

"We—"

"You've taken him to bed, haven't you?"

Anne scoffed. "*Really?* You think—"

"I don't know what to think. We're planning your *wedding*, Anne, and you're batting your eyelashes at the fresh meat in court."

"That is not—"

"Isn't it? He is new and shiny. And Hartwinn is what? Boring and worn?"

Anne exhaled. "Hartwinn is—"

"If you say the love of your life, Anne Devoy, you're *lying*. Not only to me, but to yourself," Seanna cut in, turning her sharp gaze on her.

"How can you say that? I have loved him since I was seventeen. He *is* the love of my life," Anne hissed, her eyes narrowing with each word, her hand pressing against her chest. "And you cannot talk of sniffing around new meat. I heard the duke who's visiting from Goulrich was seen sneaking out of your room."

"I'm not the one about to be wed, Anne. And if you truly love him, gods …" Seanna trailed off, shaking her head with a scoff. Her gaze turned back to the window.

"What, Seanna? Tell me?"

"You look at that fae in a way I've never seen, not even at Hartwinn. You look like—"

"Like what?"

"Like you are falling in love!" Seanna yelled, her voice echoing off the clear glass of the carriage.

Silence followed. Painful, awkward silence.

"Then your eyes deceive you."

Seanna blew a snort through her nose. "And you cannot admit it to yourself."

Anne's tongue worked over her molars. "And if I did? What then, Seanna? You think I would leave Hartwinn—"

"You shame yourself looking at him like that at dinner. You—"

"I want Henry, *yes*, Seanna. Is that what you want to hear? I want him. May Diabolus rise and swallow me whole for having a lick of desire for another man."

"You have always wanted what you cannot have."

"And why is that, Seanna?"

She shrugged, sitting back.

"All I have been told is that I'm one thing. Hartwinn's bride."

Her friend's gaze snapped to her, and confusion welled. "You're more than that, Anne. Wholly more than that."

"Then why do I feel that I'm simply the sum of a man's worth? That I'm only worth something if a man wants me. Is there something wrong with wanting to be more than that?"

A line formed between Seanna's brows. "No, there is—"

"I know I was not put on this earth to be a breeding mare nor a jewel on some man's arm," Anne cut in. She couldn't help it. The words rushed out, truth spilling from her. "Yet I have been ordered to sit down and smile, all the while being told I'm blessed that Hartwinn can give me a *nice* life. Well, I simply do not want a *nice* life."

"Why do you want more than that, Anne?"

She stared at Seanna, a tear rolling down her cheek. " A better question is why do we *settle* for that?"

"We're women—"

"We are much more than our sex, Seanna. We are powerful, with our own lands, our own riches, and I will not allow a law made by men to take that away from me."

Her friend leant forward, her face clenching in confusion. "What do you mean by a *law*?"

Anne exhaled, then explained what Albert had said, her hands balling into fists with every passing moment. When she finished, Seanna hissed a long string of curses—a rare occurrence. Her birthday was only two months after Anne's.

"No wonder Father was trying to shove every suitor at me during my winter visit to Goulrich. That's all his letters are filled with, and he hasn't accepted that I will not marry a stranger."

"You see—"

"This idiotic law is not all why you are questioning your place in this world. I know you, Anne Devoy, better than I know myself. It's him, isn't it? I bet he weaves pretty lies about how he'll give you a better life in whatever hovel—"

"He is a king's son, Seanna. He wouldn't live in a hovel."

"Yet he is not a prince, is he?"

The word "bastard" lingered between them as Anne sighed, picking at her sleeve. "He never said anything of the sort."

"You don't talk then—"

"Seanna, he isn't rolling in my sheets."

"And yet, with all you know, you still chose Hartwinn."

"I didn't know about the law until after. Hartwinn knew, but it was the king—"

"Now, what does *he* have to do with this?"

A ball of emotion caught Anne in the throat, forcing a cough from her. "He pushed Hartwinn to propose."

Seanna exhaled, piecing the puzzle pieces together faster than Anne ever could. She quickly slid beside her. "That meddling prick. He wants your lands right?"

"Yes," Anne said softly. *And me*, she added silently. *He has always wanted me. A plaything for when he is bored—not to wed or even respect.*

"Why not simply demand them? And Hartwinn is a big boy. He could have declined his request."

"I worry for what Ewan would have done to me—to Hartwinn, to Alderdeen, I mean—if he didn't get what he wanted."

"Now, Anne, he wouldn't wage a civil war. That would be stupid—"

"Not for Alderdeen. But for the border between my lands and the witches, he would." Anne let out a shaky exhale. "We know him, Seanna. He stops at nothing to get what he wants."

Seanna's hand found hers, the light tremble working its way through her fingers. "He is married now, Anne, and has been for years. Isn't that why he couldn't marry you in the first place? He would not put that alliance at—"

"You think *that* would abandon his fascination with his favourite toy?" she asked, tears leaking over her cheeks. "Not even bloody guards rushing into his room stopped him, Seanna. They stood and watched as I cried for help ..."

Anne's words faded off as she squeezed her eyes closed. The chain on that box was pulled taut, threatening to break.

"I'm here, Anne. You need not be lost to that memory. Nothing can hurt you—"

"Yet it does, Seanna. It is barbed, sticking into aching parts of me."

"And how I will share that pain with you for all my days."

"He never hurt you."

Seanna squeezed her hand. "No, but I convinced you to come to Goulrich. I introduced you. Maybe if I never left you alone—"

"He still would have found a way. This isn't your fault, and this is damned sure not mine. The blame lands squarely on his shoulders. He is the one who decided to hurt me."

"Then why do I feel such guilt?"

Anne watched as the streets of Alderdeen slowed from outside her window, already arriving at their destination. "You feel guilty because you're human, Seanna. And that monster sitting on the throne is Heylla-born, and has never loved anything but power." The carriage pulled to a stop, and Anne sighed. "I suddenly don't feel like trying on my wedding dress."

Seanna held her hand out, waiting for her to take it. "Yet we're here, and we cannot let the things that linger in our past stop us from moving forward."

Anne held back the words she wanted to say and slid her hand into Seanna's. "How did I get so blessed to have such an intelligent best friend?"

"You missed beautiful, stylish and clever—"

"And humble," Anne said, swinging the door open and pulling Seanna into the shining sunlight, leaving the darkness that had formed with their words to swirl in the carriage.

ANNE GROANED, CURSING HERSELF FOR NOT LETTING Abigail move at least some of her belongings to the lord's wing. Yet, she couldn't give up the place where she felt the most like herself. The awful paintings she had hung, the spread of amber-coloured perfumes under her mirror and the material hanging from her spewing wardrobe. There was no room for her in Hartwinn's rooms—as if, by purpose, the lord who had built Valliss hadn't wished his wife to fill the space. Maybe that was why she would return late at night after they said good night to slip between the cold sheets—to rest peacefully without the ghosts of lords past watching her every move.

The room was cloaked in darkness, only the shining moon cascading through the wide, stained glass windows. Her bed was made, tucked tightly, yet something was deposited on her sheets. Anne strode up to it curiously. It was the bottle of fae wine, sealed in shimmering gold. A note was folded next to it. She snatched it up, and in rudimentary, scratched words, it said:

For next time we are in the gardens.

—H

Anne slumped onto the bed, the bottle rolling and hitting her hip, yet her eyes never left the words. Her fingers traced over each and every one, devouring them. He could have written anything, and she would have cherished it. With a soft exhale, she collected both the letter and wine, and lowered to the stone right under her window, to the loose brick she hid all her secrets in. Grunting, Anne pulled the brick free, pulling the ancient letters out, allowing them to spill across her lap. She placed both the bottle and note in. The fading, yellowed letters were from years passed. Some from Hartwinn, some from Seanna and even ones written by unfitting lovers she had lost time with before committing her heart to Hartwinn. One by one, Anne flicked each open, reading the words, only to shove them back into their hiding place.

Pieces of memories flared, from promises of pleasure from men she would never see again to pages of excited, old gossip from Seanna to the commitment of Hartwinn pouring his adolescent heart out.

All things she once cherished.

With a heave, she replaced the brick. Her hand lingered on the stone as she prayed she wouldn't break her own heart in finding out what she truly wanted from this life.

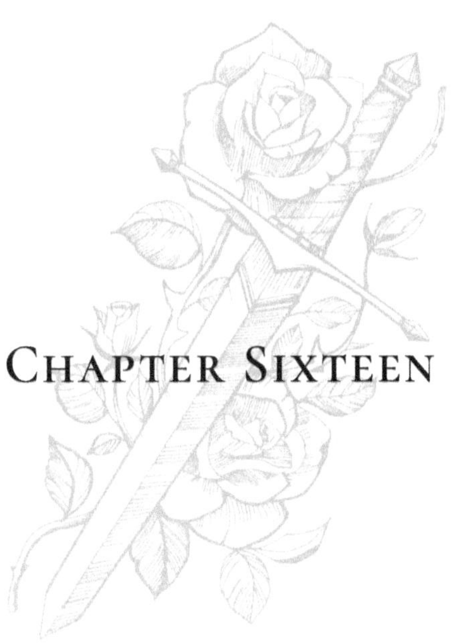

CHAPTER SIXTEEN

THE NIGHT OF DIABLOUS' COMET HAD COME WITH THE strumming of a lute and giggling wine spills across marble floors.

It was more than a stuffy party in a ballroom, but a true night of *sin*.

The great Diabolus' comet was about to fly through their skies, allowing all to give into their basic needs for only as long as the moon was bright in the night sky. As soon as the sun set and the lanterns were lit, women and men swanned out, dressed in scandalous clothing, all wearing half-faced masks—barriers to stop the Dark One finding them and punishing them for their sins when the sun rose.

A masked Anne picked around the people slung across laps and lying stretched out on the grass, a glass of warming sparkling wine in her hand, searching for Seanna and Hartwinn. Both had asked her to meet them there, yet neither were lurking in the shrubs, nor were they splashing in the fountain. Finding a low, stone bench, she plopped herself down and yanked up the velvet-laced bodice Abigail had dressed her in. The cut was lower than she had ever worn, and she had hardly the bosom to fill it, needing an even tighter corset to push up the small amount of cleavage she had.

Two manicured hands curled around her shoulders, sending her eyes wide.

"I'm engaged," Anne yelled, jumping out of her skin.

She whirled around to find a smirking, eye-glinting Seanna, a jittery-looking Henry and Cidran, whose eyes lingered over her on the bodies pressed together, whispering lusty nothings to each other. Hartwinn had his arm slung over Henry's shoulder, swinging from a half-drunk whisky bottle.

"Now, do you wish to have some fun, Annie?" Seanna whispered in her ear, breath hot with drink.

Anne matched her smirk, pulling her mask from her face. "What kind of fun?"

SNEAKING OUT OF VALLISS WAS NOT THE FUN ANNE expected Seanna to suggest, yet it filled her with an exhilarating rush that had her giggling. It had been years since they had ventured into the city without a guard lurking behind them, let alone when the whole city was lit up and people spilt onto the street to share merriment. Yet Anne knew it was more—something in her was driving her towards the city, down to the Lower where the drinks were cheaper but corners more darkened, more hidden. She wished for the anonymity she had found in the forest.

"The whole city is celebrating, Anne," Seanna said as she twirled under a flickering, dirty lamp. "Why should we hide away in Valliss?"

"What if someone recognises us, and whispers find their way up to the castle?" she asked through a giggle, pulling her hood higher, hiding her face from passersby.

Ever-brave Seanna flicked her hood back and shook out her hair. "Let them."

Anne's fingers gripped onto the hood, finding the courage to shove it back. But some of her excitement had been eaten away by that all-devouring anxiety.

Seanna groaned her name.

"What if this gets back to the castle, and it hurts—"

"Hartwinn's *reputation*? Needn't worry your pretty head. He has his own secrets, like how he snuck out that one time to Madame Diamone when he was eighteen, and we didn't see a shadow of him for three days. No one talks of that."

"Well, that was before we—"

Seanna groaned, rolling her eyes. Then, she unceremoniously shoved Anne's hood back. The flickering lantern light captured the silkiness of her loose curls, right down to that excited sparkle in her eye—the one that annoying buzzing had attempted to dim.

"See? So much better," Seanna murmured before turning to the men. "Now, if heavens forbid, we get caught, we just split up. They cannot catch us all."

A loud whistle and rowdy yell of dirty words came from a group of men across the street. Anne narrowed her eyes, feeling that uncomfortable squirm inside her, but Seanna linked her elbow with hers and, without hesitation, shot her middle finger in the air.

"Eyes to yourselves!" Seanna shouted, causing the men to herd them forwards.

"It might be a night of sin, but don't ruin it by getting locked up in the Pali for brawling," Hartwinn said, cheeks flushed.

Laughing, Anne glanced backwards. Henry was watching her as he took a sip from the whisky bottle. A honeyed warmth that burnt in his eyes dripped over her exposed skin, running right to her core.

Hartwinn stumbled sideways, blocking her view of Henry. "Annie, where shall we go?"

"You seem to be known at Madame Diamone's. Shall we go there?"

"How—"

Seanna cackled, slapping her thigh.

"You're the worst at keeping secrets!" Hartwinn exclaimed, eyes crinkling with a grin.

"Me and Anne share everything, isn't that right?"

She nodded enthusiastically. "That is correct."

"Does beautiful Anne know about that one time you got a—"

"Nosebleed and thought she had murdered someone?" Anne cut in. "Yes, that tale always makes me chuckle. All because a lover had accidentally headbutted you when you were drunk, and you woke up to a pool of your own blood and a missing body."

Seanna slapped Hartwinn on the chest. "I honestly thought I had killed him. I was already preparing myself for the Pali."

Hartwinn captured her hand and twirled her around, making her giggle, demanding she dance across the street with him. Soon, Seanna and Hartwinn were swallowed by the masses converging on the street of sin. Anne's heart picked up speed as the crowd pressed towards her as if they were a swirling wave drawing all in its path. She was sucked up as bodies pressed against her, elbows digging into ribs, boots stomping on her skirts. Air was forced from her lungs as she drowned, slippers splashing through the muck as she fought against the crowd. A hand grabbed a fistful of her skirts, and she whirled around to find Henry only inches away from her.

"I've got you, Fate."

"I ... cannot ... breathe," Anne wheezed, eyes wide.

His hand slipped from her skirts to wrap a protective arm around her. He forced his way through the crowd, shoving and pushing. They were abruptly spat out on the other side. A worn, paint-peeled sign hung over them—The Black Raven Inn.

Singing and clinking of glasses filled the air.

"I guess this will do," Henry said, dragging Anne through the swinging doors.

The Black Raven Inn was overwhelmingly loud. Laughter and lute strumming assaulted her eardrums. Rough, dirty men slouched in chairs around solid wooden tables laden with frothy ales and half-drunk wine. Plump, made-up women strode around the room to slink into laps, searching for coin.

The Black Raven wasn't a large, ornate establishment but a dark, dank inn.

Henry pursed his lips for a moment, then Anne laughed. It wasn't the place she expected to find herself in, yet it was perfect. A place for them to simply be them—like it had been in the forest. Before either knew the other's name.

Cidran fell through the doors with a curse. Straightening his surcoat, he winked at Anne and slinked to the back of the inn as if he knew what they both wanted.

Privacy.

Anne hauled Henry towards the bar, right to the ruddy-faced, moustached barman. The flickering lantern light captured her. His eyes widened a fraction as he recognised her. Anne pursed her lips, her hand digging for coins in her pocket.

"What a pleasure to see ya here tonight, my lady. What will you be having? We have wine—"

"Ale. Nothing from the bottom of the barrel either," Henry ordered, dumping a handful of coins across the worn, dented bar. "And your silence. We were not here."

"Of course. Only the best for ya," the barman murmured, giving them a rotten-toothed smile before turning to a silver tap to slosh out the ale.

As she waited, Anne's fingers drummed on the countertop, glancing over her shoulder to find Cidran had slid into a booth, surrounded by rough-looking men holding a ratty deck of cards. Anne turned back, smiling to herself. Henry's scarred, tanned hand spread out beside hers. Her hand flattened, small in comparison to his. His little finger twitched as if demanding to touch hers, and her finger stretched out, brushing ever so slightly.

Anne's lips parted as if to speak, but a drunk shoved Henry aside, demanding another drink, forcing him to stumble into her. The bartop now cut into her spine. He caught himself on the bar, his face only inches from hers. His rich brown eyes met hers, reminding her of the tall pines around her childhood home, lulling her to get lost amongst the branches. Never needing to find her way back.

"Is this a lesson?" he breathed into the tight space they shared.

Anne shook her head, her cheeks bunching with a toothy grin. "This is just ... *fun.*"

Henry's eyes searched her face with such an intensity that her cheeks warmed. He leant in and whispered, "Is it devilish that I wish I was the one who made you smile like that every day?"

Her hand rose to press against his chest as if to push him away. Instead, she fisted the material, drawing him closer. "That is just the whisky talking."

"It might be. Yet it might be the most truthful thing I have said since stepping into that castle."

Anne leant back against the bar, her arms brushing against his. He leant forward as if chasing her, their lips only a hairsbreadth distance. With each whispered word, her lips feathered over his. "We shouldn't—"

"Yet, you do not push me away."

"I …"

His arms tightened around her, caging her in tense muscle. His nose dragged over her cheek, right to the shell of her ear. In a breathy croon, he asked, "Do you ache for me as I ache for you, Fate?"

Before she could answer, a rowdy shout came from the corner, and the clattering of chairs sounded as men rose.

"You stinking fae thief. You cheated!"

Anne glanced over Henry's shoulder to find Cidran standing, hands raised in the air, smug smirk across his freckled face. Three rough men stood around him, a foot taller than him. "I'm no cheater, good sir. You're simply awful at cards."

"You cheated," a bald man with a crooked nose hissed. "And now you'll pay."

A flash of silver gleaned in the low lantern light, and a woman shrieked, launching herself across the room. The barman behind her sighed.

"Now, gentlemen, there is no need for violence. Shall we play another hand, and you can see if you can win back your coin?"

Another rough-looking man with a shaggy beard and a scar across his cheek cracked his neck, then his knuckles.

"I believe your companion is in trouble."

"Is he now?" Henry asked, gaze not leaving Anne, his knee slipping between hers.

Cidran took a step back, hands still raised. One man swung a fist, narrowly missing him. The other launched into an attack, blade slicing and slashing. He dodged and ducked—not gracefully, but with stumbled feet and grimaced flinches. Tables were upturned in the fray, and more women screamed in panic. Tankards were slammed down, and more men began to shout. Then, it wasn't simply the fae and the losers fighting but an all-out brawl. Fists flew in the air, and glass smashed.

"I believe he needs some assistance—"

"Eyes on me, Fate," he crooned, his voice a deep rumble of vowels. "Cidran will be fine. He's a general's son, after all. He can hold his own."

Anne's gaze snapped to Henry, that molten heat at her core popping and splattering at the desire dripping from his words. "And what man lets his friend fight all alone?"

That crooked smirk spread over his face as the door to The Black Raven was swung open with such force that the hinges screamed. Knights of the Silver strode in, their armour gleaming and shining, already shouting for order and calm.

Dayvis amongst them.

Their eyes met, and something akin to disappointment flared in his light blue eyes. That made Anne's heart clench and all the heat drained from her.

She hissed a curse and ducked under Henry's arm. "We have to go—"

"Anne Davoy, if you move another muscle, I will drag you to the Pali myself."

ANNE WAS YANKED BY HER ELBOW DOWN THE STILL-PACKED streets of the Lower by Dayvis. Away from Henry and his burning gaze. Away from the peering, curious gazes of the masses to a small park that sat near the looming Valliss Castle. In the centre stood a young blood oak tree that had just begun its stretch towards the looming starry night. The disappointment radiated off the old knight like a thick stench, coating her.

"Dayvis," Anne said, pulling to a stop. "Dayvis, let me explain—"

He turned to her, his face incredulous. He had never looked at her as if she was a stranger. Now, there was an unknowingness swirling in his eyes.

"Explain? You were all over that man when you wear—"

"Another's ring. I know. I—"

"At least tell me you are drunk," he said, pressing his fingers to his eyes. "I can at least forgive that."

"I haven't had one drink."

"*Anne,*" he groaned, throwing his hands up in the air. "Does Hartwinn know?"

She scoffed. "There is nothing to tell."

"*Nothing?* I may be getting older, but I'm not blind. Nor is that barkeep, or the patrons of that Heylla pit who saw you all but dry hump him."

"I didn't—"

"That is not the point, is it? Whispers contort and change until they resemble nothing of the truth."

Anne slumped against the solid oak's trunk, sliding down into its roots, her forehead falling on her knees. Dayvis let out a soft, almost inaudible groan as he lowered himself next to her.

"Do you want to tell me what's happening?"

Anne turned her head, eyes shining in the light. "I will, but you cannot tell anyone what we are about to talk about—especially Hartwinn. You must vow to me."

"I—"

"Dayvis. *Please.*"

"I vow it."

Anne exhaled, and in the next breath, began to spew the confusing, secret feelings she had into the night. Dayvis leant back on the tree, nodding and clicking his tongue. She finished with a sniff, squeezing her legs tighter, feeling a fraction lighter now that she had vomited all she had in her.

"You must tell Hartwinn."

"Old age must be taking your hearing. I cannot tell him."

"You love him?"

Anne turned to Dayvis, shaking her head. "Henry? It is far too soon to call it—"

"No, girl. Hartwinn," he cut in with an exhale, obviously tiring of her.

"Very much so."

"Then you should tell him. Allow this not to be a secret."

"Then what? I leave court? I have only ever known Alderdeen. It is my home."

"You think when this blows up, you're not going to be leaving Alderdeen? Do you think Hartwinn will let you stay after you pair sneak around behind his back?"

"I ... haven't thought of that."

Dayvis leant back, his eyes going to the sky. "You cannot have both, Anne. You cannot save one heart, thinking you won't hurt the other."

"I don't wish to hurt anyone ..."

"And that is your greatest weakness," Dayvis finished with a sigh. "You don't wish to, but you will. Who do you wish to hurt? A man you desire, who intrigues you, or the man who has loved you since you were both too young to understand what it meant?"

"Who would you choose?"

Dayvis laughed, a deep, rumbling chuckle. "That's not a question I can answer."

"You must have been in love once."

"Yes, Anne. I was very much in love," Dayvis answered softly. "Yet, she was not long for this world. But in the handful of years we spent together, I knew love. That raging fire on a cold winter's night."

"What happened?"

"She had a sickness even the healers couldn't heal."

Anne reached out and gripped the knight's wrist. "You must miss her."

"Every day, every minute, every second," Dayvis said with an exhale and a glance to the night sky. "She would have liked you, Anne."

Her chin wobbled as she fought the tears that brewed. "Dayvis, what do I do?"

"You follow that heart inside your chest, Anne, and try not to look back."

"Look back? Why?"

Ignoring her question, he stood, brushing off the leaf matter. He extended a hand down, helping her to her feet.

"Davyis, why?"

"Because you will not wish to see the trail of destruction you will leave behind by choosing with your heart."

Chapter Seventeen

Anne sat at her designated vanity in Hartwinn's wing of Valliss. She had yielded to his demand and allowed Abigail to bring some of her belongings over. Yet, the maid fluttered nervously behind her, pausing every step, bunching her hands.

"You seem ... *nervous*. Why?"

Abigail squeaked, her eyelashes fluttering. "No reason."

Suspicion rose in Anne, making her narrow her eyes at the maid in the mirror. "Tell me."

"I've been sworn to secrecy," Abigail spluttered.

Anne turned in the chair, her hand gripping the wood. "Abigail, you don't know how to keep a secret. You're the biggest gossip in this place. Now spill."

The maid pressed her lips together and shook her head.

"Anne! Come here at *once!*" Hartwinn yelled from the bedroom, saving Abigail from the grilling she was about to receive. A cold sweat broke out her skin, and that fine tremor began in her fingertips.

He knows about Henry.

Anne stiffly rose, wiping her hands on her gown. She couldn't meet Abigail's gaze as she strode past. But from the corner of her vision, she saw a smile play on the maid's lips.

Something isn't right. This doesn't feel like a death march.

Anne stepped foot into the bedroom, expecting to find a fuming, betrayed Hartwinn. Instead, a line of flickering candles was placed in a softly glowing path.

And no Hartwinn.

She slowly trod around the candles, which led her out to the lord's private garden. Pausing at the door, her eyes trailed over the candles burning brightly against the darkness of the night.

"Hartwinn?" she called out.

"Just down here," he replied from behind a hedge.

Anne, barefoot, stepped out into the night, her skirts trailing over the stairs as her toes met cold, dewy grass. Without hesitation, she sprung over the earth, jumping foot to foot until she found him.

Hartwinn stood over a spread-out rug laden with food, surrounded by only a handful of candles. He was dressed in a soft linen shirt, barefoot, his hair a mess. The Hartwinn she knew. Her heart ached as her eyes took in everything.

"What is this?"

"It's been eight months since we were engaged, Anne. I know they haven't been the easiest, but I thought we could spend the night under the stars. Talking and celebrating—"

"Hartwinn, this is..."

"Too much?" he asked, glancing around

Anne blinked as a tear rolled down her cheek. "It's *perfect.*"

"Why are you crying then?"

She sniffed, swiping the tear away. "I didn't realise how much I missed *you* until right this second."

Hartwinn extended a hand, and with a deep breath, Anne took it, allowing him to lead her over to the rug. He helped her down and dropped a warm blanket over her shoulders, settling beside her, their fingers entwining.

"You're too good to me," she said, her eyes gazing upward. The stars twinkled above her, shining bright in the night sky.

"Am I? I feel awfully rotten at this fiancée thing."

"You've—"

"Do *not* make excuses for me. I have been neglectful. I know that."

"I wouldn't say neglectful."

"What would you say?"

Anne fiddled with the blanket. "Preoccupied."

Hartwinn exhaled at her word, eyes narrowing at the twinkling sky.

"Difficult not to be. The tutors, the quiet talks with Father in his study, all of the books I was forced to memorise never prepared me for this." He paused to scratch his chin. "This is hard. All of it. I never thought—I didn't even consider that I would simply drown."

"Drown? You seem to be thriving."

"Not in all aspects, I see. Things are changing, and not just between us. This world is. And I wish to change with it. I refuse to be stuck in the past with old ideals and even worse values."

"You ..." Anne's gaze sank to their hands. "You wasted all those years only caring what your bastard of a father thought, not fully able to stretch and grow. Now, you can."

"You think so?"

"I know so," she said with a scrunch of her nose.

"I suggested you be a member of my council—"

Anne's gaze snapped to him, surprise working its way through all of the fine muscles in her face. "You did? You never told—"

"I was out-voted," Hartwinn cut in bitterly. "I wasn't aware I could be out-voted. This is my land, and my castle."

"Let me guess. Albert had whispered in ears."

"Whispered? He shouted."

Anne reached over, plucked up a strawberry and popped it into her mouth, allowing the tart sweetness to coat her tongue. "You need to be rid of him. Shall we call Father Pristone to exorcise the castle of his ghost?"

"I'm trying, *believe* me," Hartwinn murmured, eyes widening a fraction.

Anne chewed and said through her mouthful, "Explain?"

"Do I have to?" he asked with a grumbling sigh.

"I know we can discuss the elaborate courses of food for our wedding? First, we have—"

"Good gods, no. Seanna has me well-versed on how many animals are going to sacrifice themselves for our love."

"You seem to be spending an awfully lot of time discussing our wedding with Seanna."

Hartwinn dug around, searching for the ripest berry, not looking at her. Something flared in his eyes, too fast for her to catch it.

"Seanna and I have a meeting every couple of days to discuss it. To appease the council, I do make a big song and dance about how much time she takes up, but honestly, I enjoy spending that time with her. She is very meticulous, calculating, at times frightening. It's admirable. Too bad she was born a woman. She would have been a fearsome nobleman."

Anne's face turned sour at the flippant comment about Seanna's sex. She was formidable regardless of what Deus had formed between her legs.

Hartwinn winced at her reaction, misreading it. "Anne, I presumed you knew of our meetings—"

"You can spend time with Seanna, Hartwinn. Even, more scandalously, not to discuss our pending nuptials, but simply to *talk* to her. She understands more than most of the burden of a title."

"Do you think she would mind?"

Anne reached out and dragged the back of her fingers over the sharp stubble of his face. "Not a single bit. But don't fear. I won't tell her how much you simply *love* discussing lace and ribbon for the flower girls."

Hartwinn grinned to himself—not one she had truly seen before, but in glimpses and in reflections. It was his true smile. A strange feeling grew in her; not jealousy, per se, but another feeling she could not yet describe.

Hartwinn clapped his hands together, rubbing them for warmth. "Now, let me make something up for you."

"I can—"

"I will not hear it. What do you want?"

"I have a cast on, I've not lost a limb ..."

He turned to her, his face softening. "Let me look after you, at least for a *moment*."

"Fine ... *fine*," Anne said, holding her hands up. "Surprise me."

He eyed the yellowing, dirty cast. "When does that come off?"

"Freya said next week. Thank the gods. It's getting itchy," she explained, shifting the cast around to see if she could scratch the never-ending itch that had developed near the dip of her wrist. "And before you wallow, this wasn't your fault."

He reached out, hand falling on the cast. "I can't help but feel—"

"It was the wolf that scared Carrots, not you."

"That mare—"

"Is healed, and ready to ride again," Anne exclaimed, grinning, knowing he wished the same thing that Dayvis had: for Carrots to be dog meat. "Now, that's if you actually ever wish to saddle Boot and ride with me again."

He leant over and nuzzled her neck. "That's not the riding I'm interested in."

Anne giggled, pushing him away. Each touch flipped her stomach, forcing guilt to churn uncomfortably in her guts. "Now, I don't believe I'm the meal—"

"You could b—"

Anne pressed her hand over his mouth. "Not tonight. Tonight, we *talk*."

Hartwinn nodded, smiling against her palm. He reached up and pulled her hand away. He leant in, eyes solely focused on her lips. "At least one kiss. You wouldn't deprive a man of one kiss."

Anne smirked, leaning back on one hand. "I may."

"You may?" Hartwinn replied, slinking forwards, climbing over her discarded blanket. His hand pressed against the space between her crossed legs, bringing his face to hers. "You cruel woman, you torture me so."

"And I will torture you for the rest of your days."

"Sweet torture, if I say so myself."

Anne's smirk widened to a grin. It was easy, simple and uncomplicated. *Why can't my heart thud harder for Hartwinn? Why can't whatever is forcing me and Henry together gently guide me to Hartwinn instead?* None of it was fair—especially to Hartwinn. He hadn't a clue of the battle forming inside her.

"I'm suddenly famished," Anne said drily, nodding to the spread of cheese, meats and fruit. "You wouldn't let your betrothed waste away, now, would you?"

Hartwinn searched her eyes for a moment, a flash of disappointment crossing his features, but it was hidden by his eye-crinkling grin. "As you wish."

Pinching with his fingers, he laid cheese and cut meat on a slice of thick, crusty bread and offered it to her. Her stomach grumbled in appreciation. Anne leant forward and took one big bite, her eyes meeting his, a charge of heady desire filling the air.

One she squashed with an obnoxious chew.

"Now, tell me how you are going to convince that bag of bones he needs to return to his grave."

Hartwinn passed over her open sandwich, then took a sip of wine from the bottle and considered his words. "We isolate him. Force him into a corner."

"Wouldn't that simply make him snap his teeth?"

Hartwinn grinned, a feral stretch of his lips. "That's exactly what I want. I want him *desperate*. I want him plotting."

Anne chewed as her mind turned over. "So you can shame him in the eyes of the court? Does he still have shame in that dried piece of jerky he calls a heart?"

"I want to ruin him," Hartwinn said softly. "I want to make sure he can never weasel his way back into my council."

"What about the other ghouls?"

"I want them gone as well."

Hartwinn was plotting. It suddenly made sense why he never stood his ground against Albert at the party. He needed to lull him into a sense of security of feeling like he had Hartwinn in his pocket.

"You're a sneaky little viper, aren't you? You're almost as venomous as old Hicka."

Hartwinn laughed, shaking his head. "Gods forbid I ever turn into her. Now, what I truly want, Anne, is to build this city into much more than what it is today. I want it bustling with industry, farms and families. I want this place to be bursting at the seams."

"You wish to rival Goulrich, don't you?"

"No," he said seriously. "I want to *surpass* Goulrich. If I had my way, I would rule this land separate from Ewan."

"King Hartwinn Novak has a certain ring to it," Anne joked, bowing her head, hand waving.

"I like the sound of that," he murmured, thumb tracing over the lip of the bottle.

"Oh, please! If they crowned you king, they'd have to forge something to fit your humongous head."

"And you, queen. Imagine the matching crowns. What jewels do you wish for yours?"

She scoffed, finishing the bread. "I will never be a queen."

"You were born to be more than a wife, Anne. Remember that."

Anne stretched her legs out, considering his words. Was she more than a title, more than a lady wife? That question had her wrestling with her sheets nightly.

"You know, if you rid your council of Albert, Frederick ... and what's his name?" she asked, changing the subject.

"Robert."

"But they hold lands and riches—"

"And so do you. So does Henry. Why does it have to be the old blood of Alderdeen who make decisions for a new era?"

Anne reached out and cupped his face. "You're a dreamer, Hartwinn Novak. A brave one, at that, and I, for one, cannot wait to see this city bloom under your gentle, kind hands."

He turned and pressed his lips to the slow, thudding pulse of her wrist.

"My hope is that long after my skeleton turns to dust, this city will remember the lord who brought the melting pot of people together in *peace*. That any differences can be settled in council rooms with handshakes, not in muddy battlefields with the dead and dying."

"And it will be glorious," she whispered. "This utopia of peace."

"And you, Anne, will be by my side, ruling alongside me."

She shifted over, resting her temple on his shoulder, her eyes searching the night sky. *Will I, or will that driving force tear us apart, only to stitch our hearts to others? Would mine even survive it?*

Anne pressed a kiss to his shoulder and smiled up at him. "Let us ponder more about Alderdeen's future in bed."

"Does that mean—"

"Not every night. I think we still need space. But tonight, yes."

He grimaced and asked, "Why? Haven't I given you enough?"

"I don't wish to depend on you so, Hartwinn."

He shook his head, that earnest look flashing. "Anne, you can—"

She rolled her eyes and groaned. "Please, if you say I can depend on you for anything and everything, I will simply return to my chambers, much less speak to you again. You must let me do this."

Hartiwnn nodded, rising to his feet, stretching out the aches from sitting on the cool ground. "If it is just for tonight, I'm happy. Maybe I can convince you."

Anne looked up at him. "And I shall allow myself to be convinced until you snore in my ear at the bell at three in morning, and the urge to smother you becomes difficult to resist."

Hartwinn laughed as he heaved her to her feet. His fingers linked with hers as he drew her inside, where the candles burnt low, and the bed was warm. Then, Anne got her wish. They talked and talked as the moon travelled across the sky—yet their words lacked substance, meaning. They talked about everything but nothing at the same time. And as sleep dragged her down into the murky abyss of tall pines and Henry's burning gaze, Anne had a disappointing realisation—she hadn't ever been allowed to truly be herself, not since a cold governess struck her knuckles. In harsh whispers, she was told what she would be: the agreeable, subservient wife who tried everything she could to please her lord husband. That depleted, anemic version of herself was what the world saw. Not all those saw that. A pair of woody brown eyes saw her and didn't look away. As Anne tossed and turned, suddenly awake with her runaway thoughts, she didn't know if she was still that woman—or if she ever *had* been.

Chapter Eighteen

The stomp of a boot crushing Anne's toes for what felt like the seventh time that afternoon was her last straw. Her legs tangled as Henry stepped forward, missing the beat she called out. He looked pensive, bordering on uncomfortable as he lumbered around the empty throne room. His body was stiff, and all his movements sharp.

Anne's voice simmered away until she could hear Henry murmuring the steps to himself, eyes on his feet. Even that thrill of pressing skin to skin had faded with each day they had spent stumbling around. Yet, she still cherished every moment with him, even if her toes were spotted with purple bruises.

"This isn't working—"

"I nearly have it."

Anne pulled him to stop and untangled herself from his grip. "No, you don't. We've been working on this for *two* weeks. The ball is only a handful of weeks away. I'm not a miracle-worker."

Henry raised his arms, a determined look setting on his face. "Just one more time."

Anne rubbed the throbbing ache from her newly released wrist. Freya had warned her not to overuse it, that the bones may not have fused completely. Yet, she had allowed Henry to awkwardly spin her around the ballroom, pulling and yanking on her until she had begged Abigail to give her the tonic Freya had left her.

There must be something else we can do, she thought, bringing her finger to her lips.

Selfishly, she wanted to prove to the fan-waving gossips that a gentleman was peeking through the rough exterior of the sword-wielding warrior. And she wanted to be the one to shine him.

Henry dropped his arms, his lips pinched with disappointment. "I told you I don't dance."

Anne scoffed a laugh. "You said that you *don't* dance, not that you are truly *awful* at it."

"Maybe it's the teacher—"

"Me? I'm an impeccable dancer," she said, pressing her hand to her chest. Then, she reached out and poked him square in the chest. "You're the one with two left feet, and I have the bruised toes to prove it."

"Then what shall we do? I could simply not dance—"

"Not dance at the ball held in your honour?" Anne cut in, her voice incredulous. "That is utterly *ridiculous.* You will be expected to at least dance once—or twice, depending if you find the right partner." She sighed, brows bunching. "We simply have to get you to relax. Then, the steps will come."

"How will I ever relax here?" Henry asked, raising his arms. "This is enemy territory. I was trained to never relax here. To always be on guard. Never let my concentration lapse, or it means *death.*"

"This is simply a room, Henry."

"And where I felt most comfortable was in that dingy inn. But I do not believe we can return there. Not without a comet in the sky."

His words were laced with an unspoken meaning—one Anne dared not delve into.

Spiral later, she commanded herself. *Overthink his words later.*

"Henry—"

"I am not done. I want to tell—"

An idea struck her like a lightning strike, forcing her to rush to the door, cutting his words from his mouth. She grinned over her shoulder. "This is a battlefield. Not only for you, but for all those who will dance here. How about we go to the place where peace is found?"

"Where?"

"Just come. I know exactly where to go."

Valliss' stables were bustling and busy, with men and women streaming through the wide open sliding doors, carrying bales of itchy hay or leading whining horses into the small pens. Henry paused, hands going to the edge of his shirt, pulling it down a fraction. A flicker of a muscle worked in his jaw.

Anne reached out and tugged on his sleeve, waking him. "There is nothing to fear here, I promise."

He nodded, distracted. His eyes roamed over the fine hand carving nestled between the roof and the door. It was nothing like the cool, grey stone of Valliss. Even Anne, who spent more time within the four walls of the stables than in the trinket-filled sitting rooms—much to Seanna's dismay—hadn't a clue why it was so tenderly carved and cared for.

Anne cast a toothy grin to Henry and turned and walked backwards. "Are you coming? Carrots needs a brush, and she bit three stable-hands yesterday, so no one is going near her."

"A fae built this," Henry said softly. His hand rose to rest on the carved panels. His finger traced the lines.

Anne stopped and glanced up. Her eyes found a rush of horses, surrounded by leaves and vines etched into the dark, glossy wood. "How do you know?"

"This is the same one I grew up under," Henry explained as his shoulders relaxed. "The fae believe these carvings are blessed to protect the horses inside. I never thought I would see it again."

"Why?"

"Ewan burnt it down when he attacked the manor I spent my childhood in."

Anne exhaled his name, her eyes flashing to him.

"I shouldn't speak on this—"

"No, you should. We need to know what poison our king has infected this land with," Anne cut in, her hand raised to join his. The wood felt smooth and warm under her palm. She thought she would struggle to find the words to soothe him, yet the words fell from her. "This has been here longer than anyone can remember, and I believe this will be here when we turn to dust. May this give you some comfort."

He turned to her, poised to speak, yet no words left his mouth. All he did was stare at her. His gaze pierced her—not like a punch in the guts, but in the way that light punctured through a dark room, bright and radiating.

"Come, Henry. Carrots will wait for no one."

A sharp curse cut through the quiet murmuring, making Anne rush through the stable, Henry in tow. Right to Carrots' stall. A frowning, cursing young stablehand was leaning half out of her stall, climbing over the door to get away from the mare.

Anne's skin prickled as Carrots' teeth snapped in the air.

"Oi, get away from me, Rotten," he commanded, kicking his short legs to get purchase over the stall door. He fell in a heap at Anne's feet, his eyes widening as he took her in.

"Good afternoon. Is Carrots misbehaving?"

"My lady, I didn't know you were comin' to the stables today," he said as he scrambled to his feet. "She tipped her food over, and I was goin' in—"

Anne's narrowing eyes flicked to the puffing mare behind the boy. "She does that on purpose to lure you in. You must be new."

"Mylo, Lady Novak," the boy stammered, bending at the hip.

"Anne. Please, just Anne." She took a step towards the horse, reaching out for the mare's soft nose. "Now, Mylo, Carrots has a foul temper, but she loves a scratch between her eyes."

"Nah, miss, I will not be puttin' my hand near her ever again," he replied, scurrying backwards and running into the shining afternoon sun.

Henry settled next to Anne, reaching out and scratching Carrots right between the eyes. "You gave that boy a right spook, pretty girl."

Carrots batted her long, blonde lashes at him, soft puffs leaving her.

"*Ciùin*," Henry breathed with a soft grin.

Anne watched as his gaze trailed over Carrots' long face, taking her in with a wide-eyed reverence.With her cheeks heating, she realised that is exactly how he looked at her—and now she knew why everyone had seen it but her. It was obvious.

Anne cleared her throat to force the ball of emotion out. "I will get the brush."

Upon returning, after taking a few deep breaths to soothe her nerves, she found Henry already in Carrots' stall with a handful of hay. The mare munched happily as he whispered to her, low enough for her to only catch a few words.

"Are you enamoured with my horse?" Anne asked, slipping into the stall.

Henry turned to her, that crooked grin spreading. "With something, Fate."

She pushed Carrots' food-seeking head away and dragged the stiff-bristled brush over the deep dip of her back. Henry lingered close, not because of the size of the stall but because of the driving force that drew them together, a lingering hand between her shoulder blades.

The sound of the soft scratching of the brush filled the ever-growing tension between them.

"May I?" Henry asked, settling behind her.

Anne nodded, her chest rising and falling.

His warm hand trailed over the dip of her wrist, only to encapsulate hers. She parted her fingers, allowing his to slide between hers. Anne couldn't look away from how well their hands fitted together as if they were made for each other. She let the traitorous thought settle between her ears as he dragged his thumb down over the webbing between her forefinger and thumb. Her eyes traced the fleeting touch over her skin.

"You know, we have a tale in Orynile, Fate, about the song of Oryah's heart."

"Will you tell me?" Anne asked in a soft voice.

Henry ducked his head, bringing it closer to the nape of her neck. She could feel his breath cascade over exposed skin with each muttered word. "It would be my pleasure."

Anne allowed her eyes to blur as Henry took a steadying inhale and began.

"It all started when Oryah, bleeding and scared, fled to Heylla. Terrified that Diabolus would entrap her as his brother had done, she hid deep in the Dead and Dying Forest, surrounding herself with stripped, bare trees. Nothing like her glorious gardens. That was until a man found her, muddy and dressed in rags. He took her in, gave her a warm meal and a soft bed. He was kind and caring. Nothing like she had ever known, for she had only known cruelty and submission at the hands of Deus. Weeks passed, and Oryah, now not fearful of being caught, began to leave the cabin to walk amongst the trees. But everywhere her fingers touched, life bloomed—much like the feelings between her and the mysterious man. But, in her grand wisdom, she knew he wasn't simply a man, as none could live in this hellscape."

"It was Diabolus, wasn't it?"

"Yes, the Dark One himself," Henry answered, inching closer until his body met hers, warm and unyielding against soft and malleable. "The man who shared her bed, who made her feel safe, reached into her chest and ripped her heart clean from her body. As he held the still-pumping organ in his bloody claw, Oryah braced herself for him to crush it, proving he was the master trickster. To her surprise, he reached inside himself and ripped his own heart out. Tearing muscle from sinew, he held them close together, and what made the glorious goddess fall to her knees was—"

"What? What happened?" Anne cut in, needing to know.

Henry let out a huffed chuckle. "Patience, Fate. Their heartbeats timed, moving in sync. Instead of crushing it, he protected it, cherished it and honoured it."

Anne softly exhaled. "Then?"

"Love bloomed, Fate, in a world that only knew pain, suffering."

"I worry about what happens next, Henry, for I know Oryah as Deus' divine wife."

"Deus finally found her, feeling her magic through the earth." Henry's hand tightened on hers as his voice became a fraction harder. "He threatened war on Heylla if Diabolus didn't give her up. Oryah, knowing the world she had come to love would be destroyed, sacrificed herself. Deus forced her to return to the heavens to rule her great garden and be his queen. In her despair, Oryah broke her heart in two, casting one half to Diabolus so he could hold it close to his to hear the song their hearts sung to each other, and keeping the other half to remind her that she was loved, wholly and fully."

"But what of Diabolus?"

Henry's hand skimmed over her hip, only to spread out over fluttering flowers on her bodice, drawing her ever closer. "Well, he stitched that part of her heart to his so they would always beat as one."

Anne held in a gasp as the rhythmic thudding of Henry's heart drummed against the bare skin between her shoulder blades. "Go on. This tale feels unfinished."

"When my ancestors defended the Great Forest against a terrible enemy, Oryah blessed the fae with the gift she had given Diabolus: two hearts beating for one another. We call them a heart's match."

Anne let out a soft sigh as the last of his warm breath prickled her skin. Her mind raced to catch up with the barrage of thoughts that wound his words together and the thudding of her heart.

"Anne, I need you to say—"

"That is beautiful, Henry. Truly. I guess Diabolus is not all fire and brimstone then."

"He is simply misunderstood."

Silence simmered between them as thoughts tangled and snagged on the rocky ridges of Anne's mind. She turned in his arms, brush falling to their feet. Her hands skimmed over the linen shirt he wore, right over honed muscles to his forearms. A line had formed between his brows, and his shoulders were tense. He radiated a worried energy as if he had given too much away.

"Dance with me."

Henry let out a choked laugh as the muscles in his neck relaxed. "Right here?"

"Right here," Anne repeated, her hands finding his.

Without letting him think, she stepped back, and Henry mirrored her.

He never once looked away from her face.

His boots never found her toes.

They simply stepped and spun around Carrots' stall. Henry's hand slid down, falling on the small of her back. With a gentle pull, he closed the gap between their bodies until they were flush, swaying together. It was a different kind of dancing—not made for ballrooms or loud parties, but quiet moments and night-chilled balconies.

"Henry ..." Anne whispered into the space between their bodies. "Do you think a human could be a fae's heart's match?"

As soon as the words left her, that crackling tension snapped in two. Henry pulled away from her, a crevasse opening between them. His warm, honey eyes hardened, dipping from her.

"No," he replied through a clenched jaw.

"But what if it was a possibility?"

"No, Anne. It is not possible. Me and you—"

"I was *not* speaking about you and me," Anne cut in quickly, as if to cover up the strange truth that lingered in the air.

His eyes flashed to hers, and hurt brewed like a thunderstorm, threatening to pour down on them.

"A human and fae could never be a heart's match," Henry explained, shaking his head as if to convince himself. "Oryah binds the matched lives when they bond. It would force the fae to give up their long life to only live a handful of years. That is *cruel*."

Anne kicked her slipper against the soft hay. "I wouldn't wish to live if the one Oryah fated me too was not in it. That is kindness, not cruelty."

"It *cannot* be, Anne," he said firmly.

"Why not?" she asked, hating that desperate tone that made her snap her vowels.

A sharp exhale left him. "Because it would end in heartbreak, Fate. For both of them. This world is not ready for love to bloom between the fae and humans, as much as we want it to. It would be a battle every day to prove their love should be celebrated and not shunned."

Anne shook her head. "Isn't that once-in-a-lifetime love worth fighting for?"

"Be as that may, Fate, this is a fight even you would lose. And there is no dagger-throwing knight to help this time."

Anne raised her chin, setting it at a determined angle. "Then I would go down swinging, Henry Ashmore. I would give it all I had, fighting until my last breath."

"But I have fought enough, Anne. I am tired. So very tired."

"I—" She cleared her throat. "It would be worth it, Henry, even for a handful of years."

His eyes rose to hers as a small, sad smile spread on his face. "That's the problem, Fate. I know it would be worth it as it torments me at night as I toss and turn, aching for it. I dream of it every time I close my eyes. It lingers on every stray thought, catching me in the chest. It would all be worth it. Yet, I hesitate, finding reasons for it not to work, creating scenarios in my mind that only make me panic. The battle still remains in me, and I do not know if I can fight what is inside of me *and* the entire world."

Henry stepped back, lips pressed together as if he spoke too many truths. Anne followed him, her hand reaching for his. But he scurried back from her touch, slipping from the stall.

Anne and Carrots rushed to the stall door, only to watch him stride through the stable, only pausing to glance up once, then disappearing into the light, never looking back. Carrots butted her head against her arm as if she was demanding she run after him. But Anne simply stood there and wondered why, of all things they had spoken of, that was what Henry decided to lie to her about.

He was fighting. He was fighting with all he had.

CHAPTER NINETEEN

Anne cut Dilon off with a sharp wave of her hand as she pulled to a stop right in front of Hartwinn's war room. In her fist was a crumpled scroll, and within her was a burning anger. She exhaled and inhaled, her shoulders rising with each breath. There was no shoving the feeling down. Not now. Not after it was so out of control, boiling over the edges. She plastered a strained smile across her face. Dilon's face bunched with apprehension.

"I beg your pardon for my shortness, sir. I simply received terrible news, and I need to speak with Hartwinn at once."

"No need to beg, my lady. He is currently in session with his council. He has been for hours."

"Perfect. They should hear this as well."

Dilon nodded, opening the door a crack. Arguing voices flooded the corridor as Anne slid through.

Hartwinn's war room was large and spacious, filled with leather lounges. A table sat in the centre with high-backed, uncomfortable-looking chairs, parchment spread across the smooth, glossy surface. On the walls were painstakingly painted scenes of hunting dogs and gallant knights in shining armour. A fire blazed, creating that uncomfortable wick of sweat on her skin as she stood at the closing door. Only one set of eyes turned to her—Henry's.

Their eyes met, and a spark crackled through the over-warmed air.

"Hartwinn, I bel—'

"They shouldn't have too much say in where they are going," Albert croaked from his chair, cutting Henry off. "They are refugees, after all. They should be happy with what they get."

He spoke as if Henry were not in the room—no wonder blades were drawn.

"But the rocky outcrop? No, we should give them the Westryn District. Far enough out of the city that they can congregate," another councilman said, "And close enough that they can edge the city."

"Gentlemen, I believe we—"

Hartwinn leant back, still not taking notice of her. "Westryn district is where I envisioned all along, yet I wish for Henry's kind to mingle—"

"Lady Anne is in the room," Henry said, standing. Just as she had taught him.

The scrapes of chairs—all but one, Albert's—filled the room.

"Anne, what a surprise! You've caught us in an impasse," Hartwinn said as he rounded the table towards her, his arms outstretched.

She strode towards him and shoved the crumbled parchment at his chest. "He sits on my land's borders."

"Wait, what? Who?"

"Our glorious king."

"Anne—"

"Were you going to wait until we were handfasted to give him allowance to my lands, or will you give the order now?"

"I have no—"

"My men have spotted Ewan's forces gathering on the borders of my ancestral lands, and I will *never* give him permission to cross into them."

"I haven't the faintest ..." He took the scroll, rolling it open, his words fading as his eyes narrowed at the letter. He cursed softly, returning to his chair, eyes glued to the missive.

"He doesn't need your *permission*, you daft girl. He is the king," Albert said with a scoff, turning his milky gaze on her. "It would be best if you left this for the men to discuss."

"I do not recall asking for your advice, sir, nor do I wish for it," Anne said tersely.

"Yet, here you are storming in here as if this castle is already yours," Albert said, waving his wrinkled hand at her.

"It is mine. This is my home, and this is Lord Hartwinn's council room, not *yours*."

"You have yet to prove your worth to the court."

Another sick, hand-clenching wave of anger rose. Through an exhaled breath, she asked, "And how do I do that?"

A sick tilt of his lips appeared as he replied, "I think you're very well-versed in that, Anne."

Hartwinn's eyes shot up over the scroll, but before he could speak, Henry rose. Indignation flared and flickered over his features. He leant over the old man, lip twitching upwards. "You say anything like that to Lady Anne *ever again*, and you will meet your god before you are due to."

"Hartwinn, control your beast," Albert snapped, his voice wavering.

"Henry, please," Hartwinn said, raising his hand.

He returned to his chair, his body tense, eyes narrowed on the talking skeleton. His hand rested on the table, his forefinger tracing a split in the wood from where he stuck his blade.

"Now, Lady Anne has an esteemed place in this court, Albert, as my soon-to-be lady wife and the mother of my children. She may wish to discuss matters that are befitting of her station—"

"Befitting of her station? She should be discussing which flowers to have at this farce of a ball, not war. She is a woman, and she's far too *emotional* to even be considered of any use. Look at her raging and pouting."

Anne's eyes flashed to Hartwinn as Albert's words punched her in the guts. *Just a* woman. *Hartwinn's wife, the mother of his children. And that's all I will ever be—at least in this court's eyes. Yet, that's all I've ever wanted. So why would him saying those words ever hurt me?*

"Lady Anne is intelligent, quick-witted and loyal. You speak of her as if she hasn't a brain between her ears," Henry said with barely restrained anger. "She has every right to question why your king is lingering close to her lands."

Hartwinn's eyes returned to the scroll. "This *doesn't* mean he will march, Anne—"

"And it doesn't say he comes in peace, does it?"

"War is an art form many women do not understand," Fredrick said softly with a condescending nod.

"I understand it plenty, sir. Yet, when was the last battle any of you saw? Aside from Henry, of course."

"I was in the—"

"Yes, the Great Battle of Widows Peak, and your valiant efforts gained us, what? A plot of land which sheep graze on."

Hartwinn placed the scroll on the table. "Anne—"

She took a step towards his council. "You forget that Hartwinn and I had the same tutors. Lord Novak demanded it. I know each and every battle you won and *lost*, Albert. Shall we drag a skeleton or two out of y—"

"That is enough, Anne," Hartwinn cut in sharply. "We do not need you goading these men. We are trying to better this city, not set it alight."

"Hartwinn—"

"I shall deal with this. You should retire for the evening."

"You will not dismiss me like I'm some petulant child—"

Hartwinn rose, pressing his hands on the table. "You've been given an order, Anne. Now, go to bed."

She stood, rooted to the spot. He had never spoken to her in such a tone before, especially not in front of his council. Anne knew she had gone too far, pushed too hard and expected too much. She allowed that flicker of hot emotion to control her instead of smothering it.

And she didn't regret a single word.

"Please, Anne. Do not make me ask again."

His words unrooted her, causing her to sprint from the room. As the door closed, Anne heard the vile words leaving Albert's mouth, "You'll need to take a cane to that one." Then, the crashing of wood against stone and men yelling.

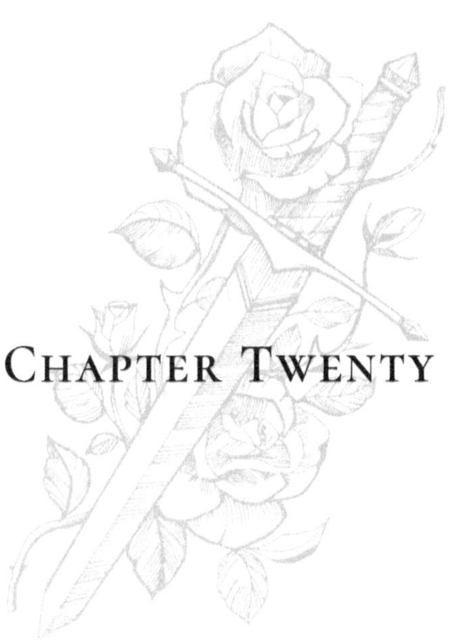

Chapter Twenty

The ground was damp, soaking through Anne's slippers as she stomped through the night-fallen garden. The laced edges of her skirts captured the settling dew as she drew closer to the looming walls of the castle. Reaching out, she dragged her fingers over the rough, moss-covered stone. Valliss had never had iron bars on it until now.

"Deus damn you, Hartwinn," she muttered, voice thick with anger.

Turning, Anne slid down the wall, allowing her skirts to poof out like an over-iced cake. Closing her eyes, she reclined her head until the chignon at her nape, made of pins and gems, crushed against the rock. The dirt under her fingers was cold, damp, forthcoming to her digging. She wanted to burrow away, run towards the home she had left when her parents had died. Did it even exist anymore, or would she find an abandoned house with overgrown vines cutting through the walls and cobwebs in the corners?

A presence settled over her—one that smelt distinctly like fresh rain, cut timber and old leather. She breathed him in, allowing what it sparked in her to settle deep in her chest.

"It is far too nice of a night to be alone, wouldn't you think?" a voice asked, rumbling with humour.

Anne cracked an eye open to find Henry standing over her, his unbound dark hair curtaining his high cheekbones. He looked flushed, jittery. His eyes, darker in the nighttime, matched the twinkling sky above. A crooked smirk curled on his face, making her lips twitch upward.

"Much too nice. Care to join me?" Anne asked, patting the ground next to her.

Henry sighed and sat down, resting against the stone. His long legs brushed over the vast material of her skirts. He glanced at her, then down at her dirt-encrusted fingers. "Planning an escape route from that torrid display?"

"If only it were that easy."

"What do you mean?"

She dragged her knees to her chest, resting her cheek on the knobbly part of her knee. "You see, there is a gods-awful law."

"A law?"

Anne sighed. "As the first of the wars was starting, noblemen were dying in troves, leaving mothers, daughters and sisters with riches, lands and titles. A wave of women were gaining power, and the king's father wouldn't have it. So, he decreed a law that women could not access their own inheritance until they turned twenty-five. Unless—"

"They marry before then, and it goes to their husband," Henry finished.

"Correct," Anne punctuated with a pop of her lips. "So, masses of women who should have held their families' titles were married off. Some as young as thirteen."

"And they call us barbaric," Henry muttered. He glanced at her sideways and added, "And I presume you are an heiress to an enormous fortune, as well as vast properties."

"Correct ... again. I'm a duchess, to be exact."

Henry looked away, a tight look flashing on his face. "Hartwinn ... He loves you, Anne. He wouldn't simply allow that."

She frowned at him, annoyance bubbling in her. "So that justifies him relegating me to a life of child-rearing and boring balls?"

"I never said—"

"I'm wholly certain of Hartwinn's feelings for me. But would that love for me risk civil war? I don't believe so." Anne sighed. "And I don't wish to marry because they believe they have a *right* to me or my lands."

"What are you saying?"

She rolled on to her knees to face him, allowing the tirade of angry thoughts she had held in to spew out. "When I marry someone, it'll be because I cannot stand to think of a morning where I don't wake up beside them. I'd rather burn with desire, ache for him, than feel only a flicker of a flame. And don't get me started on children. I will have them when I choose to, not because I'm forced to—"

Henry interrupted her rant with a soft exhale. "Love, Anne. You want *love*."

"I am in love," she snapped defensively.

He shook his head, his hands smoothing on his thighs. "You are not *in* love with him, Anne."

Her gaze snapped to Henry, denials ready to fall off her tongue. Instead, she drew an unsteady breath in.

"Then is that asking too much?" Her eyes rose to the sparkling, twinkling sky, only to return to Henry. "Is being in love with the man I marry too much to ask?"

He searched her face as something she couldn't name roared to life in his gaze—one that slid over her chilled arms, embracing her. One her heart leapt on and held tight.

"No. That is not too much to ask."

A tear rolled down her cheek as her jaw trembled. "Then why does it feel *impossible*?"

He raised his hand to brush the tear from her, but it dropped into his lap instead. "I ... don't know, Fate."

"And Hartwinn thinks of me as the same knobbly-kneed seventeen-year-old who kissed him in a maid's closet, but I'm not." Anne's hand spread over her racing heart. "I'm a woman with womanly desires and a half-intelligent head on her shoulders."

Henry's gaze dipped to her lips. "I do not see a girl. I see a woman— a smart, caring dreamer, but a woman nonetheless."

Tears rushed from her eyes in surprised blinks. She hadn't expected him to say that.

"You ..."

"I see you, Anne," Henry said softly. "I see *you*."

She pressed forward, closing the space between them. Her lips pressed against his. She was desperate to touch him, to feel the thump of her heart push something outside of that wallowing worry around her body. He reached up and gripped her biceps. There was a slight tremor in his hands. Anne thought he was going to drag her closer, but instead, he gently pushed her back, breaking them apart. Henry released her reluctantly, finger by finger. She dared not read too much into it.

He scrubbed his jaw, looking torn. "We shouldn't have done that."

She rubbed the tears away with her palm. "You should know better than to tell me what to do."

"You cannot lose yourself with me, nor hide from the heartbreak in my arms. This is not a simple roll in the hay. This means more, and I cannot allow it to mean more."

"Henry, please," she whispered as more salty droplets rolled down her cheeks. Anne wasn't beneath begging, but she knew it wasn't her he was resisting. It was the slip of metal on her finger or the new one around his neck.

"I need this alliance to work for my people," Henry choked out the words as if he didn't believe them himself.

"And I complicate it?"

"You ... *complicate* it?" He paused, searching her eyes. "You are something else. Nothing I have ever encountered. But, I need to put my people first, to find them a home. My king has demanded it, and I cannot disappoint him."

"At the risk of your own happiness? Your own desires?"

Henry closed his eyes. "Yes."

"I see ..." Anne said, scrambling to her feet. The rejection turned her bitter, angry. "And what? You will keep longingly staring at me across the dining table?"

He rose, shaking his head. "If it makes you uncomfort—"

"And *what*? Am I only worth something when I'm nameless in a forest?"

Henry's face hardened, jaw set. "And you seem to only want me when you are drunk or crying. Am I just a distraction for a bored lady? Or have you grown tired of Hartwinn rutting between your—"

Anne's hand flew, slapping Henry across the cheek. The skin-prickling noise filled the air. "You brute, how *fucking dare* you!"

"How dare I?" Henry bent at the hip, anger flaring in his nostrils. "I am not the one about to get fucking married, but talking of love and smelling the way you do."

"Smelling the way I do?"

"You smell intoxicating, ruinous," he snapped, growling. "I cannot stand it."

Anne shook her head, taking a few steps back towards the castle. "If you cannot stand me, and I'm the complication, I should leave."

Henry let loose a few ragged breaths. "Anne—"

"What?" she asked, whirling around. "What do—"

He pressed his lips to hers. Not a shy, chaste peck. He devoured her, sucking all the meat from the bones, leaving her aching and bare. A whisper of a groan came from Henry as their lips parted and met in more fervent kisses. He tasted of honeyed, smokey warmth as if she'd drunk a glass of whisky. Worse, he tasted *right*. Anne's hand went to his chest, tangling in the lacing of his shirt, feeling the cold gold mix with warm skin under her fingertips. She stepped him backwards, legs entwining. With a sharp turn, Henry had her against the wall, pinned by his hips. His hand roamed her as if to remember each dip and curve of her body, only to slide down her skirts, yanking them up. Her soft skin was caressed by the cool night air, waking her from that feverish dream.

"Wait—"

"Good goddess, Fate," Henry murmured against her temple, breath cascading over her prickling skin. "I *ache* for you."

It took all her willpower to press her hand to his chest and push him back a fraction. "Not here. Never here."

Henry nodded, brushing his lips against her forehead. "When? Where?"

Anne swallowed, her mind whirling. "The Black Raven Inn. Tomorrow at midnight."

He reluctantly pulled away, only to lean back in and press a kiss to her lips. "I'll be there."

She stood for a long while after he had left, heat draining from her bones, right into the damp earth below her, waiting for that sick, stomach-churning feeling of betrayal to rise. For the tears of regret to come. And as the moon travelled across the sky and right into the early morning, neither ever did.

CHAPTER TWENTY-ONE

THE DOOR TO ANNE'S BEDROOM CRACKED OPEN, AND THE beam of light cut through the dim of her room. Hartwinn stood in the doorway, the collar of his shirt open, shirt untucked. But the stench of whisky didn't follow him. Anne rose quickly from the drawer she was digging through, realising she was still fully dressed, not in the night-gown he would expect her to be in. She racked her mind for an excuse, but all the useless organ could do was remind her that midnight bell would toll any minute, and Henry would be waiting for her.

"Anne?" Hartwinn called out. "You're still awake."

"Hartwinn," she said quickly. "What are you doing here?"

"I ..." he spluttered, stepping into the room. "I thought I could come watch you sleep for a while."

Anne blinked at him, confused. "What has happened?"

He exhaled, scratching his chin. "I've just got word that Ewan sent men to raid a village that held rebel forces. Only fifty miles from the border of my land. Far enough from here he didn't think I'd find out."

"Good gods," Anne breathed. "Did any—"

"No one, Anne. No one survived." Hartwinn sniffed, his hand working harder on his chin, tears shining in his eyes. "Not even a single woman or child. They burnt the village to embers."

Anne's hand slapped over her mouth. A soft gasp came from her.

"I could have stopped it—"

"Nothing could have stopped it," she cut in, taking a step towards him. "Ewan will do as he pleases, as he always has done."

Hartwinn pushed off the doorframe and into the room, his hand threaded in his hair. "That is what I'm fearful of, Anne."

"We're so far away from Goulrich, we might as well not exist. Isn't that what your father said once?"

"He will turn his eye on us one day, and I worry for that day."

Anne slid her hands over the tight material of her pants. "But we cannot worry for that day, or we will be worrying for nothing."

"I know yesterday was unpleasant, and I said I would give you space and time—"

"But you wish to stay here?"

"*Please.*"

Anne bit down on her lip, casting her eyes to where the flickering lights of the Lower were beckoning her. But that bubble of betrayal had finally popped in her lower belly, coating her insides. What seeped out was that bitter, anxious feeling. That's when she knew she had to stay.

Hartwinn needed her.

That churning emotion was drawing her back into that familiar, safe embrace she always had known—and maybe, should never have left.

Anne strode to her bed and kicked off her boots. "Are you joining me or what?"

Hartwinn crossed the room and plopped himself next to her. His hand found hers. She was sure he could feel the slick stickiness of her betrayal on her skin. That he would know.

"Is this all right? I know you wish to slow down—"

"This is good."

"Good."

Anne stared at their hands, the mismatch so much more evident now she had held a hand that fit her perfectly. She cast the thought to the pit of tar in her guts, watching it slowly sink, then disappear.

Hartwinn's eyes took her in, frowning in confusion. "Why are you dressed?"

Anne tensed and wet her lips, scrambling for an excuse. She was taking too long, and he would see through her lies.

"I was going to see Carrots," she said, her words coming out in a jumble.

His brow rose. "It's almost midnight."

"And what were you doing in your office at this time?"

"Working. And at least I wasn't sneaking out to see a *horse*," Hartwinn joked, shoving her with his shoulder.

"Sneaking out? I wasn't sneaking out. The stables are *in* Valliss," Anne said hurriedly.

He stared at her, causing her heart to launch into her throat. Then, his face cracked into a grin. His laugh—which used to create flutters in her stomach but now turned to lead sinking into that abyss with her runaway thoughts—echoed around the room.

Anne didn't like how easy it was to lie to him.

"You and that mare, I swear. If I were a jealous man, I would have sent that horse away years ago."

She smiled at him, the corners strained. "Thank Deus you're not. Now, shall we get ready for bed?"

"Can we stay up awhile? Or we can go see Carrots—"

Anne shook her head, standing. The demand to move was overpowering her, or else she would spew more than words at their feet.

"We should stay here. The less we get the stablehands gossiping, the better."

Hartwinn stood up, following her around the bed. He caught her hip with a hand, dragging her into an embrace. Tucking her under his chin, he brought her close to his chest. A fleshy cage surrounded her on all sides, and she felt like a trapped rabbit, slamming her furry body against the bars.

"Hartwinn—"

"You soothe a part of me, Anne," he murmured into her hair.

"I do?" she asked, the most honest thing she had said to him in days. "All I feel like I do is give you a headache."

"A wanted headache—"

"A headache nonetheless," she cut in, pulling from him.

Anne's hands gripped her shirt, yanking it from her pants. She glanced at him over her shoulder, his eyes glued to the shadows of her body through the linen.

"Anne—"

"Are you going to climb into my bed with your boots on?"

Hartwinn exhaled, yet he didn't move. "Do you wish—"

"For our clothes to remain on? Yes, I do," she cut in, flicking her own boots off.

Disappointment tinged her movements, yet that feeling of her betrayal was a heavier weight to bear, forcing her to drag each limb.

"I want you to want me ... And Anne, I don't think you do."

Her fingers tangled in front of her. "That isn't—"

"True?"

"That's not what ..." Anne exhaled. "I don't know what I want."

"Something has changed," Hartwinn murmured with an exhausted sigh. He flopped back onto the bed. "Something between us."

She sat beside him, tucking her hands between her knees. "I think I'm deciding who I wish to be in this world."

He cracked an eye at her. "Who do you *wish* to be?"

Anne threw herself back next to him, flinging her arms above her head. "I don't know."

"Well, when you find out, introduce us. I may like her more than you."

She rolled her eyes and let out a giggle. "More than *me*? Impossible."

Silence enveloped them. Both stared up at the soft canopy material gathered above her bed. Her eyes found the timeworn carvings they had etched into wood, their names squished together. A string of worried thoughts filled her mind. *Is Henry sitting at the bar, waiting for me? Is he turning to the door every time it swings open? Or is he drowning his sorrows in a near-empty tankard, or losing himself between another woman's legs?*

"Do you think people can change?" Anne asked softly.

Hartwinn looked at her—really looked at her with that sharpness he reserved for his council members. With a sigh, he answered, "I truly hope so, or we're doomed."

SLEEP HAD TAKEN THEM CAPTIVE, DEMANDING THEIR EYES shut and allowing the sun to rise on another day. Their bodies sought the warmth the other radiated, tangling limbs. Yet as her bedroom door swung open with such force, it launched both from the depths of their slumber. And from Anne's bed.

Dayvis strode in, not even dressed in leathers, but in a linen shirt and leather pants, surrounded by his lieutenants.

"What in the Deus' name are you doing storming in here?" Anne breathed, holding her chest as her heart thundered against her rib cage. "What time is it?"

"Hartwinn, we need to speak *now*."

A dishevelled Cidran shouldered through the men, his eyes flashing. "Where is he? Where is Henry?"

"What do you mean? Someone, please tell me what is going on," Hartwinn asked, rubbing the sleep from his eyes.

Cidran's gaze fell on Anne, confusion making a line form between his brows. "He is not in his bed, and he hasn't been all night."

Hartwinn's own brow furrowed, his eyes working in their sockets, only to rise to Anne, who still wore the shirt and pants she had intended to sneak out in. Confusion, then that disastrous, knowing emerged in his silver pools.

"Someone better start speaking and—"

"Henry was in the Lower at an establishment called the Black Raven Inn. It seems one of the local lads lost a father in one of the battles against the fae. He decided he wished to make Henry pay for his people's crimes."

Anne exhaled, taking a step toward. "Is he alive?"

Dayvis pursed his lips, barely holding in his disapproval. "He was stabbed."

Hartwinn cursed, his hand scrubbing his jaw as Cidran exhaled, his eyes flicking between Anne and Dayvis. Anne stumbled towards the door, her anguish propelling her forward. She pushed through the crowd of men that made her spacious bedroom feel cramped, erupting into the corridor. Her trembling hands gripped her knees as she hunched over, demanding air enter her lungs. Ignoring her command, the suffocating band squeezed her rib cage so tightly she worried her ribs would shatter.

This is my fault, Anne whispered silently. *This is all my fault.*

A hand fell to her hunched spine. She glanced up at Dayvis, who stood over her, concern written all over his aging face.

"He is alive, Anne. Barely, but alive."

Relief flooded her with such force that tears leaked from her eyes, dripping on the stone beneath her feet.

"And just so you know, he called for you. Over and over," Dayvis said in a hushed tone. "I've never seen anything like it. It was as if he was fighting to get to you, Anne. The healers had to knock him clean out. I think he thought you'd be in that pub, and the men would turn their attention to you."

She straightened, scrubbing the tears from her cheeks. Her eyes roamed the walls, taking nothing in. No words fell from her. There wasn't anything to say—and Anne had lied enough for the night.

"It appears you've made your decision."

She glanced down at her chewed, bloody fingers, then up at Dayvis. "You'd think I would have, but I remain as torn as ever."

He clapped her on the shoulder. "If I were you, I'd decide before more blood is spilt."

Chapter Twenty-Two

Three whole days had passed since Dayvis had woken them in the middle of the night with horrible news. And not a single note, letter or missive to say Henry was alive and well. Anne had chewed the skin around her nails raw. Someone was talking about silks and lace in the stuffy drawing room she'd sequestered herself to. It had the best view of the only entry into Valliss castle. She took nothing in, only nodding and responding in the lapses of conversation. Her mind was firmly set on Henry, yet Hartwinn lingered on the periphery.

A knock on the door sent her scrambling from the window, shoving past tailors and dressmakers holding out golden, glimmering fabrics. Cidran stood in the corridor, his unruly curls springing from his crown. Even his clothing was wrinkled like he had slept in it.

He looked worn, tired.

"What is it?" Anne asked, her voice hushed. "Is he ..."

"Alive," was all Cidran said wearily.

Anne sagged against the doorframe with relief, but her heart picked up pace. Glancing down both sides of the corridor, Cidran removed a letter—really, a hastily folded note—from his pocket. Her own gaze followed his, then snatched the piece of paper from between his fingers, hungry for any words from Henry.

He cleared his throat and ran a hand over the springing curls. "He's been asking for you," he said in a low voice.

"Hartwinn isn't letting me out of the castle. Not until the men who attacked Henry are captured," she replied, holding the precious letter to her chest. "I cannot simply scale the walls and stroll down to the Medicus Tower, now, can I?"

Cidran smirked. A mischievous light flared in his hazel eyes. "You will find a way out. Now, I must be off. I have my own letter to write."

With that, he turned on his toe and strode down the corridor, whistling.

Anne leant on the door and took a steadying breath. The rough parchment scraped against her skin, almost as if she could feel his caress. *That's if he ever desires to touch me again after taking a dagger in a pub that I never went to.*

She shoved the note down the front of her corset and allowed a plan to form in her mind. Whirling on her toe, she barked into the room, "Now, let me see that muslin!"

THE TENTH BELL RANG THROUGH ALDERDEEN IN A DULL, bellowing toll, making Anne fling back her blankets. She was fully dressed in soft brown leather pants and a billowy blouse. Feigning a sickness, she had dismissed Abigail early.

The folded letter sat on her bedside.

She hadn't dared open it yet. Not with a wild plan running through her mind, excitement coursing through her veins. She snatched up the note and muttered to herself about being brave.

Unfolding it, her eyes ran over the scrawled letters, ink drips and smudges, a smile curling on her lips.

Anne,

I write to you, knowing I have survived my first night after receiving quite a nasty walloping by some local men, much to my embarrassment. You see, I was deep in my cups after I knew you weren't coming. I do not hold any ill will towards you for not coming. Things are ... complicated for you. Heylla, they are complicated for me.

But if you could spare a moment, I would ~~love~~ ... no, I mean, I would enjoy the company. Cid has been a dreadful nurse, moaning about his betrothal as if he is going to the gallows. Both being romantics, I think you and he would get along. He wishes to marry for love, but his father has other ideas. Maybe you both can complain together, openly and loudly. Then, maybe, someone will hear and sweep you away, running off into the sunset, but I presume you would miss this life, and these people you've surrounded yourself with ...

I'm rambling even in this letter.

The healers say I will be in the Tower for a few more weeks. I am already itching to leave. You see, I am not a man who is used to stillness. I do not believe I have ever been still.

Anyway, if you could do me the honour of visiting me, I would be very appreciative ... and it is the least you could do for someone who you stood up on our first night together.

H.

P.S. My favourite flowers are roses, if you wish to bring some to my bedside.

P.P.S. I hope you are not fretting over me too much.
P.P.P.S Give Carrots a scratch for me, I miss my pretty girl.

Anne could have squealed, but instead, she traced over the swoops and dips with her forefinger. Her smile spread even further until it met her eyes. She hadn't smiled so widely for what felt like an age. Henry's written common tongue was stilted and formal. His letters were rudimentary, rushed, but she could hear his voice, that deep rumble, as if he had pressed his lips to her ear.

By Deus, he has tried. And that is enough for me.

Anne slipped from her bed, jammed her feet into the scuffed boots, fastened the cloak around her shoulders and strode to the window. She shoved it open, allowing the cool night breeze to envelop her, cooling her racing thoughts.

Climbing over the windowsill, she realised she'd need to jump. Her window was almost six feet from the damp soil. Pressing her lips together to stop the scream, she pushed herself from the safety of her bedroom. The ground rushed towards her, and by some miracle, she landed on her feet. But a painful shock ricocheted up her shins, making her hiss and wobble. Her eyes darted around. Nobody had seen her, allowing a sigh of relief to leave her. No one should be walking the gardens, not at that time of night.

Anne pushed through the hedge, snapping small branches in her path. It spat her out onto the great expanse of green grass. She half ran across the lawn, cloak billowing behind her. Slipping between the rows of thorny bushes, she spotted what she was looking for. A dark red rose. Anne plucked it from the branch, careful not to prick herself. She twirled the flower in her fingers, allowing the heavy floral scent to permeate her nose as she breathed it in, a grin spreading wider.

And now I'm truly ready.

A pair of footsteps crunched up the gravel path. Anne's eyes darted back to see two men talking in hushed tones, cloaked by darkness.

She had nowhere to hide.

She had to scale the wall.

Hoping they would be too engrossed in their conversation to notice a woman climbing above them, Anne sprinted towards the mossy stone. She shoved the tip of her boot into a crumbling piece of mortar. And with the rose between her teeth, she hauled herself upwards, muscles crying out at the sudden strain. Their hushed words floated and drifted up to her ears.

The men were talking directly below her.

"You promised you would do it *right*," a male snapped. She recognised the croaking tone. *Albert.* "And all you've done is mess up."

Anne froze, forcing her fingers to strain, eyes widening.

"I'm not a fuckin' priest of Diabolus. You don't get silver service with me," a coarse, crude voice said. "All you wanted was him messed up—"

"You stabbed him."

"He broke two noses and an arm. He was fuckin' anglin' for it. I got him in the shoulder, not the fuckin' guts. He isn't going to die. Now, where is the coin you promised?"

Anne clung to the stone, not daring to shift a muscle. Sweat pooled, making her grip slippery. She prayed to Deus that she'd stay attached to the wall and not fall onto the heads of those men.

The jingle of coins filled the air.

"I've paid you. Now get out of here before you're recognised."

"Recognised?" the man barked a laugh. "I presume none of these fuckin' fancy nobles have been to the whorehouses I go to. You know, you promised me more than to beat the shit out of a fae. You promised me that pretty blonde as well."

Anne's breath wheezed out, strangled by her own fear.

"You were promised nothing but coin. Now, go before I change my mind and call for the guards."

Bodies shuffled, and the wall shook as someone slammed a body against it.

"Unhand me—"

"Now, now, you know I don't take threats well. If you rat me out, you'll be the one with a knife in your guts, and I'll have your pretty little wife screamin' my name before you're even fuckin' cold in the dirt."

Anne's boot slipped, making her already straining fingers scream. She hissed a curse around the rose.

More clinking of coins.

"Fine, fine. Go get yourself a whore on me."

Albert muttered under his breath and strode away, gravel crunching under him. Anne wasted no time scurrying up the wall, grazing her palms. She needed to be up and over before anyone—including the two conspiring below—saw her.

When Anne finally reached the teetering top, slipping into the dark, narrow walkway, she realised she had dropped the rose in her haste to climb the wall. As she glanced over the edge, in a sliver of moonlight, a man stood, rough-faced, scarred and hulking. A man she wouldn't forget any time soon. His eyes burnt in the darkness, staring directly up at where she was only moments before, her lost rose in his fingers.

Anne had run the entire way to the Medicus Tower, not stopping for a single second to catch her breath. The marvellous feat of architecture loomed over her, cutting through the deep purple night sky. The sight had often awed her in the daytime, but in the darkness, it seemed to grow bigger, more menacing. Her body was sweaty, pooling in hidden crevices, and her palms were oozing blood. Pausing at the archway, she attempted to steady her heart rate. Winded, tight stitches twisted her in guts. Her mind was still running, attempting to answer the questions it kept asking her.

Why? Why? Why?

Anne shook her head, freeing herself from the thoughts, crossing the empty courtyard. With a shove, she pushed the wooden door open and was immediately dragged into the warm, citrus scent of the corridors. Candles burnt on the walls, casting the wide reception area in an orange glow. Freya, holding a lantern, emerged from the darkness, squinting at her. Her apron was dirty, and strands of her hair had slipped from the bun at the top of her crown. She looked tired, yet concern etched between her brows.

"Lady Anne? What ails you? You should have called me to Valliss."

"I'm here to visit a patient."

Freya's face pursed like she had sucked a lemon, shaking her head. "It's way beyond visiting hours. Come back in the morning, and not after the tenth bell has tolled."

Anne took a step forward, right into the light of her lantern. "Please, I must see *him*."

Realisation dawned on the healer's face, then her lips smoothed into a thin, disapproving line. "This is awfully peculiar. No one informed us about your visit to the fae emissary, and it appears you don't have a chaperone."

"I need not for a chaperone, being nearly twenty-five," Anne said, raising her chin. "I'm a woman, not some giggling adolescent."

The healer raised a brow. Her eyes lowered to the glistening diamond on Anne's finger. "I mean no offence. We are aware of the pending nuptials, and I wish not for nocturnal visits to Sir Ashmore to bring shame to you. I will call for the Silver to walk you back to the castle. It's not safe to be on the streets this late."

Anne bit down on her lip. Her plan was slipping through her fingers. She took two quick steps towards Freya, her fingers tangling at her front, brows meeting. Anne knew how desperate she looked, but she didn't care.

"I ..." she paused, wetting her lips. "I wanted to see him. You know, make sure he is alive and well. While Lord Hartwinn is kind and understanding, I couldn't divulge to him that I was visiting a man—let alone a fae male—in the middle of the night. I believe he would be quite upset."

"That assumption would be correct."

Anne sighed, eyes dancing over the flickering flame.

Truth, she decided right then and there. *I will tell the truth.*

"I just wanted to have a precious moment with him without the eyes of the court on us."

The healer's face softened as she lowered the lantern. "Anne—"

"No bother," she said, waving her hand. Her stomach dropped, disappointment weighing heavily inside of her. "Please tell him I came, that I tried to see him and that I will be in our—I mean his—spot when he returns to court. There is no need to bother the Silver. I can make my way back to Valliss."

She turned, blinking back tears. *What a waste of a—*

"Wait, Anne," Freya said with a soft urgency, making her glance over her shoulder. "Damn Oryah. If you get me in trouble—"

"I simply found my way in here and to him," Anne assured, nodding. "No one let me in. I will wear the punishment, I swear."

Freya took a step forward. "You know he is *fae*, right? This—whatever it is—will only end with heartbreak or you being shamed and driven from Hartwinn's court."

"Why? Why are they the only options?"

"That is the way it is—"

"And what if '*the way it is*' is wrong?"

Freya searched her face, lips pursing again. Anne could see the cogs ticking in her mind. Without another word, she turned on her heel, lantern flickering, and strode up the corridor. Anne rushed to follow her, leaving her tangled mess of thoughts on that shining, citrus-smelling floor.

Chapter Twenty-Three

Anne had thought she'd feel absolute relief when she saw him, yet all she felt was that sweaty, grimacing guilt. Henry sat up in a bed, surrounded by fluffed pillows, his long hair unbound, falling around his shocked face.

"Fate? Are you truly here?"

She stepped into the room, allowing the door to close behind her. "Hello, Henry."

He struggled up, pushing himself up with one arm, sheets slipping lower to reveal his naked torso. Twisted, raised scars marred his skin, starting from his last rib to over his shoulder, running down his spine.

He had been burnt. Quite severely.

Their gazes clashed as something—something *dangerous*—sparked between them.

"You look well," Anne stated matter-of-factly. "For a man I presumed was dead."

"Is this a dream?" he choked out.

She cocked her head and circled around the bed. Her footsteps were slow, deliberate. Her fingers trailed over the messy bedsheets. "Do you dream about me, Henry?"

"I ..."

She slid up on the mattress, allowing her hip to meet his. "You do, don't you?"

He swallowed hard and dipped his chin once.

And I dream of you, Anne almost confessed

She watched as his hand glided over the sheets, and with the faintest of touches, skimmed over the dips of her knuckles.

"I can assure you, you're not dreaming. I'm here in the flesh," she quipped with a wink.

"How?"

"The walls of Valliss castle are surprisingly easy to clim—"

"You scaled the *fifteen*-foot walls to come see me?" Henry asked, his voice a fraction shrill.

Anne's smile dimmed. "Of course I did—"

"You could have hurt yourself or fallen."

A flicker of annoyance rose in her. "I wouldn't have—"

His free hand poked her slim arm. "You have no muscle tone. You cannot get by with simply sheer will."

Anne raised her brows, leaning in. Her hand trailed the soft linen of the sheets, right along the edge of his leg, stopping just short of his exposed skin. "I can do a lot with simple sheer will. Muscle isn't every-thing, you know."

Her eyes sank to the honed dips of his stomach for the briefest moment. Then, she glanced away, cheeks warming as a singular dirty thought filled her mind. *Gods, he'd look magnificent pumping in—*

"But you seem to be enjoying looking at them."

Anne groaned, rolling her eyes, but that smile never returned. She needed to tell him and unload her truths instead of weaving lies.

"Henry, I'm sorr—"

"No. I believe I owe you an apology. I should not have kissed you in the garden, let alone asked you to bed."

Anne's eyes dipped as his words forced a breath from her. "I see."

Henry's hand reached out and lifted her chin. His gaze searched hers, and she didn't see a single speck of regret or desire. Just wide-eyed reverence.

"Do not allow that worry in you to twist my words, Fate. All I want to do is kiss you and more. Goddess, that moment is seared into my mind. I dream of it, my mind wanders to it without me knowing. But I should have waited until you had made up your mind about who you wished to love. I simply complicated it by kissing you."

"Henry—"

"Which means I understand why you did not come—"

"You're such a fool, Henry Ashmore," Anne said, tears welling. "A stupid, handsome, caring fool."

"What?"

"I wanted to kiss you, Henry. I've desperately wanted to since the day we met in that forest. The feelings I have for you complicate my life, but that kiss, Henry, was a shove I needed. Yet the guilt I feel is eating me alive."

"Hartwinn—"

"Is a part of it, but more so, it is that you got hurt because of me."

"Not because of you, Anne," Henry said, shaking his head.

"You wouldn't be here in the Tower if I—"

"It would have been worse if you had been there, Fate. Those men were animals. I fear for what would have happened if you were there."

Anne suppressed a shiver, her mind lingering on the conversation she heard. *Not yet,* she decided. She didn't wish for him to be dredged in pain or sadness.

"Besides, you seemed *awfully* bored in your letter."

"Much like you are at those *awfully* long dinners."

"I'm not," Anne exclaimed with faked outrage.

"Your face says otherwise, Fate."

She choked out a giggle and gave him a gentle shove. He caught her hand, turning it over. Grazes, fresh and oozing, stared back up at them. Flecks of stone and dirt sank into her wounds.

Anne went to pull away, but he held on tight. "It's nothing—"

"You should never have shed blood for me."

"I would bleed myself dry for those I care about, Henry. One drop is nothing," Anne whispered, her lips barely parting.

"One drop is *everything* to me."

They were close—too close—their lips mere inches apart. She knew he ached for hers as much as she did his. To touch for a fleeting moment.

A fool's dream.

Emotion sparked in her eyes, and her lips parted. "Can I—"

Henry didn't let her finish her sentence before he leant forward, pressing a kiss on her forehead. Anne's grip on the sheet tightened as she let out a quiet sigh. She hadn't expected him to kiss her. If that was all they could do without falling deeper, she would savour it. Yet that sticky tar of betrayal had congealed around her organs, bubbling and bursting, forcing her to pull away—far enough that it cooled the tension, but not off the mattress. The diamond flickered as she twisted it around.

"I didn't think you ..." Anne's voice was soft, hesitant. Her face pinched. "I didn't think you survived. No one would tell me anything, and I was scared the last words we would ever exchange were ones of anger. That I wouldn't know how to find you ..."

"Find me?"

"Your grave, Henry. I was worried I wasn't able to find your grave ... to say a proper goodbye."

His gaze shifted away, across the dark, sparse room to the window, while her eyes lingered on the shining rock on her finger.

A single tear glistened on her cheek, falling onto her twisting hands. Anne took a deep breath in and began, "I thought—no, I wondered if you had left this earth, maybe I would feel it. That we shared something in that forest that goes beyond the gods themselves. But I felt *nothing*. No pull, no driving force. Just an overwhelming fear that you had given up your life for someone like me. A simple, bored lady. You matter, and I don't ..."

Sobs devoured the rest of her sentence—ugly, shoulder-shaking sobs.

Henry groaned, pushing himself forward. With a tentative hand, he cupped her cheek, thumb rubbing the building wetness away. Her hands darted to his, holding on. Her eyes shut tight, squeezing the last of her feelings out and down her cheeks.

"You matter. Now look at me."

Anne shook her head while still squeezing her eyes closed.

"Look at me," he repeated more firmly.

She cracked an eye open at him, and he shared a small smile with her.

"I have fought on battlefields against armies with more iron than all the fae lands combined, and I even survived my childhood with my brothers nipping at my heels. A knife to the shoulder won't be the thing that sends me to Oryah's great gardens."

"You promise?"

"I vow it."

"It wasn't some drunk thug who stabbed you, Henry. He was sent by that walking skeleton, Albert. He knew you would be there, that I would be. Someone is whispering our secrets."

"Who?"

"This court is full of gossips. Anyone could have seen us and told her lady. Then, they told someone else."

"We need to tell Hartwinn—"

"No," Anne cut in sharply. Her heart jumped to her throat at the simple suggestion.

Henry winced at her tone.

She exhaled, smoothing her hand against the soft sheets. "Just not yet. I'd rather ensure Hartwinn's aim is true when he finally vanquishes the undead haunting Valliss."

"I would ask to be returned to court, but I fear facing Freya's wrath if I rip my stitches."

"Do you want some company until then?"

Henry met her gaze, and for a moment, Anne allowed herself to be lost in the woods of his eyes. She felt the soft beams of sun splash across her skin, right to that soft, mossy smell filling her nose, and even the feeling of steady solid trunks under her fingertips.

The tips of his pointed ears turned a flushed pink as he answered, "I would love that, Fate."

Chapter Twenty-Four

The chattering of women filled the drawing room with its wide windows and bulky, ornate furniture. The steaming cups of tea were passed around, and fine-needle embroidery was discarded as the spread of scandalous secrets began.

There was power in gossip. Anne had quickly realised that when she was thrust into court mere moments after she debuted. Gossip was protection from a world not made for women. Spreading tales of men who mistreated their wives, to suitors who had frequented gambling dens spilling more gold than sense who vied for dowries of the richer ladies of court, to even which healer would rid one of an unwanted child. Yet, that is how Anne's own secrets were spread, putting Henry at risk.

"I heard—"

"Well, Abigail told me this—"

"And then she said—"

The mutterings blurred into one as Anne glanced out the window, eyes on the gravel path out of Valliss Castle. She ached for those gates to groan open, and for Henry to gallop through. He was still not well enough to return to the castle—something about an infection from the rusty blade.

Seanna leant back, resting her chin on her fist, her eyes glazing. She deplored the gossips of court, yet readily devoured any information given to her.

"Well, my husband said—"

"What has that walking, talking skeleton said this time?" Anne asked, cutting in. She turned her gaze to the plump, brown-eyed Edda.

"Anne, please, would you mind not calling my husband a skeleton—"

"A ghoul then? Someone alert the Silver, for we have a member of the undead walking the halls," Seanna cut in, giggling.

A whispered laugh spread through the women as Edda narrowed her eyes and jutted her chin out. She was loved by most of the nobles, but Anne knew that she had clawed her way up through the ranks in court, only to be married off to the oldest man, who had cast three previous wives to the grave from pushing out his children. At least Edda had not yet endured the privilege of their marital bed.

"Fredrick was telling me the fae has made all these outrageous demands," another woman said, leaning in with her brows lifted.

"Like what?" Seanna asked, straightening a fraction.

"All sorts of things. What land they should have. To allow them in the guilds. Can you *believe* it?" Edda answered, disbelief evident in her tone. 'My darling Berty said they should just accept their place and go toil our fields. I must say I agree with him. You cannot come here looking for peace, then make demands."

"They didn't come here. Hartwinn invited Henry," Anne corrected, turning her near-empty tea cup around. "He wanted to foster peace."

"Regardless, they should not be so picky. Heylla, they'll be asking to marry our women next," Edda said sharply, nodding to the others, who hummed in agreement.

Anne sucked her teeth, narrowing her eyes. "Wouldn't we be luck—"

Seanna stretched with a groan, cutting her off before she could strike up an argument with Edda. She leant over and plucked a biscuit off the tray as a wicked smirk spread across her face. "You know what I *heard* about the fae?"

"What?" Edda asked quickly—far too quickly.

"Yes, Seanna, tell us," Anne said, distracted. Her eyes lingering on the buxom brunette, who squirmed under her keen gaze.

"I've heard they are impressive lovers, with more impressive"—Seanna wiggled her eyebrows—"*swords.*"

The women broke out in blushing giggles, and Anne looked to the ceiling. Those traitorous thoughts emerged in her mind.

"Seanna, you are truly wicked," Edda said through a giggle. "Do you think—"

"Oh, we all know he would be a right-good lay, toss you around like a flour bag," another woman said.

A wave of something akin to jealousy rose in Anne. She stomped on it.

He was not hers, nor was she his.

"I bet it's all talk," she said, plucking the biscuit from Seanna with a grin. "Like most men."

Another wave of giggles and scandalous murmured conversation filled the room. Until sharp shouts and baying horses came from outside. Anne stood and rushed to the window, pressing herself against the glass, only to be followed by a stampede of the chattering women.

Astride two chestnut mares were two men dressed in warrior's leathers, swords strapped to their hips. One long and lean with raven-black hair, all angles and lines, and the other hulking, broad and with such orange hair it glowed in the afternoon sun. Hartwinn's guards surrounded them, hands on weapons.

"Good gods, who are they? Now that one can throw you around," Edda said with a barely concealed lust, her hand resting on her ample bosom.

Seanna leant on the windowsill, gazing down at the men with an amused look on her face. The orange-haired man turned his head and glanced up. She exhaled so softly Anne almost missed it.

"Shall we find out?" Seanna murmured, shoving the window open.

"Seanna—"

"And who do we have here?" she called out, her voice ringing clearly through the air.

All the men in the courtyard glanced up to see the noblewomen of Alderdeen peering down at them.

"I am Wyn Neverclove, and this is Pietra Villarreal. My, what lovely ladies they have here in Alderdeen. Who do we have the pleasure of gazing at?" Wyn called back, a cocky, self-assured smirk spreading on his face.

Anne instantly disliked the man. Yet giggles came from behind hands and flicking fans.

"The future wife of the lord of Alderdeen, sir," Anne called back flatly.

"Or maybe your future wife, if you are lucky enough," Seanna added, a smile spreading across her face.

Pietra shaded his eyes with a large hand and simply stared up at her. His face was hard, yet the corners of his lips twitched upwards.

"If Oryah blesses us—"

"Gentleman, I see you're being welcomed by the roses of the court," Hartwinn said, emerging from underneath the window. "You have finally arrived for the ball."

Wyn slipped from the horse, landing on his feet nimbly. He pushed a stray hair back from his face, exposing a pointed ear.

"Another fae," Edda said almost disappointedly behind Anne. "Soon, they will be crawling over Alderdeen like cockroaches."

Anne didn't look away as Wyn saddled up to Hartwinn, his steely gaze skimming over the young lord. "Now, where is Ashmore?"

Chapter Twenty-Five

Anne's laugh reverberated around the small room, escaping her in quick gasps. She leant back on the foot of the bed, her cheeks aching from the grin she had been wearing since she stepped into the Medicus Tower.

It had been three weeks of scaling walls and late nights that bled into morning.

Time that was as precious to her as jewels or gold.

A spread of half-eaten cheese and bread and an empty flask of wine sat between them, all stolen from Valliss' roaring, busy kitchen. The warmth of the wine heated her chest and loosened her tongue, causing her to want to spill secrets that should be kept locked away.

"You're such a liar, Henry Ashmore," she joked, screwing her nose up at him. "And an awful one, at that. That cannot be true."

Henry grinned at her, showing a row of crooked but white teeth. "On my honour, Lady Anne. I tell only the truth."

"You lost your virginity to a princess from Moonmire? Please, that's unbelievable."

"Her kingdom is only a boat ride away, Fate. Not even that long of a journey. Only a handful of weeks."

She sat back. "Now you're going to tell me you've been there."

"No. She was visiting my father, and—"

"You caught her eye, being young and virile?" Anne finished with a flurry of giggles. "I would think she would have been right impressed with the matter of moments you spent together."

Henry pushed her with his foot, his eyes twinkling. "It was longer than a moment, thank you."

"Possibly—maybe the *second* time."

"Well, then, what about you? I presume you are not ..." He cleared his throat as if suddenly embarrassed. His hand rose to his braid, pulling it over his shoulder. "A *virgin*."

Anne pressed her lips together, stifling a grin. Hers wasn't a summer fling, nor was it even that romantic. If anything, she realised, it was a *cliche*. A handsome stablehand and a handful of painful moments in the hayloft, only for him to pat her on the rear and ask if she enjoyed it.

"For someone so experienced, you're a right prude." She leant forward, plucking up a piece of cheese and popping it in her mouth to chew it obnoxiously. "A prim, proper *prude*."

"I am not."

Anne's eyes locked with him. It was a dangerous game, and she was determined to play it.

"Prove it."

The words settled between them, charging the air with such tension she could feel it spark over her skin. Henry's grin turned slightly feral, making her breaths come harder. He leant forward, his hands caging her to the bed. His gaze dipped to her waiting lips, then, with a slow, agonising pace, he dragged it upwards. He leant in closer until she could smell the soft berries of the wine on his breath. He brushed her lips once, forcing a sharp exhale to leave her and a throb to form between her thighs.

Tension snapped as the door swung open. Henry slumped backwards, taking shallow breaths. From the corner of her eye, Anne could see the bulge straining against his pants, only adding to the arousal thudding around her body.

Freya, wearing a frown and a dirty healer's gown, stormed in, making Henry drag the blanket across his lap.

"You have to go, Anne," she ordered. "Now, before it's too—"

"Freya, where have you run off to?" Hartwinn called down the hallway in a playful, singsong voice.

Anne cursed, clambering off the bed. She turned in tight circles, searching for an exit. Her eyes settled on the window.

"You cannot go out there," Henry hastily whispered, almost reading her thoughts. "We are far too high, and we have had far too much wine."

"*Wine?* Then you are almost healed, Henry. We may have to discuss discharge plans in the morning," Freya snapped, narrowing her eyes at the fae warrior. "Under the bed. He won't see you."

The thud of boots sent Anne scrambling to the floor, crawling on her belly. She pressed her fingers over her mouth as the metal springs groaned overhead.

Henry's face came into view. "I'll see what he wants, Anne, and try—"

"Quickly, get into bed," Freya interrupted. "And hide whatever Lady Anne has given you. I dare not allow Hartwinn to make assumptions about what *services* we provide here."

Anne giggled into her hand, but her amusement was cut short as soon as she caught sight of Hartwinn's shining boots entering the room. She squeezed her eyes closed and sent a prayer to Deus that she wouldn't be found.

Anne's breath was hot and heavy against her palm as she watched Hartwinn stroll around the small, plain room, his boots clicking over the stone. The springs of the mattress creaked as Henry shifted on his bed. His feet found the cool stone floor, readying to stand.

"A midnight feast?" Hartwinn asked.

"Yes, I need to eat more regularly. Isn't that right, Freya?"

The healer gave a stiff answer and excused herself.

"Please, don't get up on my behalf. I'm glad to see you're alive and well."

"It will take more than a dagger to send me to Oryah, Hartwinn. You know that. To what do I owe this pleasure? It's beyond midnight."

"I was walking in the lower city, as I do most nights. You see, sleep is elusive, and I sleep much better after a stroll. And I was wondering about what we have been discussing and reflecting on—"

"Me being stabbed? I do hope you have not lost sleep over it."

"We haven't found the assailants yet."

"And you most likely won't," Henry said. "If I was a betting man, Hartwinn, I would think those men were out looking for me, not simply intolerant of my presence."

"What are you saying?"

Anne shifted under the bed, annoyed. *He is telling him about Albert without any evidence—or exposing what I've learnt.*

"It seems someone wishes for me to run back to Orynile with my tail between my legs."

Hartwinn scoffed, sitting. "You don't frighten that easy."

"No, I do not," Henry said seriously. "That was not simply a brawl at an inn. It was planned, considered."

"Heylla's rats, I think you're right," Hartwinn cursed, the wood cracking as he sat back. "Who?"

"Who do you think?" Henry asked flatly.

"He wouldn't—"

"He would, Hartwinn. He is a scheming old fool, thinking the laws do not apply to him."

"Do you have proof?"

"Yes—"

A sharp yank of his leg hairs from Anne made Henry hiss and kick his heel back, narrowly missing her.

Hartwinn's boots moved. "Henry, are you all right? Shall I call for—"

"No, just an ache. The stitches are tight, you see. But, no, I do not have proof."

"We can't act without proof. But what I cannot work out is what were you doing there?"

"Having a drink."

"No, at that specific inn. Isn't that the one you and Anne were found in?"

"On the night of the comet?" Henry asked with faked confusion. "Goddess, I had so much whisky in me I'm surprised my organs weren't pickled."

"Henry—"

"It was the anniversary of Kitra's death. I merely wished for a quiet night to drown my sorrows."

The men were silent, contemplative.

"My apologies, Henry, I didn't mean to pry."

"No apologies needed. The day has come and gone. The sun rose and fell. And by the next day, the hurt was a fraction less."

Hartwinn let out a laugh, breaking the tension. "I was surprised to hear you lost the fight, Henry. What did they call you again?"

"The wild wolf," he answered a fraction stiffly.

Anne reached out and traced two letters on his calf. *W. W.*

"That's right. You're a fearsome—"

"I *was* a fearsome warrior, Hartwinn. Not anymore. I do not believe I will pick up a sword again."

Hartwinn groaned as he stood. "Don't speak so quickly, Henry. I believe we shall see you raise your sword again. Now, rest up. I expect to see you back at Valliss soon, especially now that we have your fae brothers stirring up the inhabitants."

"My apologies. Wyn Neverclove can be—"

Hartwinn barked a laugh. "I do remember how he was, even from all the way back to when I was a child. He seems to have learnt to hold his tongue. Even Dayvis is impressed by him, talking about recruiting him to the Silver."

"Wyn would never leave Orynile," Henry said almost bitterly.

"He will," Hartwinn said with a hopeful tone. "I have a good feeling about this, Henry. Right in my guts. I swear to Deus, I do."

"We shall see. I believe he will only give me a headache," he said with a sigh.

"Then he shall be *our* headache, if he decides to stay. Good night, Henry."

"Good night, Hartwinn. I do hope you get some rest," he replied.

Anne froze, waiting until she couldn't hear the clip of his boots anymore. She crawled out from under the bed to find Henry looking down at her unimpressed face.

"You told him."

"No. I merely planted a seed. Now, are we going to finish this wine before Freya kicks me out of the Tower, and we have to go back to asking each other silly questions at the dinner table?"

Her fingers tangled in front of her. "A better question is, who is Kitra?"

Henry froze, the long, lean muscle in his shoulders tensing. "She was ... my wife."

"You were married. When?" Anne replied, cringing at the words leaving her mouth. "Hartwinn never said—"

"It was a long time ago, Fate," Henry finished. "So long ago that memories of her have faded around the edges, and now, she is simply another ghost who haunts me."

Anne took a step forward and asked another cringe-inducing question. "Did you love her?"

Henry took a long time to answer. Long enough for Anne to start to fidget, shifting on her feet. Cruel taunts ricocheted around her skull, bouncing off to echo in her ears.

That was a dumb question. Of course he loved her, he married her, idiot.

Finally, his eyes rose to hers. Through the hints of pain and hurt, that soft, radiant look shone through. It reached out as if it grew fingers, arms, and brushed over her lips. A trail of warmth was left in its wake. Warmth she had only felt deep in that forest.

"I thought I did, but now, I am not sure," Henry whispered.

Chapter Twenty-Six

A hooded Anne stood under the looming Medicus Tower, sharp in the night sky, light flickering in the rectangular windows. It could be their last night to simply be Anne and Henry before they had to return to the fleeting glances and polite conversation. She had come earlier than ever before. The tenth bell hadn't even rung yet, and she risked being recognised. But every fluttering heartbeat and tense of her muscles was worth it to spend a handful of moments with him.

Anne took a steadying breath and strode through the front door. None took notice of her—or simply averted their gaze—as she climbed the spiral stairs. Her boots were loud as she walked down the bare, sterile corridor right to the room Henry had been allocated. She knocked on the door, glancing up and down the hallway.

Waiting and waiting, yet there was no answer.

Her heart picked up pace, and that faint, anxious buzz began just behind her ear. She jingled the door handle, finding it locked.

Anne stepped back, her hand falling from the cold metal. Her eyes roved over the worn wooden door, not seeing a single thing. She would have known if he had returned to Valliss.

What if something happened?

What if the infection got worse, making him sicker?

What if Albert sent an actual assassin to force Henry from this world?

Would I know?

"Miss, ya all right?" a voice asked from behind her.

Anne whirled to find a boy no older than twelve, standing with arms full of soft linen towels. He had a kind, open face that she thought would always have a smudge of dirt on it. With narrowed eyes, she recognised him. It was the same boy from the stables—Mylo.

"Hello again, Mylo. I'm looking for the man who was in this room."

He shifted his load and cocked his head. "Hello again. What's his name?"

"Sir Henry Ashmore."

Mylo blinked at her, then his eyes dropped over her and then rose. "Interestin'."

Anne raised both her brows at him, waiting for him to explain. But he didn't. He simply turned on his toe and said over his shoulder, "Are ya comin' or what?"

Anne exhaled and rushed after him.

He kept sneaking glances at her as he led her down corridors and through rooms, delving deeper inside the Tower than she had ever gone.

"What are you doing here? I thought you were a stablehand."

"I'm many things, my lady, as I presume you are." He paused at a random door, then nodded to the crack in the wood. "This should be his room, but you—"

Before he could stop her, she shoved through the door, desperate to be in Henry's soothing company—but more desperate to see he was alive and well.

What she discovered made her cheeks warm and her jaw unhinge, popping open.

Henry was naked, sprawled in a shallow tub of steaming water, steeping in the bitter stench of medicinal herbs. One long, powerful leg dangled over the edge, his muscular, scarred back to her. But what caught her breath in her chest was what he swirled between his fingers.

A ribbon—one she must have left there after one of their nights together.

He whispered her name in a long exhale as he reclined his head. His breathy words didn't flutter between her legs, but right to her heart.

He thought of her as much as she thought of him.

Anne cleared her throat.

Henry sighed, dragging his body from the water. Rivers cascaded over his skin, running down over his pert rear. Those twisting, raised burns covered half his bare spine, as did scars from a life lived. He held a hand out without turning.

"Boy, pass me a towel. Wait"—a deep inhale and a long exhale—"*Anne?*"

Still not saying a single word, she took a step forward. Her breath came out as soft, quick pants as anticipation grew in her, devouring all that led her there. Her hand rose and dragged up the divot in the centre of his back, only to dance over the twisted, warped burns that marred his skin. He almost growled in response to her touch. But not in pain.

"What happened here?"

"I was burnt."

Anne pressed her hand to the scars. "How?"

"I was getting children out when King Ewan razed the forest around the stronghold. He somehow knew where they were hiding, and commanded his army to begin there. A few burns are nothing to keep our children safe."

"How many?"

"What?"

"How many children were hiding?"

Henry exhaled. "Forty-five."

Anne's hand went to her mouth to stifle the gasp that came from her. "He was going—"

"To burn every single one," he finished. "He knows our offspring are precious to us."

Without a second thought, she kicked her boots off and slipped into the tub behind him, her skirts floating through the herbs and soap swirling in the water. Her other hand traced another tempting route— one lower—more fraught with that aching need. Over the deep ravines of tortured, honed muscles of his hips to the splattering of rough body hair. Until he caught her wrist before she dared sink lower.

"You are *glorious*, Henry Ashmore. A few scars don't change that."

He placed her palm directly over his beating heart, the organ fluttering against her. "I am nothing compared to you."

Anne pressed her face to his warm, faintly scented skin, squeezing her eyes closed. His thumb found the bony divot of her wrist. And with one fleeting touch, Henry had warded away that anxious, choking feeling.

"What are you doing here this early, Fate? I did not expect to see you until after the midnight bell."

"I don't know—"

She stopped herself. That was a lie. A rotten lie.

With a steadying breath, she confessed, "I *need* you, Henry Ashmore. More than I have ever needed another."

Henry remained silent. That wasn't the answer he wanted. She knew it. It confused things, muddied the water. But that water was never crystal clear. Not for them.

"You make me feel safe in a world where all I have been is frightened," Anne confessed, pressing her forehead deeper into his spine. *The world inside my head,* she added silently.

"I make you feel safe?"

"More than anyone ..." Anne whispered.

She could hear the breath catch in his throat. "*Fate.*"

"Please, Henry—I know. I know this will never work out. That this is simply a fantasy. But can we pretend in this room that this world will allow us to be in love?"

"This will break your heart."

"And yours, Henry? Will it not break yours?"

"Anne, my heart is already broken. Yet, I find it fracturing with every passing moment I am not gazing into your eyes, kissing your lips, hearing you laugh or moan. You remind me of a time before my heart was pieces in my rib cage. A blissful time."

"Then, shouldn't we allow ourselves simply to be for—"

"For what? *One night?* We both know this will never simply be one night if I take you to bed. You and I will forever be drawn to each other. I cannot cast you to a life of pining and longing for me. It is not fair."

Anne exhaled. Henry was right. If he allowed her into his bed, she would crawl over broken glass to return. Yet, she couldn't—no, she wouldn't—give up. Not on this budding thing growing between them, and definitely not on him.

"No," she said sternly.

"No?" he echoed, glancing backwards.

Anne knew he was slipping through her fingers, so she allowed the truth to tumble from her, falling where it may. "I want *you*, Henry Ashmore. I want *us*. I want *this*. Even if we have to run away and live in a cottage in the forest or board a boat to flee Zeroth for distant lands, I will have you."

His chest rose and fell against her as if he was letting out a sigh of disbelief.

"You are young—"

"But I'm not stupid. I know what I want."

"And that is me?"

She squeezed him a fraction tighter. "Yes."

"What of Hartwinn?"

Anne was silent for a while, searching for the right words—none too callous, dare she sound heartless and unfeeling, but none too light and gentle so as to not confuse either of them.

"He will understand after we explain everything. He is not an unkind man."

"He will, but you will shatter his heart, Anne."

"And yet must I give up mine to save him? All because years ago, our fathers made a deal—"

"It has grown to be more for him. You know that, Anne."

"And yet I feel I may have outgrown him," she said without thinking. Her words were harsh, and not what she truly wanted to say.

"Say that again, Anne. That was cruel—"

"I want more than a flicker of a flame. I wish for a roaring fire. Destructive but beautiful. Ever-consuming. Yet as the embers drift away, new life is sprouted."

"Anne ..." Henry warned again, yet there was no bite to his tone. "You know I want you."

Her hand slid a fraction lower, making him hiss a sharp breath through his teeth. "Within these walls, can we pretend that you're simply Henry, and I'm simply Anne? Nothing outside these four walls matters. Not while we allow ourselves to dream of a life together." She paused, pressing her cheek to his spine. "Shall we simply damn ourselves to Heylla and allow what our bodies are aching to do?"

"You temptress," Henry whispered before letting her hand free.

Her fingers skimmed over curled body hair, right to a hardness wrapped in velvet. Her hand pumped over him once, then twice. Until Henry whirled around and grabbed her face. Their eyes met, and the air crackled with such tension Anne worried a lightning storm would form above them, striking the ground.

"May the Dark One be kind to our souls."

His lips crashed into hers, kissing her with such force she almost fell out of the tub. Tongues parted, swirling together. Hands roved and roamed.

A slash of cool water up her skirts had Henry breaking their intense embrace.

"We should get out, lest I drag you into the swirling depths with me."

"And ruin Aranea silk? This is made from a specific—"

"So no ripping it from your body?"

Anne laughed, slapping him across the chest. *"Absolutely not."*

She splashed out of the tub first, right to a pile of linen on a small table. Fighting the grin that worked over her face, Anne's heart sung, but the most distracting was the hot throb of arousal thumping through her.

She had never been so needy, so feral for a release.

Turning back, Henry had found whatever clothing he had stripped to cover his groin. Her eyes devoured the spread of rough body hair, the rippling muscles, finding the nearly healed wound marring his shoulder. She wet her lips with a roll of her tongue, almost tasting that pure male, salty flavour.

Anne wanted him trembling and whimpering her name, all but begging for release. A mighty fae warrior brought to his knees as she, a human girl, sank to hers. There was a certain power to it—one only she held, and it was rushing to her head.

"Fate," he whispered. "I can smell ... what you are thinking."

She held the towel out to him, her gaze capturing his. "Then, you should know how much I want to do this with you."

That soft, marvelled look had spread on his reddened face. Even so, the lingering sign of worry furrowed his brow. His heart and head were clashing, and Anne didn't know which would win—unless she gave him a shove.

"Get out of the tub and sit on the bed. You said I only ever want you when I'm crying or drunk. Well, I'm sober, and have not shed a single tear. "

He reached out and took the towel. "This is a bad idea."

"This is a terrible idea, and yet, you haven't asked me to leave."

"I do not wish for you to leave."

"Then bed, now, Henry Ashmore."

In a flurry of clean linen and a splash of water, he perched on the edge of the makeshift bed, covering a hardening bulge with the towel.

Anne's pace was painstakingly slow. Her hands dragged over her pounding pulse to curve over her breasts. Henry watched with bated anticipation, shifting as if wanting to rise and meet her. She shook her head, slowing the tracing of her body even further. "*Stay.*"

Anne reached out, her fingers sliding up his tensed thigh. Henry's eyes fluttered closed, his hands clasped to the edge of the mattress.

Neither of them were going to last long. That ache had been growing for far too long.

Her hand brushed over the towel, making his hips buck. Gripping the material, she dragged it over the same journey her fingers took. His thick manhood sprung out, hard and eager. Anne murmured to herself about the absolute surprise that the rumours were true.

With a bite of her lip, Anne lowered herself between his knees, allowing her hands to roam over his body, trying desperately to memorise the feel of him under her palms. Her hand pumped him once, hard. A bead of moisture slid under her thumb as she swirled it around the tip.

"Do you think I could take every inch of you?"

"*Good Goddess,*" Henry whispered in a low whine. "Anne, you are going to drive me *mad.*"

Anne grasped him right at the base. She captured his gaze, beaming that hot, honeyed desire up at him, letting the wanting, the desire for him pour from her pupils into the tense air between them. And he returned it tenfold. Henry's hooded eyes oozed need at her, wrapping an invisible hand around her chin, holding her. Anne's tongue flicked out greedily. He gasped sharply, and his eyebrows met in the middle.

With a smirk, she sunk her lips over the thick head of his manhood, making him release a groan from somewhere deep in his chest. His hand slipped to the back of her head, fingers tangling in her hair. She sucked and swirled the length of him with a fervour she could only describe as *enthusiastic*.

Anne wanted him groaning and bucking into her mouth with abandon.

Anne wanted to see him wild, frenzied.

Anne simply wanted him. All of him.

She watched his head fall back and his eyes close. Her lips popped off his manhood with a satisfying sound. "Eyes on me, Henry. I'll stop if you look away. Do you want me to stop?"

Henry shook his head, brows meeting. He almost looked panicked, as if she would leave him in that state between building pleasure and that messy thrusting of release.

"Then don't look away," she murmured, before lowering her head again.

Anne went from the fast rolling of her tongue around the aching tip to choking him down in gagging gulps, which made Henry whimper her name and tighten his hand. She was slick at her core. Her own release was a distracting throb, forcing her to shift her thighs together, seeking any sort of friction. Yet Anne didn't stop. Her hand didn't wander.

Only moments before, she wanted him wild, but suddenly, she desperately wanted to ruin him for anyone else. Never would he find another who could bring him to the edge of pleasure and cast him off in such a way he'd be falling for not mere moments, but hours.

"Gods, Fate," Henry murmured. "You take me so well."

Spurred on by his praise, Anne dipped and sucked, her hand working in tandem. Her nails dug into his thigh. The tense of his lower stomach as he thrusted into her mouth became more rabid, sloppy.

He must be close.

"Anne, *fuck*," he muttered through a curse. His tangling fingers yanked at her hair, sending a hot sear around her scalp. "I'm about to—"

A deep, almost growl cut off his words. Then, a hot surge of saltiness hit the back of Anne's throat, making her gulp him down. She endured until he was fully spent, leaving him aimlessly thrusting, spilling all he had.

Anne grinned up at him, wiping her mouth on her sleeve. Henry leant forward, his hand pulling her head back. Angling her face to his, he dragged a thumb over the sharp edge of her jaw, then over her now-swollen bottom lip.

"This wicked mouth will have me on my knees, begging to take it again."

Anne's grin turned mischievous as she shifted her thighs together. The tension still brewed in the air as if those clouds were waiting to pour down on them.

"You would look good on—"

Before she could finish her sentence, his mouth was on hers. His tongue broke through, not caring where it had been before, mixing her sweet honey with the salty tanginess of him. It wasn't a savoured kiss. It was a needy, haphazard mess that she relished in.

It hadn't finished with Henry finding his release. It had only just begun.

"On your back," he ordered gruffly, pressing his forehead to hers. "I need to know if you taste like you smell ..."

Anne's brows almost hit her hairline as she sunk onto her rear. Gripping her silky skirts, she slowly dragged the wet material up her calves, right to her knees. "Do you now?"

"Stop teasing me and show me what is mine. *Now.*"

Anne bit down on her lip to stop a gasp leaving her, knowing it was his desire speaking. Even so, she allowed that bubble of hope to grow within her.

She was his—all of her was his. To take, to touch, to do whatever the Heylla he wanted to. More than that, she belonged to him. That thundering organ flooded her body with more than lust. Another emotion that grew in the spaces of her heart: love.

"Needy, are we?" she murmured with a smirk, dragging her skirts higher.

Henry growled a curse and launched himself at her. He forced her to the rug beneath them as their tongues clashed, as her hands roamed and gripped onto sweating skin. With a grumbled curse about clothing, he shoved her skirts up around her waist. Fingers trailed over her splayed knees, slipping down the soft skin of her inner thigh to circle around her damp underwear. She released a sharp exhale as her core clenched in need.

Her release was near, and Henry hadn't even touched her yet.

With eager hands, he yanked her undergarments to the side, finding her wet and glistening. He released a shaky breath, teeth almost puncturing his bottom lip. His eyes rose to hers. Something had softened the lust, but the filth that left his mouth had her almost groaning in need.

"By the goddess, Anne, I'm going to fuck that ring right off your finger and replace it with my own." He slipped his fingers through her folds, teasing her entrance. "This is mine. Tell me. Say it."

She groaned, her hips jerking. The promise of release had almost sent her rabid. "It is yours, Henry. All yours."

With a feral grin, he dove between her thighs to end that tortuous ache with a swirl of his tongue. Her legs locked around his head, frantic for him to take her to that edge and toss her off. His hands found the dip of her knees, spreading her wider, only for him to devour her with the ferocity of a man starved.

Her release rose quickly and forcefully inside her, sending that pulsating pleasure through her entire body. He was returning the same vigour she had shown him with each swipe of his tongue. A finger slid inside of her. Feeling no resistance, he fitted another, then another. Until she felt that aching fullness that only his manhood could erase.

"Henry," she cried out, her voice loud in the quiet of the room. "Good gods, *fuck*—"

His hand snapped over her mouth, her cries spilling between his clenched fingers. Yet, he still didn't cease the constant licking and sucking—not until Anne was tossed over the edge and crashed onto those rocks. Her body contorted and her hand snapped to his, forcing it more firmly over her mouth—a way to muffle her moans of absolute pleasure. Tears leaked from her eyes, meeting his clenched fingers. Not ones of sadness, but of that overwhelming, giddy feeling of joy.

Anne sagged to the rug as a naked Henry rested on her stomach, both well and truly spent. Pleasure had been wrung out, leaving no drops. Her fingers found the soft point of his ear, only to smooth over his crown, over and over. Henry's eyes fluttered closed, and a softness emerged on his face—one Anne had never seen before.

Neither spoke.

There was nothing to say.

Words they would say to each other would only hurt, and Anne didn't wish for this to be drenched in pain. She craved that slow fluttering growing in her belly and that giddiness that had her head spinning.

A fist slammed against the door, and a rambunctious voice called out, "Oi, the walls are thin, Ashmore. The Tower doesn't need to hear you and your hand becoming acquainted."

Anne let out a stifled giggle as Henry groaned, hiding his face in the bunched material of her skirts. Yet she didn't move, nor did she stop the soft, trailing fingers up his spine. She found him staring up at her. And for the first time, she saw something akin to hope in those woody pupils. It made tears blur her vision of him.

I will protect your heart, Henry Ashmore. Not a single part of it will crack. I vow it to the heavens and right to the pits of Heylla. I will guard it as if it is precious gold, and I a dragon, she silently promised.

CHAPTER TWENTY-SEVEN

ANNE LOUNGED BACK ON THE DEEP CHAISE IN THE SITTING room with the perfect view of the entrance. None had asked her why she preferred that room, and none questioned it. Her sloppy, half-finished stitching was cast to the side, her fingers picking at the skin around her nails. Anne's gaze was locked on the window, waiting impatiently for Henry's return.

She wanted to see him.

Yet, her eagerness was tinged with treason and treachery. She hadn't slept properly since their night together, tossing and turning, haunted by dreams of Hartwinn crumpling and casting her out into the cold. She couldn't even stand the thought of him touching her. That he'd smell another on her and know someone else had given her pleasure. Yet, her heart sang at any stray thought of Henry. The feelings clashed within her, iron screaming against iron. Neither winning or losing.

"You've been staring longingly out the window for hours, Anne. What seems to have caught your attention outside?" Seanna asked, squinting at her own embroidery.

"Nothing," she said with a sigh. Her eyes shifted to her scabbing hands. "Nothing at all."

"So you're not waiting for a certain fae warrior to return? It's today, isn't it?"

Anne's gaze snapped to her friend. "I don't know what you're speaking of."

Seanna reached over and struck her on the shin with the hard wooden part of her hoop. She clipped one of the many bruises she had developed from climbing the wall, forcing a cursed hiss and her hands to slap to it.

"I thought we didn't lie to each other."

"I'm not—"

Another whack of the hoop.

"Fine. Fine, I'm waiting for him. What of it?"

"What of it?" Seanna exhaled. "You're engaged, for one, Anne Devoy. You cannot be pining for a man when yours already walks these halls."

"I simply enjoy *talking* to Henry—"

"I'm sure all you've done is *talk*," Seanna cut in curtly.

Anne frowned at her. "He isn't rolling in my sheets—"

"But you may be rolling in his?"

"I'm not."

"You're a liar, Anne. A terrible one, at that—"

"We kissed," she cut in, her words coming out in a hushed, harsh whisper. "Is that what you want to hear? He kissed me like he was drowning and I was air, and then I sought him out, Seanna, in the darkest part of the night, and allowed him to feast on me."

Her friend had frozen, her hands losing their grip on the hoop. "*What?*"

"I ..."

Anne's words faded off. The truth had spilt between them, staining the delicate bonds of their friendship. Seanna reached for her, taking her hands and drawing her closer. "You cannot grow feelings for this man. You simply cannot."

"Tell that to my heart."

Seanna leant down and spoke to her left breast. "She is engaged to another, you rotten fool."

Anne huffed a laugh, shoving her away. Her heart wouldn't even listen to her own commands.

Seanna sat back, her eyes not rising from where her hand was smoothing over the velvet. "Regardless of that, you cannot be with him simply because of what he is."

"What he *is*?" Anne repeated sourly. "What is he, then, Seanna?"

"A fae," she whispered the word as if it were a curse.

Anne searched her friend's face with confused sweeps of her gaze, and all she saw was misguided fear. She feared Henry. *No, that isn't it,* Anne realised. She was scared *for* her, for what their narrow-minded world would think of a lady of her noble birth loving a fae warrior—the wild wolf, at that.

"Are we any better?" Anne asked, her words puncturing the air. "Our valiant king is simply the *victor*, but what of the innocents who have fallen on his soldiers' iron?"

"Anne—"

"Maybe we aren't any better than any of them—vampyre, witch or fae. Maybe we are *worse*."

Seanna gasped. "You cannot believe that."

Anne shrugged in reply, throwing her hands in the air. "I don't know what to believe, Seanna. Not anymore."

"Then we must believe the king knows what he is doing—"

Anne scoffed, clicking her tongue. "I will never place my trust in that man. All he does is infect this land with hurt, then poison it with his need for power."

"You'd be careful who you spout this shit to."

"Why? You think he can hurt more than he already has?" Anne shook her head, answering her own question. "Nothing can hurt me."

"You are wrong, Anne Davoy," Seanna said, her jaw shifting. "He can hurt the ones you *love*."

She almost snarled. "He wouldn't dar—"

"Why can't you simply just love Hartwinn, Anne?" Seanna cut in with a pleading tone. She pushed off the chaise to stand over her, bottom lip trembling. "Good Deus, you know, women would literally kill to have him even glance at them. Yet you throw it away, for what? Something new—"

"Something *different* than what I have ever felt for Hartwinn. This feels real, Seanna. This feels right. I cannot explain it. A golden string is leading me to Henry, and I'm determined to follow it."

"Then what? You will have thrown away all you have build here—"

"I don't know!" Anne shouted, her hand slapping over her mouth. A tear escaped from the brewing, meeting her clenched fingers. That was the truth. She didn't know what would happen if she chose Henry. Would she lose all she had been born to do, or would she gain more than she could ever imagine?

Anne's hand fell to her lap as her eyes dipped from her panting friend. "My heart battles my head every day, every hour, every second. Hartwinn is all I've known, but Henry ... He allows this flame inside of me to burn brighter, blowing precious air to keep it alive, cherishing it."

"Then you will leave me! Run off and cast me to these wolves!" Seanna shouted in reply, truth spilling from her like an upturned glass. That's when the tears in her eyes slid down her cheeks. Her voice wobbled as she said, "You're all the family I have, Anne. Don't leave me here *alone*."

It all clicked into place. "If Hartwinn sends the fae away—"

"You'll go with them, I know you will. Anyone with eyes can see how you look at him, and anyone with a heart would understand." Seanna sniffed. "But that would mean—"

"Leaving you here, with the wolves snapping at your ankles."

Seanna tucked a stray strand of inky black hair back into the neat chignon and nodded.

Anne took two quick steps and, without any hesitation, wrapped Seanna in a tight embrace. "Alderdeen is my home. It will always be my home. I will always return here, even if I need time and distance to mend the hurt."

Seanna wiped her tears with her sleeve. "What if the fae court is—"

"Nothing will keep me from returning. And why would I leave when my sister is here, all alone, without someone to get into mischief with? There is more wine to steal and rooms to break into."

Anne's words forced Seanna's tears to overflow again in heaving sobs. She simply held on to her friend, allowing her tears to soak into her blouse.

"You couldn't possibly do that to her."

Anne tightened her grip, silently whispering, *I'm sorry, I'm sorry, I'm sorry.* She had lost herself in the feelings that grew for Henry—and left Seanna to face that bitter, icy storm by herself. She had been a rotten friend, and an even worse sister.

"Come with us if Hartwinn casts us from court."

"And what? Live in a cottage with a brood of children and three goats? Or worse, go to that crumbling fae court?"

Anne smiled and nodded. "We can go wherever we wish, Seanna."

"We could drink fae wine and braid ribbons into our hair," she replied, her lips twitching upwards.

"Watch the men spar ... *shirtless*," Anne crooned, winking.

With a giggle, Seanna's shoulders relaxed. "Dance barefoot under a full moon with nothing but our underwear on."

Anne reached for her friend's hands and said softly, "Love the men we wish to."

Seanna's cheeks warmed to a pretty pink, her normal direct gaze averted. Anne searched her face, tears drying. "Something has happened."

Her friend let out a deep, long exhale, her slim brows pinching. "You've simply been absent at dinners, so I have struck up an unlikely friendship."

"With who?"

Seanna shook her head. That fleck of worry marred her eyes. "Pietra."

The name shattered the thin ice that had formed between them, letting the rush of drowning emotions out.

"You hypocrite—"

"I'm not in *love* with him, Anne. You left me waiting each night as you climbed over the walls. He is half-deaf from a battle with Ewan. I don't believe he can fully hear me, but we talk."

"How do you know that?" Anne asked softly, frowning at her friend.

"I—"

"How do you know I was climbing walls?" she repeated with more force.

"Hartwinn told me. Confided in me."

"He knows—"

"That you're sneaking out. Yes."

"Anne—"

She stood abruptly, cutting her friend off, rushing to the window. A carriage rolled down the road, wheels crunching on the gravel, coming to a stop outside the doors of the stables. The door cracked open and Henry clambered out, followed closely by Cidran, holding his hands out to steady his friend. Anne's breath hitched in her chest as he glanced up. They locked eyes, and that brewing tension pulled taut.

A small smile spread across his face—one he seemed to reserve for her. Yet, Anne couldn't return the grin.

Without another thought, she pushed from the windowsill, right past Seanna and out the door. Her friend rushed after her, shouting for her to stop, to come back, to understand.

But Anne couldn't.

She threw herself down corridors and dove through gossiping maids. The instant her hand found the cool metal handle, she wretched it open. Sunlight caught her in the face as she rushed towards him.

He knows.

Chapter Twenty-Eight

Golden sunlight cascaded over the pair as if Oryah shined down on them, capturing that gleam of his hair and the warmth in those deep brown eyes. Anne rushed towards him, her body covered in sweaty apprehension.

He knows.

Henry straightened as she approached. His eyes drank her in as the tips of his pointed ears warmed to a flushed pink. Her hands tangled in her skirts so as not to reach out to him. Yet he seemed to inch closer, his fingers rose to brush over her cheek.

"Anne, *ciùin*," Henry said, his voice hushed with concern. "You look flushed and wild-eyed."

"Henry—"

"And, I wonder why that is—"

His elbow found Cidran's stomach. He shot a glare over his shoulder, to which his friend returned a smirking wink.

"This isn't a time for jokes, *Cidran*." Anne took a tentative step towards him. With a low whisper just for him, she said, "I will always worry for you, Henry. Especially now."

"Fate—"

The door to a stall swung open, and Hartwinn strode out, face tight with surprise to witness them together, then smoothing into that polite grin. He clapped Henry on the shoulder, then pressed his lips to her cheek.

"Ah, Annie! I see you're already here to welcome Henry home."

"Of course, Hartwinn. It's a simple kindness for a guest who was attacked in our city."

"And I presume those late-night visits to the Tower were an extension of that kindness?" Hartwinn asked flatly, his smile fading into a cool glare.

Anne stiffened, her whole body breaking out in a warm, uncomfortable sweat. She blinked at him, her lips parting as her mind scrambled with not a coherent thought forming between her ears.

He knows.

Anne stepped towards him, shaking her head. "Hartwinn—"

"Impressive, if I do say so myself. I don't think many could climb those walls. But you did every night. I couldn't even get you to learn how to throw a punch."

"You had people following me?"

Hartwinn dusted the hay from his pants and sighed. "Yes, Anne. Albert suggested it after he said one of his servants saw you two kissing—"

"And you believed him?" she asked incredulously. "The man who hates women, who hates me."

"Not at first. But when I found you dressed the night Henry got stabbed, I grew suspicious."

A rush of fiery anger bubbled the betrayal that settled deep inside of her. Yet, it wasn't her own betrayal that coated her in bitterness this time. It was *his*.

"This is a disgusting invasion of my privacy, Hartwinn."

"Good *gods*, Anne. You were spotted scaling the walls late at night when you know good and well that rebels are being hunted down and executed. I had to make sure—"

"What?" she cut in, stepping back from him. "That I wasn't a rebel? I have only ever shown loyalty to you, to this court."

"Loyalty. Is *this* what you call loyalty?"

Anne lowered her eyes, swallowing the words she wished to spit at him. He was right, yet those words hurt to hear. She hadn't shown him any scrap of loyalty.

"Besides, Anne, everyone—including those in Goulrich—know there is no love lost between you and Ewan—"

"And, why do you think that is, Hartwinn?"

"He acted untoward—"

"He simply didn't act untoward, Hartwinn. He *raped* me," Anne confessed, her voice wavering, a stray tear rolling down her face. "He used his divine, ordained power to force me into his bed."

Gasps surrounded her. That undercurrent of anger dissipated, and what replaced it enraged Anne. It was delicate, placating, as if she would break into a thousand pieces at any moment. But she was not delicate—pretty and fine-boned, but not delicate. She was forged in iron, struck by the expectations of this world until they made her into what they desired. It wasn't her secret to bare alone anymore. She shouldn't have to hide in shame for what a man decided to do to her, nor would she ever again.

"I would never put Alderdeen at risk. *Ever.* This is my home as much as it is yours, and I hate that you ever considered it."

"Once I found out, I—"

"Then what? You simply thought I was just a *whore* over a traitor? Do you think so little of me?"

The anger from his confession should have made her lash out in sharp jabs and sharper words, spitting venom at him. But all it filled her with was such wallowing sadness it had escaped down her cheeks.

"I was just trying to protect you."

A choked laugh left Anne as she shook her head. "Protect me? You want to control me, Hartwinn. That is *very* different."

Henry looked at Cidran sheepishly. "We might take our leave—"

"*No,*" Both Anne and Hartwinn said simultaneously. "Now, you listen here—"

Hartwinn snapped out and grasped her elbow, cutting off her words. With a sharp yank, he dragged her closer. The fabric of her sleeve dimpled under the pressure of his grip. Something akin to fear flashed inside of her, cooling that fiery heat.

Anne had never feared Hartwinn, yet she had never pushed him that far.

Henry took an involuntary step forward until Cidran slapped a hand across his chest.

"No, Anne, it's time you listened. You will accept that I had you followed, as I have accepted that you were most likely sneaking into his bed. But that is now in the past, and I will forgive you for your dalliances."

"*Dalliances?*" Anne repeated softly, attempting to pull herself from Hartwinn's grip. "Do you think that's what this is? An indiscretion?"

"You've always crawled into everyone else's bed but mine. Isn't that right, sweet Annie?"

Her gaze flashed to Henry. She needed him as much as she didn't wish to. This was spiralling out of her control, and soon the fire in her body would set something ablaze. And she worried it would be her heart —or, more devastatingly, Hartwinn's.

Henry straightened, rising to his full height. In one long stride, he was flush against Hartwinn, peering down at him, cold and icy. "Unhand her, my lord, and resist smearing her character any further. Much to your assumption, Anne has not crawled into my bed, but was simply a night nurse to keep me company while Cidran rested. As any good lady would do."

Hartwinn's arm fell from her, and all he said was, "You better take a step back, Henry."

"Or what?"

Hartwinn's eyes narrowed as the edges of his lips pulled down. "You're here bargaining for refuge for your people, are you not? It would be a shame for your father's spies to see you fail."

Hartwinn's threat lingered in the air, sharp and deadly as a drawn blade.

Anne clenched her trembling hands and shook her head at Henry, her face softening. Her heart was sparking alight, burning in her chest. She would not put her own wants and desires over the lives of the fae, not for all what Henry sacrificed for. Instead, Anne shoved all the feelings down, suppressing them with all that she had until that meek, pleasant wife she had been trained to be was the mask she wore. But the mask didn't fit right anymore. It rubbed raw on her cheeks, and she could hardly see out of it. Still, she pressed on.

Her shaking hand rose to Hartwinn's arm. "Please, Hartwinn, you don't mean that. Shall we all take a breath? I believe this conversation has gotten us all heated. You were simply protecting me, as you always have. I shouldn't have allowed myself to get swept up with the excitement of it all."

Henry's brows furrowed in confusion. Her words backflipped and tumbled from what her gaze was screaming.

"Yet you have wounded me with your words, Anne, let alone your actions."

Her tongue worked over her molars. "And I'm sorry for that. I was simply angry—"

"And then you threw what Ewan did right in my face as if I was somehow complicit in it."

Anne's eyes glazed as she nodded. The chain that was wrapped around that box rattled with such ferocity that a link cracked. A wisp of a shadow slid from it, allowing a haunting memory of his lips against her ear, grunting, to manifest. That constricting band around her ribs tightened until her breathing was shallow and useless.

"That shouldn't have come out in angry words. For that I am sorry," she wheezed out.

Hartwinn reached up, but his hand dropped away. "I never knew he did that to you, Anne."

That made her vision sharpen and flash to him. "You never *knew*? That is a boldfaced lie, Hartwinn Novak."

He threw his arms in the air. "I guess we are both lying to each other now."

"You knew exactly what he did when you watched me crawl into men's beds, trying to get a scrap of what he took from me from every nightmare that would shake me and half the castle awake, or when I would jump every time someone would mention his name. You *knew*."

Hartwinn took a step towards her, his face softening. "I never knew, Anne. You have to believe me."

"Then why did you think I was scrambling for some sort of power over my body, over my own pleasure?"

"Because you're a woman, Anne," he said simply. "Power is not given freely to your sex. Many women have to *scramble* for it, using whatever means necessary."

"That—"

"Is true," Hartwinn finished, his brows bunching. "And I'm so sorry that it's the way of this world."

"What if that is *wrong*?"

"Then we must change it," Henry said.

That frightening anger had drained from Hartwinn as Henry's words simmered over him. Now, she recognised the man standing before her. It was her Hartwinn. The one she called her best friend, the one who so desperately wanted this world to be different.

"But I have power, Hartwinn. I do," Anne said, as if she was trying to convince herself. Tears started afresh.

"This is a rotten, horrible world, Anne, but even a queen would have to bend the knee before her king," Hartwinn said, an apologetic look spreading across his face.

Cidran scoffed, shaking his head. "Not every queen."

"And not every woman should be forced to her knees," Anne added.

Hartwinn sighed, glancing towards Valliss. "Come, Anne. It's time you returned to where you belong."

"Where is that exactly? In your bed?"

"By my side. As my wife, but more than that, as my oldest *friend*."

Henry stepped forward. "Hartwinn, let her—"

Hartwinn whirled around, shoving Henry. He stumbled back into Cidran, his eyes flashing to Hartwinn. Hurt was all she could see. Hurt she placed there. Hurt she had forced between the men like a sharp embroidery needle digging into delicate skin. All due to her useless, damning heart.

"Stay out of this, Henry, and away from *her*," Hartwinn threatened with a pointed finger. "You're here to bargain for your people, not take our women, you hear?"

Henry scoffed, shaking his head. "You are sounding like Albert, Novak—"

"How dare you!" Hartwinn hissed, taking a step towards him.

Henry's hands lashed out, gripping his shirt, dragging him closer. "How dare *I*? You rub her name in the dirt, then expect her to crawl back to you. This is not the man I thought you'd become."

"Is that what she did to you, or is that what you *wished* her to do?"

"If you say another word, Novak ..." Henry's knuckles whitened as the sharp scrape of teeth ground his jaw.

His shoulders rose and fell as Hartwinn searched his face, realisation widening his eyes. "You ... and her? Of all people, Henry, *her*?"

"Do not say it, Novak. Do not make it true," Henry said, his voice softening. "*Please.*"

Cidran muttered under his breath and shoved himself between the men, pushing them apart. "Gentlemen, I think that is enough for today—"

"What don't I know?"

Neither said anything, their eyes averted.

Anne stood staring at both of them, lips pulled into a tight grimace. She turned and cast her icy glare on Cidran.

"It is not my place to say, girl."

Anne shook her head as that icy chill of sadness sizzled the fire in her veins. She had created such a mess, shattering all she knew. But she hadn't a clue how to sweep it up, how to put the pieces together, gluing them. Yet, it would still bear the cracks, the chips.

Anne whirled on her toe and strode right towards Carrots' stall. Her shaking hands grabbed the bridle that was hung next to her door. With a slam, she flung the bolt back, making Carrots throw her head in fright.

"Anne, please, don't run," Hartwinn pleaded from the door of the stall. "We need to talk."

"I need space—"

"And I've given you so much that another has slid in."

Her fingers paused for a second, readying to spill the truth to him, only to have her hands work faster until the last of the buckles of Carrots' bridle were done up. Without another wasted breath, she flung herself onto the mare's back, yanking her reins until she turned in tight circles. With a kick in her sides, the mare flew from her stall. The men scattered as Carrots drove through them, snapping her teeth. Anne wouldn't stop, not until she was deep in the Sliva Forest and she could force back in all the words she had said, all the feelings she had allowed to bubble upwards. She knew, like that fragile trust she shattered, nothing would ever be the same. Anne would never be the same. Yet, a set of hooves slammed behind her, following her through the streets of Alderdeen, right into the forest that held her heart.

Chapter Twenty-Nine

The Sliva Forest was a blur of emerald greens and deep browns, not from Carrots' speed but from the tears that spilt down Anne's cheeks. Her breath was coming hard and fast as they darted around trees, and her shining hooves thundered through the scrub. Anne yanked hard on the reins, forcing Carrots to skid to a stop. Shrill whinnies filled the air as the mare threw her head around. It was as if she could feel Anne's bleeding emotions.

Rumbling, dark grey clouds had formed overhead, threatening to soak her through. The sharp sting of rain began to pelt against her skin as if shards of glass were falling from the sky.

"Woah up, girl," Anne commanded, yanking on the reins. "We have to turn back—"

A crack of lightning lit the sky, only to rattle the earth beneath Carrots' hooves. Anne's turbulent emotions and the horse's panic sent her into a frenzy, kicking and arching her spine as she bucked.

Both Anne and Carrots hated storms.

Anne leant forward, tangling her fingers in her horse's mane and squeezing with her aching thighs. The skies opened, drenching her. Rain ran over her cheeks as if the heavens themselves shared the ache in her chest.

"Don't you dare throw me, Rotten. You'll break my neck this time!"

Henry, riding bareback, erupted from the tree line. Strands of his hair whipped around his face. Even his clothing was rain-spattered, stuck to his body. With a strange grace, he slid off the rear of the speckled white and tan gelding, slamming to the ground. He rushed towards the kicking, snapping mare, his hands held out.

"Henry! Careful—"

"*Ciùin,* pretty girl. *Ciùin.* This is nothing but a downpour—"

Lightning split the sky in a blinding crack of light. Rain spattered, falling in fat drops over them, drenching them.

Carrots began to step side to side, hooves splattering the squelching mud. Her ears flicked and turned, waiting for the groan of the earth. The mare's coat was sticky with sweat, coating Anne's clenching thighs with itchy hairs. Her muscles twitched underneath Anne's tense body as if readying to launch herself right into the tree line. Henry took a quick step and grabbed Carrots' bridle, spooking her. With a final throw of her body, Anne was unseated, only to tumble to the squishing mud with a grunt. Luckily, she landed on her shoulder and not her healing wrist.

"I know, sweet girl. She shouldn't have ridden you so hard."

Carrots whined in agreement.

"Traitors, both of you," Anne murmured from the mud. "Are you going to help me up?"

"I think you can get yourself up this time, Anne."

She winced as she pushed up onto her elbow. "What are you doing here then?"

Henry glanced down at her with an unimpressed raise of his eyebrows. "What do you think?"

Anne sighed, resisting the urge to flop down into the cool, gritty mud. "That was simply *awful.*"

"That's a way to describe it, Fate," Henry replied with a snort.

"And how would you describe it?"

He stared into the mare's eyes, his hand smoothing over the softness of her snout. "That reality has finally found us."

Anne sat up, flicking mud from her bare arm. "You don't believe—"

"If that outburst from Hartwinn shows us anything, Anne, it is that what we wish can never be. We have been dancing, spinning around our feelings for weeks, until—"

"The other night," Anne finished.

"I felt such guilt—"

"And I am drowning in it, Henry. A part of me knows what we did wasn't wrong, but the other part of me is louder, screaming at me for it," Anne said with a shake of her head. "And it was I who came to you, demanding pleasure as if it were owed to me. If anyone should feel guilty, it is *me*."

Henry let out a soft sigh. "I felt no guilt for taking you, Anne, nor for the pleasure we found in each other, but for the fact that I wanted to march into that castle and *demand you* as if I had some right to you. As if you and who you are were not tangled in this court. For once, I cared about what I wanted, not what my people needed, or this damned treaty. I wanted you."

"Then why, Henry?"

"For this world is not ready for our love, Fate, and this is the only part of my life I did not wish to fight for. I am so tired of fighting, battling this world for what I want—"

"That is *horseshit*, Henry Ashmore, and you know it," Anne snapped, standing. Her dress was dirty and ripped from the stray branches. The rain was seeping right into her skin, chilling her. Anne hand pressed against her rapid heartbeat. "This is worth the fight. More so, I'm worth the fight. But we don't battle just for us. We battle for all those who have been told the world will never accept their love."

Henry's eyes had filled with tears, yet none fell. Carrots pressed her head to his chest. "But I am scared."

Anne took a step towards him, her hand pressing down harder. "Do you think I'm not? All I know is Alderdeen. All I know is Hartwinn."

"Then you should go back to him."

"*No.*"

Henry sniffed, his brows pressing together so tightly a deep crevasse formed between them. "We are doomed, can you not see that? I am that knight from your song, longing for a princess he can never have. But I do not know if I can stand under your window watching you smile and laugh without scaling that wall and climbing to you. The pull is too strong."

Hope flared in Anne's chest in a single warm spark. She reached out, her hand falling on his forearm. "You feel it too? There is a supernatural force driving us together, Henry. We shouldn't ignore it."

He angled his face from her as a single tear rolled down his cheek. "You need to go back to Hartwinn. Be his wife, have his sons and forget all about me."

Anne searched his face for a scrap of truth, finding none. "Is that what you want?"

He fell silent as the rain poured down around them, soaking them through.

"If that is truly what you want, Henry Ashmore, vow that your heart doesn't beat for me, and I will return to him. I will never darken your door ever again."

Henry groaned, backing away from her, dragging his hands over his face, pushing the strands of hair back. He looked so terribly torn, and yet, Anne had such clarity she wondered if she should have felt the same emotion.

"I cannot, Fate," Henry said as if it were his final confession before meeting those gallows. "Is that what you wish to hear?"

"Henry—"

He took a step towards her, his broad face clenched, cheeks wet with tears. In those woody eyes was desperation she had never seen. "I cannot stand the thought of your precious heart being given to anyone but me. But what truly sends me mad is all we will miss—waking together, seeing you smile before you can practise it, having you in my sheets, memorising each curve, scar and freckle of your body. Heylla, even the thought that another man's child will grow in your belly sends my blood boiling. My heart is fragile, broken and utterly *yours*."

Anne's breath hitched. She hadn't expected that; for the truth to come with such unwavering, heart-clenching emotion.

"But I cannot lose another again," he said, shaking his head.

"You will not lose me, Henry. I prom—"

"Losing Kitra almost killed me, and I will break my heart sooner than love again."

"Then why tell me that I hold your heart? Why demand I go back, knowing I will always look for you in crowded rooms, across ballrooms and on cold balconies?"

"I do not wish to torture you so—"

"But you're doing it, holding a bloody dagger, carving and carving at my flesh. This heart beats for you and only you."

Henry grew still, his chest barely rising. "You cannot mean that, Anne. You will thank me for this one day."

"I will *never* thank you. You showed me that my life is more than tightlaced ball gowns and even stuffier ballrooms. You opened my eyes to a woman I could be, yet you ask me to simply return to the woman I was."

"There is no future for us. Not in this world. You would be shunned, outcast from a life you loved, a place you call home to wander this earth. That will only bring bitterness, resentment. This is a path we cannot go down, even though it is singing to us ..."

"What about—"

"No," Henry said, wavering. His face was hard, eyes glazed. "The answer is no. Now, go back to your betrothed and forget about me."

Anne glared at him before snatching up Carrots' reins. With a grunting swing, she clambered up onto the mare's back.

"You will let me in one day, Henry Ashmore, and I will get to cherish that broken heart of yours," she said, her voice cracking. "Yet, I know the gods will break my heart instead."

He looked up at her, and the flare of hurt, mixed with such wretchedness, almost had her slipping from Carrots. Almost.

"There were many hearts broken today, Fate, not just yours," Henry said before slapping Carrots on the rear, sending her galloping into the rain.

Chapter Thirty

Anne stood at her own bedroom door, soaked through, a muddy trail of footprints behind her. She knew Hartwinn sat beyond the wood, and she had little in her to fight with him. Her head spun, Henry's words twisting and morphing between her ears until they took on a different tone. A different voice, cruel and unkind.

With an exhale, Anne shoved the door open, only to find Hartwinn locked in an embrace with Seanna. He was resting his head on her shoulder, and her arms were wrapped around him. Nothing rose in Anne—not even hot indignation at the hypocrisy of Hartwinn's actions.

Nothing.

She was empty, a void.

Anne had given all she had to Henry, and he left it out to spoil, rusting in the rain.

Seanna's eyes opened, only to find a wet, frowning Anne staring at them. She stumbled backwards out of Hartwinn's arms as if she was caught doing something she shouldn't have been, even though they had embraced more times than Anne could count.

"I'm glad you found a place to rest your head, Hartwinn, but can it not be my best friend?"

He straightened, not looking at her. "Where my head should rest is now my business, not yours."

Anne sighed. "Can we not do this tonight? I'm exhausted, wet and in a foul mood."

"Worn out, are you?"

The hidden meaning of his words slashed at her, but the blade never found flesh.

Even Seanna cringed at his words. "Hartwinn, that is enough—"

"If you both must know, all we did was *talk*. Henry sent me back to you, Hartwinn. He doesn't want me."

He exhaled, confusion bunching his brows for a moment. "Want you? He has little choice in the matter."

"And yet I'm here."

Seanna's eyes flashed between the pair. "I should—"

"No," Anne said softly. "We should have a witness for when Lord Novak makes his demands heard. Isn't that right?"

Hartwinn cleared his throat and straightened his spine. "You've had your fun, now whatever you had with him is over. No more lessons, no more sneaking out, no more picnics in the garden. You will be polite but distant at all formal events. Henry shall continue to dine with us until his men arrive, but you are not to engage with him. Do you understand?"

Anne's eyes rose to his as her jaw worked side to side, willing the tears to dry. She knew deep down that nothing would keep her from Henry, even if he didn't want her.

"I understand."

"You will be marrying me, Anne, as our fathers wished. We will join our great houses—"

"Yes—"

"I'm not finished. If I find out you have gone to him, in any capacity —lovers, or even as *friends*—there will be consequences."

"What will you do?" she asked, a tear rolling down her cheek.

"Don't force my hand, Anne, and you won't find out.

"And we will be getting married after the ball. No more stalling."

Seanna gripped his arm, but he stood unmoved. "Hartwinn, I think you need to calm—"

"That is *final*. No more arguments, for I don't wish to hear them, nor do I wish to waste my time further on this conversation."

Anne simply nodded, exhaustion eating away at her.

Seanna exhaled at the harshness of his tone. She shook her head, crossing her arms. "Now, I never thought I'd hear your father's voice leave your mouth."

His eyes flashed to her, hurt forming in the thinning of his lips. "I do *not* sound like him."

"He is hurt, Seanna. I've hurt him." Anne paused, attempting to steady her voice. "And he is our lord. He may speak how he wishes."

Seanna cocked her head at her, narrowing her eyes in disbelief. "He will not. I will not stand here and allow him to speak to you in such a tone."

Anne's lips parted as another set of silent, salty drops travelled down her chilled cheeks.

"Bed. *Both* of you. That is a command. And tomorrow, you will be moving into the lord's wing—"

"No, I will not," Anne said softly.

"That wasn't a request."

She scrubbed the tears from her cheeks. "If you demand we marry, we shall live as other nobles do. *Apart*. I shall come to you at the opportune time to create an heir, but I shall remain in my room every other night."

Hartwinn exhaled as if she had punched him in the guts. He hadn't expected that; he had expected her to fawn and coddle. For things to go back to the way they were. But they never would. Because Anne left her heart in that forest, in the care of a man who said he could never love again.

"Now, if you don't mind, I wish to bathe and go to bed. I fear I might catch a chill if I stand here in wet clothing for much longer."

Hartwinn ran a hand through his hair and strode up to her. "You forced my hand, Anne. I had no choice."

"That's what you don't understand, Hartwinn. You've always had a choice, given to you by Deus, himself, but you decided to rip the only one I have away. Who I choose to love."

Her words hung heavy in the air, making him launch across the room away from them. He paused at her door. "I must know, was he worth it?"

Anne didn't turn, but her face crumpled as more tears rushed down her cheeks—another stab to her heart. She let out a shaky breath as she met Seanna's concerned gaze.

"Yes," was all she could say.

The door slammed behind her as Anne crumbled to the ground in a sloppy, wet mess. Seanna rushed to her, collapsing in front of her, drawing her into her arms. A howling sob left Anne as she clung to her best friend, nails clawing. Her heart hadn't cracked but splintered in her chest, blasting shards right into her aching flesh.

"It will be all right, Anne," Seanna soothed with a rub on her back. "He will forgive you—"

"But will I ever forgive myself?" she asked, pushing off her friend. "I ruined everything, Seanna. Shattered it with careless hands. Now, the man I love cannot love me, and the man I respect and call my best friend cannot stand me. I have ruined it *all*."

CHAPTER THIRTY-ONE

ANNE STOOD IN THE OVERCROWDED, OVER-PERFUMED ballroom next to a laughing, smiling Hartwinn, who was talking to Wyn Neverclove. An iciness grew between her and Hartwinn. Even at a distance, it chilled her skin. It made all her smiles tight, and her jaw clenched.

Neither had spoken, not truly. Polite, stilled conversation, but nothing of that night, nor of her betrayal. It had become a habit, ignoring the festering until the skin split and weeping, oozing feelings bled out. Yet, neither could hide, as it was only days until the ball. The nobles of Alderdeen were filling each nook and cranny of Valliss, which meant lavish parties and dizzying nights that led into the mornings, not long nights of talking and arguing.

"Good Deus, Wyn," Hartwinn said through a laugh.

"No word of a lie. I stood in front of a real-life, breathing dragon—"

"Do you mean a lizard, sir? Dragons are extinct, hunted by our forefathers for their scales."

"And yet, I still bear the scar of our entanglement."

They'd become fast friends, unnerving Anne. She surveyed the dark-haired male with obvious disinterest. It wasn't because he was fae. He was cocky, smirking and worst of all, annoyingly charming, thinking he could get away with anything with a flash of teeth and a wandering eye. The women of court loved him—or lusted after him, more like it.

Anne took a sip of her wine, casting her eyes to the milling crowd. That was, until she saw Henry entering the gilded ballroom, a slight stumble in his step. The world grew quiet as her eyes followed him across the room. His arm was flung over Cidran's shoulder, who had a pensive, concerned look across his face. Anne gripped her fan tighter as Henry reached out and gripped a bottle of wine, yanking it from a bewildered servant. He brought it to his lips and greedily gulped it down.

This isn't what I taught him, Anne thought. *Not at all.*

The hulking Pietra crossed the room to him from his quiet corner with a fan-fluttering Seanna.

"And here we go," Wyn exhaled, linking a thumb in his sword belt. "He can't handle his liquor at the best of times. He will be a blubbering, ranting mess soon."

"Don't speak of him—"

A sharp glare from Hartwinn cut Anne's words off, making her grind her jaw. He was drawn into another conversation, leaving her alone with Wyn. His eyes crept over her body, smirk widening when she crossed her arms.

"I've heard the most interesting whispers about you, my lady."

"And you think you can speak to me?"

"An orphaned duchess with more lands and money than sense."

"This isn't very interesting gossip, sir. It is a well-known fact that I'm a well-endowed heiress. I'd be telling the person—"

"And you were giving lessons to a certain Henry Ashmore."

Anne raised her chin, pursing her lips. "I was simply informing Sir Ashmore of how this court works. That is all."

Wyn saddled up next to her, leaning close enough for her to feel his breath on the shell of her ear. "What really interests me is what lesson on manners had him kissing you with his hand up your skirts ..."

"I don't know what you—"

"I'd be careful of that one, my lady. He'll get you fat with his child and let you die pushing his son into this world. He only cares about proving to his father that he is worthy of the crown."

Anne's hands screwed up into fists. "That isn't true. He would never—"

"Then ask him about Kitra—his *wife*, the supposed love of his life. She was radiant, beautiful and totally devoted to him. Their love could have been a tale whispered around campfires and in halls such as these. If only he was as devoted to her as he was to leading his father's armies."

Anne felt as if someone had pinched and twisted the sore, aching part of her at the simple mention of Henry, let alone another loving him so deeply.

Wyn leant back, huffing a scoff. "He didn't tell you?"

"He has told me everything, Wyn Neverclove. Now, if you would take your leering eyes and lewd words and go fu—"

"What are you saying to her, Neverclove?" Henry slurred from behind them.

Anne whirled around to see both Cidran and Pietra holding a flushed, hooded-eyed Henry back.

"The things you should have told her."

"How *dare* you!" Henry snarled.

"We simply spoke of Kitra, that is all," Anne said quickly.

"And how much you loved her," Wyn added on.

Henry's eyes fell on Anne, a flash of something akin to hurt flaring, only to be quickly replaced with anger. "You spoke of *her* in these halls?"

"*Ciùin*, Henry," Pietra rumbled, his voice deeper than Anne had realised. "This isn't the place to discuss this."

"She was my *sister*, and I will speak of her as much as I wish to. I will not let her be forgotten to time, nor will I let people only know her as your *wife*," Wyn snapped, hurt washing away that smirking, crooning charm.

Cidran groaned, rolling his eyes as if it was a sore spot between the men that was constantly pressed. "Wyn, can we not—"

Henry forced himself forwards, fighting against the tight grip, almost rabid. "You think I have forgotten? I wear my grief as an iron shackle around my throat. I loved Kitra, Wyn, but Oryah had other plans for her."

Wyn clicked his tongue as he recoiled. "Oryah? *You* left her alone and pregnant to fight an unwinnable war. She died crying out for you."

Henry wavered, his eyes becoming glassy. "And it haunts me."

Wyn smirked, but this one was full of pain. He nodded to a scowling Anne. "Well, at least you've found somewhere to lay your head. Does she suck cock as good as—"

Anne swung with a closed fist.

She had never punched anyone before, and it bloody hurt. Pain blasted down her wrist, right from the crack of her knuckles against his jaw. Anne curled around her throbbing hand, cursing. Tears rushed to her eyes.

"Good gods, do you have a jaw of steel?"

Wyn straightened, his hand clasped to his cheek. Amusement lit his grey eyes. "Your hook could use—"

His words were cut from him as Henry slammed into him. Henry's fist crashed into Wyn's face with a concerning crack of bone against teeth. Wyn stumbled back, tripping on his own feet, but Henry rushed him, arm swinging to meet the hard slab of muscle of Wyn's guts, knocking the breath from him. Wyn quickly righted himself and drove his forehead up, slamming into Henry's cheek bone.

Henry shoved Wyn backwards, a red-stained snarl curling his lips. Their eyes clashed as both men drove forward. Blows landed, finding purchase, and missed swings soared through the air. Legs tangled, tumbling to the ground. Wrestling for control, Henry spat curses as Wyn barked demands.

Anne whirled around, searching for a guard, a Silver, but she only found curious and disgusted looks. None moved to stop the men fighting until Dayvis and Hartwinn pushed through the crowd, flanked by guards.

"Stop! Stop this at *once!*" Anne demanded, turning back. "Henry! Stop!"

"What in Heylla are you two doing?" Hartwinn's voice cut through the chaos. "Fighting like commoners at a pub in the Lower?"

Henry slumped to the stone, his lip bleeding, cheekbone swelling, but a wild, bloody grin spread across his face. Warmth pooled where it shouldn't. He was fearsome, feral, but something about him, bloody and charged, was alluring, arousing. His gaze found not the seething lord but her. A wildness was all she could see in his woody brown eyes as if it had awoken something in him. Hartwinn stepped into her view, making Anne's eyes dip.

"Guards, seize them."

Wyn remained flat on his back, arm across his face, knuckles bust open, not moving. Henry scrambled to his feet, palms out. His eyes rolled like a wild stallion cornered, readying to lash out in flying hooves and snapping teeth. Anne had to do something, anything. She shoved past a guard, whose hand lingered near his sword, to stall on the edge of the circle of iron and leather trapping Henry.

"Leave it for the training ring," Hartwinn ordered. "Then you can wallop on each other."

Albert, the bag of bones, slid up next to Hartwinn, eyes gleaming. *This is what he wanted*, Anne realised. *Fae brawling in the ballroom, showing the court what brutes they really are, proving him* right.

"Might I suggest, my lord, the old cells under the castle?" he crooned, hand to chest. "No need to send them all the way to the Pali for them to sober up."

"I'm hesitant to agree," Dayvis said, shaking his head. "The Pali is far more appropriate."

"I agree. Take them to the Pali. A night in those cells should sober them up. Both of them. And see this as a warning, I will not tolerate fighting in my court. My father, a man of violence, would have, but I'm different." He turned to Albert, his simmering gaze falling on the elderly man. "No one shall raise a fist to another in these halls. Now, guards!"

Henry backed up, arms jutting out further. His eyes searched for escape, but his body tensed as if he would fight his way out. Anne exhaled and let her legs take her forward, allowing that force to drag her to him.

Gasps came from the women, and a hissed curse from Hartwinn.

Her fingers trailed over his raised arms until she pressed her palm against his chest. Henry's whole body was vibrating with how hard his heart was beating. His wild gaze snapped to her, and for a moment, she saw the beast that lurked below his skin.

The wild wolf.

That animal didn't scare her but thrilled her.

Anne reached up and brushed over his bruising cheek, tucking a strand of hair behind the point of his ear.

"*Ciùin*, Henry. You're not on that battlefield, not anymore. You're here with me. No one here is going to hurt you. I won't let them."

He let out a shaky exhale and whispered, "I am trying. I am scared, Anne—"

Rough hands grasped him and yanked him from her. It was almost too much. It sent him snarling and straining to get back to her. Casting a frantic glance backwards, Anne watched Henry be swallowed by the crowd, her eyes never leaving his direction.

Chapter Thirty-Two

Anne stood over the green-tinged, hungover Dayvis with her arms crossed, frowning. She was still in her nightgown, and he was in the crumpled clothing from the night before. The breakfast before him was picked at, discarded, as were the crumb-infested plates around him in the empty dining room.

She had missed breakfast for the first time in years.

"Anne, please," Dayvis groaned, rubbing his eyes. "I simply cannot this morning."

"Where are they?" she asked, crossing her arms tighter.

He cast her a weary look. "Who in the heavens are you talking about?"

"You know exactly who I am talking about."

Dayvis grumbled and reached for his goblet, but Anne was faster, scooping up the cup and draining in two gulps. He stared at her, perplexed. She let out an unladylike burp and dumped the empty glass on the table.

"You need to be sober today."

"And you don't?"

Dayvis slumped back. He looked exhausted. His bloodshot eyes had smudges of purple underneath, and he looked slightly gaunt as if he wasn't eating well. "Tell me what you want, Anne."

"I want them free, and I want you to look after yourself. You look like *shit*."

He cast her a haughty look. "And they will be, at the pleasure of his lordship."

"When has Hartwinn indicated their release?"

"At his—"

"Before or after the ball *held* in Henry's honour?"

Dayvis stared at her—really stared at her. "You've chosen, haven't you?"

Anne raised her chin to the vaulted ceilings, gaze trailing over the golden beams, over the fine, painstakingly painted portraits. Had she chosen?

You have, the small, quiet voice whispered, which sounded suspiciously like her own. *But he doesn't wish to hold your heart, as he has loved another more deeply than he does you.*

Anne frowned at the voice. *I will not be jealous of a dead woman. Henry is allowed to have loved before me.*

"I ..." she hesitated, for saying the words made them real.

"Love makes us choose a path we never thought we would walk."

"Is it worth it to stray down that path, not knowing where it leads?"

Dayvis reached over and took her hand. "That is the most wondrous part, Anne. It doesn't matter where the path leads because you'll have taken the hand of the one you love and ventured with them. That's the point of this life—not the end destination, but the journey."

Anne arched her brow at Dayvis, a smirk curling on her lips. "You're surprisingly wise for a knight."

"When you've spent many years being very unwise, Anne, you learn a thing or two."

Her eyes filled with useless tears. Nothing would come of her crying. She tried to blink them away, but one fell.

"You have chosen," he repeated.

Anne took a deep breath, allowing the bravery to fill her lungs—and for once, that worrying buzzing noise didn't fill her mind.

"I don't think my heart would allow me to choose another."

Dayvis grinned and leant back further in his chair, linking his fingers. "I knew it."

"How?"

"I saw you swing at Wyn. Lousy right hook, by the way. The girl I knew would never.

She would have been worried about upsetting someone for not looking demure, meek. You *are* changing."

"For the worse?" Anne asked, concern lacing her tone.

Dayvis laughed, shaking his head. "No, for the better. Now, you should go to him."

"I cannot simply waltz into the Pali—"

"He isn't in the Pali, but in the dungeons."

"I thought—"

"Maybe a certain lord wished for a certain nobleman to think he was going to the Pali ..."

"What has happened?"

"A trap was laid, that is all. We were simply waiting for a rabbit to jump in, but none did." Dayvis dug around in his pocket, producing a set of iron keys. "You'll need these."

"Hartwinn—"

"Was going to release them tonight. He thought the time together may cool their ire towards each other."

"How will I—"

"I lost them after I had my fourth whisky," he explained, shrugging. "How careless of me."

Anne knew no one would believe Dayvis to be that sloppy, yet she snatched the keys and held them to her chest. "Thank you."

"You can thank me when you live a fulfilled life, Anne. Now go before the guards check. I made sure they will only come down at the eleventh bell."

Anne leant down and pressed a kiss to his scratchy cheek. "Your wife was a lucky woman."

"I only know love because of her. Now go!" he ordered with a clap.

She sprinted from the room, knowing exactly which dress she would wear.

ANNE HADN'T BEEN DOWN TO THE DUNGEONS BELOW Valliss. Not even as a curious teenager. They usually laid empty after they sent all criminals and prisoners to the Pali. She walked down the stone corridor, fingers trailing along the old, rusted bars. Her boots splashed in the still water between cobblestones, keys clenched tightly in her other hand. For a moment, she wondered if they ever held anyone down there. *Perhaps a madman? A dangerous prisoner? An evil witch? Or was it a sad soul accused of a crime he didn't commit?*

Shaking the thoughts from her mind, she continued down the mossy, damp corridor, hearing the males argue before she even found them standing chest to chest, battered and bruised.

"Gods, you have not changed a single bit in the years I have been away from you," Henry spat at Wyn. "Stubborn and thickheaded. I pity the woman you end up shackled to."

"Pity me? I pity that poor blonde who is infatuated with you, you miserable old sod. All you'll do—"

Anne cleared her throat and crossed her arms. "Now, now, boys. It seems you still cannot get along. I might leave you down here until you do."

Henry froze, stiffly turning. Surprise was written all over his face as he stared at Anne, mouth agape. Wyn poked his head out from behind Henry, a smirk spreading. "If all gaolers look like you, then I'll—"

A stray fist into his gut cut him off, leaving him doubled over and groaning.

"What are you doing here?" Henry asked, shoving Wyn away.

Anne raised her hand, the keys slung around her pointer finger. She gave them a tempting shake. "What does it look like? I'm freeing you."

Henry strode up to the bars, his hands enveloping the cool iron. His eyes danced over her, making her chest warm. She definitely hadn't forgotten the wildness she saw when he was bloody and feral on the floor of the ballroom—nor when she had slid her fingers between her thighs later that night and cried out Henry's name into her sheets as her release crashed into her.

His gaze warmed, curling up one corner of his lips. "What are you thinking about, *mo chridhe*?"

Steam could have bellowed out of Anne's ears with how hot her cheeks got. Her eyes darted to him, and for a moment, she allowed the flicker of remaining lust she felt to fill her irises. Henry's brows twitched upwards as his lips parted.

Exhaling, she mouthed the word that felt foreign, wrong on her human tongue.

"What does that one mean?"

Henry pressed his forehead to the bars, that crooked, breath-stealing smirk spreading across his face. The lighter flecks of gold in his eyes glittered. His hand lazily slipped through to brush her lips, only to drop away. "Nothing at all."

Wyn snorted behind him, but remained silent.

Her fingertips danced over the tender-looking flesh of his cheek. Henry's eyes fluttered closed as a small exhale slipped through his parted lips.

"You pair really went at it, didn't you?"

Henry captured her fingers as if to press a kiss to them but looked like he thought better of it. "Worry not for me, Anne. Death is a dear companion. We have done this dance before. My end's not near, nor will it be in this cold, damp dungeon or even in this castle. I will die in the arms of the woman I love."

"You promise—"

"I vow it," he whispered, finally pressing that fleeting kiss to her fingertips.

"I told you I will always worry for you, Henry—"

"Good goddess, *please* let me out before you decide to run away together, and we all end up in a cell," Wyn cut in with a deep groan.

Anne scrambled back. "I forgot you were there, Wyn."

"I *figured*," he murmured.

With a clang of keys and a few mis-starts, the door swung open. Wyn shoved past Henry, right to Anne. There was something in his eyes —something that burnt with the truth.

"Take a step back—"

"You feel it, don't you?"

"I feel nothing towards you."

"No. Not me. *Him*," Wyn said, pointing at Henry. "You feel it like a shove between your shoulder blades, driving you to him."

Henry shook his head. "Wyn, not here."

"Then when, Henry?"

He rushed towards Wyn, gripping him by his shirt. "Go."

"You need to tell her—"

"Do not ever tell me what to do, Neverclove."

Without even looking at her, Wyn glared up at Henry. "You will kill him, Anne. You and your puny human lifespan. That's if he ever grows the bollocks to bond with you. For now, he will sniff around you like a desperate pup wanting a scratch."

"*What?*" Anne asked, confused.

Wyn's feet left the ground as Henry drew him upwards to his face. His lip curled as his nostrils flared. Wyn's eyes narrowed, but a shimmer of fear appeared on his features.

"You better make yourself scarce, right now. That is an *order*."

Henry shoved him backwards, making him stumble right into the wall. Wyn straightened, his hand curling into fists, knuckles whitening.

"*Pòg mo thòin*," Wyn spat before turning on his heel and storming to the exit.

He left them alone with Anne staring off into the distance. Her heart slammed around her head, drowning out her spiralling thoughts.

I will kill Henry.

"*Kiss my arse?* Good goddess, he is still such a *child*," Henry murmured with an exhausted sigh.

"Is that true?"

"Anne—"

"If we were to be bonded, would you *die*? Is it because you've already lived longer than a human lifespan? Would you rapidly age? Tell me."

Henry took a while to answer. The longer he remained still, contemplative, the more Anne's mind began to form her own rambling, panting conclusions. She strode right to Henry and turned him to her.

"Answer me."

"My life would be bonded to yours, Anne. I would only live a human lifespan. You know this. I told you."

"That is—"

"*Romantic*, isn't it? That is what you said, right?" Henry cut in with a half-smile.

Anne shook her head, her hand rising to his heart. "You will die—"

"After we spend the rest of our lives together. I will age as you do, and not like some awful ghoul."

"And if we do not bond ..."

Henry shrugged. "I shall live hundreds of years."

"And you'd give that up?"

He turned to her. His gaze had warmed, burning directly into her. And she had her answer. Henry took a step towards her, forcing her to take a stumbling step back until her spine hit the cool wall. Her hand grasped at the stone so as to not reach for him—or was it to steady herself? She couldn't tell.

Anne should have said goodbye to him and returned to Hartwinn. But she and every god watching knew that would never happen. Not ever again.

Henry's body, broad and masculine, loomed over her as his forearm met the stone above her. His towering presence didn't frighten but roused something deep inside of her. He was close enough for the smell of musk, waxed leather and unwashed man to waft off him. He didn't reek, but the opposite. She couldn't help but draw him in, right down deep into her lungs, allowing him to settle there.

"I'd give up a thousand lives for you, Anne. For you, I'd give up *everything*."

"But you said you didn't wish to hold my heart—"

"I only said that as I was—"

"Scared?" Anne finished.

"*Terrified*, Fate. Terrified I would give my heart away, only for it to shatter into a thousand pieces."

Anne lowered her gaze, and the question slipped from her before she even considered the words. "Like it was by her?"

Henry lowered his forehead against hers. "I loved Kitra, but I was not ready to be anyone's husband."

"But Wyn—"

"He was my best friend, and I killed his sister. He has every right to be angry, furious and hateful with me."

Anne exhaled, her eyes finding his half hooded, glazed as if trapped in a memory.

"I thought the campaign Sundryl sent me on was only going to be a few weeks, not the months slogging through mud and blood I had to endure. The *Slanaighers* said it was safe for me to leave, that the babe wouldn't come before I got back. I never thought ..." He paused, loosening a breath. "But the battle turned into a war, and I was trapped, unable to return to her. That wasn't even the worst thing. I was so caught up in warring that even the letters I sent weren't full of love and longing, but of battle and pain. Words I should have sent to my father, not my pregnant wife."

"What happened?"

"By the time I got word she was birthing, she was gone. She died alone, in a cold marital bed, taking our precious son she loved so much with her to the great gardens. And it's all my fault."

"Henry—"

"I say my heart is the one I wish to protect, but it is really yours, Anne. If I hold it, I will crush it." Henry sniffed, tears tracking down his cheeks. "Wyn is *right*. I do not deserve the love you have for me."

Silence echoed. Anne could even hear the drip of water splashing on the mossy rocks, harmonising with her sharp inhales.

"And, that is where you are *wrong*, Henry Ashmore."

"What?"

Anne's chin wobbled as she battled the lump in her throat. "You deserve my love, not because you've hurt and suffered, but because you've been brave too ..."

Her words were stolen with a soft exhale as tears fought to spill.

"To what?"

"To travel this world with half a heart."

Henry shook his head, his brows meeting. His hand tentatively rose, placing it over her thundering heartbeat.

"My heart has a match, Anne, and I believe it lives in you."

"Oryah, with all her divine knowledge, has brought us together. As if it was—"

"*Fate.*"

Anne laughed as tears rolled down her cheeks. Her hands captured his face, letting their gazes meet, to dance, to search, to allow that overwhelming feeling to flood the space between them. He gripped her hips, holding on tight. Tighter than ever before, as if he wasn't going to let her go. Still lurking in those woody forests was disbelief.

"Do you truly wish for someone like me to possess your precious heart?"

That handful of words dented her building joy. Each one was tinged with sadness, that deep-rooted self-loathing. She wished she could do something—anything—to cut those roots away, only to replace them with something that grew deeply, but didn't draw life from the soil but gave back.

"You already do, Henry. I was simply minding it for you to come and take it."

"Are you sure, Fate?" he whispered, his voice a fraction wobbly.

"I have never been more sure about anything in my entire life."

His shoulders heaved as a soft sob escaped him. Anne didn't let him go, nor did she speak. Her words couldn't combat those barbs that cut deep into his own heart. Only time and the love she wished to shower him with would unhook those thorns

What Anne did was kiss him, pressing her lips to his over and over, hoping Oryah would hear their hearts singing to each other, as hers did for Diabolus. And unlike their tale, Anne and Henry would be together.

Soon, their kiss turned hungry, with aching want, tongues swirling. Henry's knee slid between her thighs. Anne's hips rolled and bucked. Her hand leapt from the stone to the hard muscle of his back, clawing at him. Rough, powerful hands seized her waist, forcing her to drive down on the long muscle of his thigh. Their kiss broke in heaving moments, only for Henry to drag his mouth down her throat, tempting her with scrapes of teeth, then returning to her mouth, devouring her once more.

Anne gently pushed him away, not wanting them to get too caught up with each other, and having him take her against a wall.

Henry rested his forehead against hers. "What are we going to do?"

Her hand encapsulated his cheek, thumb stroking. "We will be together, even if I have to tear this world apart. I will have you, Henry Ashmore. Oryah made you for me. I will not give that up."

A droning bell rang—the eleventh bell. Soon, Hartwinn's guards would be crawling all over the place. Anne turned her face to the creeping sunlight from the small windows and the truth morning usually brought. The truth was that she'd do anything he wanted her to do.

Jump, and she would ask how high.

Run, and she would ask how fast.

Love him, and she would ask how endlessly, how deeply.

Is it desperation to be loved or is this growing into something more?

Anne craved to be with him in whatever sense—friends, lovers, even enemies. She wanted to loathe him, love him and long for him in every breath she took on this earth and in every lifetime she was cast to.

CHAPTER THIRTY-THREE

ladies, lords and everyone between, all descending on Alderdeen, hungry
vultures, readying to pick the bones of the city dry, filling themselves for
the next city they flocked to. However, Hartwinn was ready, bracing for
their sharp beaks and claws with free-flowing wine and never-ending
platters of delicious, mouth-watering meats, roasted and crispy vegeta-
bles, wedges of cheeses and bright, sweet fruits. All ready to be
devoured.

Valliss' makeshift throne room was glowing with hundreds of
candles, flickering and casting an orange glow over all who ventured in.
Rainbows of blooms filled the gaps that candles were not shoved in.
Even a swaying troop of strumming lute players backing a warbling
singer filled the air with soft siren songs of love.

It reeked of Seanna.

Yet, she was nowhere to be seen, when normally she would be
preening and purring.

Anne paused at the entrance, the herald of the court's deep baritone
voice ringing out into the dim of the room announcing her arrival. She
hadn't a chance to even take one step before Edda swooped in, slipping
her arm through hers, pulling her deeper into the masses of people. That

uncomfortable tightness in her chest emerged as they shouldered their way through.

Edda leant in and whispered, "We must bow before the true queen of this land—"

"Hicka—"

"Is making an *appearance*," she finished, her brows rising.

Anne let Edda drag her to the corner of the room where the elderly woman was holding her own court. Surrounded by women all vying for her attention sat Lady Hicka with more gold on her fingers than in Hartwinn's coffers, even dressed and powdered as if she were from a different century. Lady Hicka outranked even Seanna, thanks to her late husband. But Anne knew not to be fooled. Hicka may have had deep-set wrinkles and knobbly joints, but her green eyes were clear, unclouded by age. She was sharp-tongued and quick-minded. One wrong step and one will lose her favour, which would mean social death in Alderdeen.

Hicka turned her shrewd gaze to a grimacing Anne and beckoned her over with a sharp wave of her fan. Edda dropped into a curtsy, while Anne simply stared at the woman.

"Hicka."

"Anne."

Hicka took no notice of Edda, who was scraping at her swollen ankles.

"I've heard the most peculiar rumour about you."

"You must be bored out in your country manor if you are talking of me."

The old crone reached over and poked her in the chest with her fan. "There are whispers that you've been seen consorting with a fae male."

Anne softly laughed, flicking away her fan. "What tall tales you've heard."

"Those rumours—"

"I have much more exciting news, Miss Hicka," Edda cut in.

Hicka turned her eyes to the young bride. "What is it?"

Edda swallowed—one never interrupted Hicka, even Anne knew that—but she was far too keen to impress the woman. She continued, "Well, I know who stabbed him and who commanded it."

Anne grew tense, her gaze rising to Edda. "*Who?*"

"Well, my darling Berty, of course. He wishes this riffraff to leave Alderdeen—"

Anne rushed her, gripping her by the shoulders. "Are you daft? Henry could have been *killed*."

Edda wiggled in her tight grip. "He will bring his scum—"

"Your *precious* Berty is the scum, infecting Hartwinn's council with hatred and disgust. Henry is nothing like the tales we have believed. He is kind, caring and wants to better this city. And what does your husband want?"

"You only believe that because you're the whore spreading your legs for him," Edda spat right back, her tone full of disgust. "I saw you. I saw you and him rutting like commoners in the gardens."

Scandalous whispers surrounded her as the ladies of Alderdeen waggled more than their fans.

"That was *you*? I knew it."

"And I told everyone, including poor Hartwinn. You don't deserve to be the lady of Alderdeen. A woman of your *class* should never sit next to such a powerful man."

Anne's upper lip twitched, feeling that hot rise of anger. With a sharp exhale, she shoved Edda back, fighting the urge to swing her fist as her vision turned red.

"You and Albert belong together, Edda," Anne spat as if that was the dirtiest, filthiest curse she could imagine. "You call me a whore, yet who is it who sold her body for absolutely no power? *You.* Albert will never see you as anything more than a brooding mare, and if you dare speak up, he will beat that fire out of you. The sooner he meets Deus, the better it will be for you."

Edda's eyes grew wide as an ugly snarl emerged on her once-pretty face. "At least I wasn't seen leaving King Ewan's chambers in nothing but my underthings, only to beg the healers of Goulrich for a *certain* type of tonic."

Anne's jaw clenched in response as fans waved more furiously than tongues.

Edda's words held a knife to her, forcing her to spew out insults. But she would plunge that blade further, right into her squishy insides. Her hand snapped out, latching onto Edda's elbow. She drew her in closer so she could whisper in her ear. "And I hope when that walking skeleton ruts into *you* with his shrivelled manhood and pumps you full of his barron seed, you think of the pleasure you witnessed between Henry and me, and how you will never feel a wick of it in your pathetic life."

Edda scurried back, ripping herself from Anne's grasp. "I will not stand here and be pitied by a sullied whore like you."

"And I will feel no sting from the words of a hateful woman like yourself." Anne raised her chin, allowing herself to inhale her truth and exhale the fear that had kept her silent those years. Yet, her hands still trembled when she continued, "If you all must know, I didn't go into Ewan's bed willingly. He forced me. And if I did beg for a tonic to rid me of a child created in pain, may Diabolus rise and swallow me whole."

Silence echoed after her confession.

Edda glanced around, searching for allies and finding none, all eyes lowering from hers. She had gone too far, pushed too hard—but so had Anne. It would have been simpler if they simply slogged it out, landing punch after punch. However, it was a battle of highly strung emotions, which only clashed over and over. None would come out victorious. Only that awful ache in Anne's head and the regret for using such sharp words would win.

"You will pay—"

"I won't, Edda. Neither of us will. That is a simple fact. These women will gossip about us, but neither of us will face a hangman's noose for this. Unlike your husband, who ordered the attack of a crown prince—"

"He is *not* a prince."

Hicka leant forward, finally speaking. "Henry Ashmore may be bastard-born, but he has royal blood in his veins. His father, Sundryl Ashmore, High King of the Fae, and I are old acquaintances, and I think he will not take kindly to those who threaten his son's life. He has marched onto a battlefield for less."

Edda's face paled, and her eyes widened before she threw herself into the throng of people, pushing past Seanna in such a hurry she almost lost a slipper.

Seanna shot her a confused look. Anne's eyes rose to the hulking, stoic man standing behind her. His hand hovered on her shoulder in a familiar way. Did they simply bump into each other, or had they come together?

"What in Heylla?" Seanna mouthed.

Anne cast her a tight grin and turned back to Hicka, who was eyeing her off as if she were a precious jewel, all while she tapped her fan on her lips.

With each silent second that passed, the fury faded away, and she waited for that bitter taste to coat her tongue. But it never came. She had nothing to hide, and especially not the love in her heart.

All the women sat straight-backed, eyes glued to the old crone.

Waiting. Watching.

Until Hicka threw her head back and cackled. Laughter filled the once-tense air, allowing a friendly, jovial lightness to replace it.

"I've been waiting for someone to humble that girl for *years*!" Hicka exclaimed, slapping her knee, laughter still pouring from her. "And I have finally witnessed it. I thank you."

"You're welcome," Anne replied hesitantly.

Women began to chat and laugh, turning away from them, leaving Hicka and Anne to consider each other.

"You, Duchess Davoy, seemed to have grown a backbone."

"I've always had a backbone. I just never knew how to use it."

"And that's what happens when you fall in love. You change. Sometimes for the better, and sometimes for the worse"

"I'm not—"

"Please, if I had not had witnesses spotting you two dancing in a stall or him riding into a storm after you, I would believe your lies. A lady of noble birth, falling for a fae warrior. That is the stuff of ballads, of tales, not of reality. But yet, it has happened here in sleepy Alderdeen."

"You don't seem disgusted by the idea."

Hicka flicked her fan out to wave across her face. "I have seen much worse things than two idiots falling in love."

"I don't know what to say."

"Say nothing, and go inform your lord of the treason that is occurring under his roof, or—"

"Or?"

Hicka leant in closer, and a wickedly impish smirk spread on her face. "Or find your lover and give me and my ladies something to talk about for the rest of the year. Your choice."

She stared at the old woman. *My choice ... And I have chosen.*

She curtsied and returned an equally wicked grin. "I do hope you have tea to soothe your throat from all the talking you will be doing."

Anne turned on her heel, her emerald green skirts flaring around her. She raced over to Seanna, who was eyeing Hicka with a nervous tilt to her chin. Like all the women in court, she wished to impress the old crone.

"I've got to go—"

"Anne, what is going on? Edda was crying—"

"And I couldn't care less. I'm going to find Henry. He owes me a dance."

"I think he owes you much more than that," Pietra said. "He owes you his life."

"And what does that even mean? I feel like someone has turned off the lantern and left me in the dark," Seanna said, a slight whine to her voice.

"I can explain—"

"I will explain later."

Anne and Pietra spoke in unison.

Seanna let out a choked laugh and turned to Pietra, poking him with her fan in his broad chest, then turned it on Anne. "You can explain now, whereas you will simply inform me of what happened later."

Anne nodded, pressing a kiss to her friend's cheek, and pushed into the slow-moving throng of people, allowing the wave to force her forwards. Her eyes searched for him in every face, peeking into each corner, simply allowing that golden string to tug in her chest until it led her right to him. Henry was leaning against a wall, ranting to Cidran. He was dressed in fine leather and soft cottons—exactly what they had spoken about. He wasn't a man for silk or velvet, but steel and sweat. The leather gripped his body in a way Anne found nearly indecent.

God gods, he is unholy, Diabolus-made, and I want him so terribly.

Henry's hands waved and pointed. Cidran simply shook his head and laughed. They glanced at each other, and before Anne knew it, embraced in a tight, backslapping hug. She dared to take a step closer, loitering on the peripheries of the crowd, allowing their conversation to flow to her.

"I see blue sky on a hot summer's day in her eyes, Cidran. That's all it reminds me of every time I even glance at her. Like when we were young men. You know, the day we decided to go to the lake—"

"And you spent the whole time floating, seeking answers instead of getting a glimpse of the wood sprites bathing."

The corner of his lip quirked upwards and Anne's mouth mimicked his. "All I remember is the elder sprite threatening to gouge your eyes out if you ever dare to spy on her girls again."

"And you never got the answers you were searching for, did you?"

Henry dropped his gaze, but it rose almost immediately as a true grin spread on his face, crinkling his eyes and rounding his cheeks. He sparkled with life. He was so full of it, that precious thing, that Anne could feel it seep out and embrace her. That simple smile would be seared into her mind to play in her dreams and linger in her thoughts for the rest of her days.

"I did, Cid. You said yes, and I will never have to question it again."

A toothy grin stretched across his freckled face. "You will always have me, Hen."

Anne took a step closer and cleared her throat. Both men turned and exhaled. She knew she was a vision in emerald green and gold. Yet, as Henry's eyes worked up her frame, Anne felt seen—truly looked at. Not for the dress she wore or the jewels against her skin, but for who she was.

"I know who ordered the attack—"

"We all know who did," Henry said softly. "Hartwinn is waiting for him to slip up—"

"His wife just confessed to all the noblewomen of the court. There is his cheese for the trap."

"And for the life of me, I cannot find a single part of me that cares about that right now. All I wish for is a dance with you."

"With me? Henry, you were almost—"

"By the grace of the goddess, I wasn't. Now, I will not waste another moment. Will you allow me the honour of dancing with me at *my* ball,

Fate?" he asked, holding his hand out. "For I wish to dance with no other."

Anne exhaled and allowed a smile to spread over her face. "It would be my pleasure."

Henry glanced back at Cidran, nodding for him to join them. He shook his head, pressing his hand to his breast pocket. "I have a letter to write to a witch. It seems I've been inspired."

Henry drew Anne closer, allowing his hand to settle on the curve of her waist. He leant down, and for the briefest moment, his lips brushed along the taut muscle that ran along her shoulder to her neck, setting her on fire.

"Don't do anything I wouldn't do!" Cidran called from behind them.

Anne laughed as Henry pulled her towards the dance floor. Couples were spinning and stepping with a casual ease. He swallowed almost audibly, and cast her a wobbly grin.

He was nervous.

Anne pushed onto her toes and whispered in his ear, "Just like we did in the stall. Nothing more, nothing less."

"You and I have very different memories of what occurred in that stall, Fate."

Anne's cheeks warmed as her hand slid into his. She pulled him onto the dance floor as the song changed—the same one they had practised.

"Now—"

"Eyes on you, and relax," Henry finished seriously.

Anne watched with barely contained glee as he steeled his face into what she expected to look when he stepped out onto the battlefield. She burst out laughing as he twirled her around. Never once stepping on her toes nor ever looking away. They simply flowed, their feet exactly where they were meant to be.

"You've gotten good," Anne whispered.

Henry turned with her in his arms and whispered back, "Only because I have the right partner."

The entire world seemed to disappear, fading into nothing, for only they mattered, and no one else. His hand trailed down her spine to firmly grip her waist, dragging her aching body closer. Their eyes never parted, never once looked away. That soft, fluttering worked its way up her chest, to settle around her heart—not making a home, but *going* home. It was always supposed to be there.

There will be no other, Anne thought silently. *Not for me, not ever.*

He leant in, his lips a feather touch over the shell of her ear. "You are glorious, *mo chridhe ...*"

"What does that mean?"

She felt his lips stretch into a grin against her as he whispered, "My heart."

Anne exhaled and replied, "And yet, I'm nothing in comparison to you, *mo chridhe*—"

A hand locked around her raised elbow, tightly, yanking her away from Henry. Shattering the moment they shared, into a thousand pieces, crashing around their feet. Anne followed the arm up to an enraged Hartwinn. His eyes weren't full of rage, but that heartbreaking hurt.

It was time, they had to tell him.

"What did I say—"

"I was telling him the information I learnt. That is *all*. Now let go of me."

Coward, the small voice whispered. *You coward.*

Henry cleared his throat. "We were trying to be less obvious—"

"By practically dry humping each other on the dance floor?" Hartwinn cut in with a hissed whisper.

Anne's lips parted in outrage. "We were not."

Before she could fight any more, Hartwinn was already dragging her away from Henry, who stood torn, his hands fisting by his side, eyes never leaving her.

"Enough, Anne. Enough of this. I forbid you from seeing him—"

Anne fought his tight grip. "Forbid it? You cannot forbid me from doing anything, Hartwinn Novak. I'm to be your wife, not your slave."

Hartwinn had pulled her into the cool night, right to the balcony. He let her go with a shove. "Do you think I'm a fool, or do you simply treat me like one?"

"Yes, I danced with Henry."

"Anne—"

She threw her arms wide, tears rushing to her eyes. "What do you want me to say?"

"The truth. For once, the *truth*."

Anne clenched her jaw, pinning with a desperate look. "The truth? I love him, Hartwinn."

"You *love* him?" he whispered, his face crumpling. "Anne, you—"

The earth rocked beneath her feet, as a hot blast exploded in the sky. Stars rained down, lighting Hartwinn's eyes, and the hurt that Anne put there. Anne whirled around, hands slapping over her ears, as more colourful bangs popped in the smoky air.

"Dragonfire," Hartwinn explained, from behind her. "Something Ewan's men discovered from one of their many battles. It's a by-product of—"

"The fae—"

"And, what about them, Anne?" Hartwinn said with a weary sigh.

Anne turned to glare at him, her body tensing with another crackling pop. "They're going to be *frightened* of this. Did you not think that this is what Ewan used on *their* battlefields? That they had heard enough explosions?"

"Anne, I never thought—"

"That is your problem, Hartwinn. You think too deeply of the things that don't matter. Oh, and by the way, Albert's daft wife, Edda, just confessed that he was the one who ordered Henry's attack. How is that for evidence?"

"Hicka just told me. He and his wife are to be banished in the morning."

Anne exhaled and strode to the door. She cared not for Albert and his hateful schemes.

Only for *Henry*.

Her eyes searched for him, but only saw a sliver of his dark hair fleeing through the doors of the makeshift throne room. But what made her exhale was Pietra, eyes wild, backing up. Seanna stood in front of him, her hands out. A guard approached him, and with one frightened swing, he slammed his fist into his face. More guards shoved and pushed the crowd apart.

Anne stepped inside, and a flood of noise hit her square in the chest. Pietra was shouting, and Seanna was matching him, demanding he listen to her not the sounds of battle echoing inside of Valliss. She was pleading, but that sharp command was evident. But Hartwinn's guards voices' were a deep, baritone, fighting over her, simply ordering him to get a hold of himself.

None had seen what the fae had, and yet no scrap of empathy was heard in their voices.

It disgusted her.

Anne finally had made it to where the guards stood around Seanna and Pietra.

"They are here, Seanna! They are coming for us!" Pietra shouted, eyes roving seeing ghostly enemies. "I must protect you—"

"Pietra, you listen here, right *now*!"

His eyes flashed to hers.

"You're in need of some fresh air, aren't you? Shall we go for a walk amongst the roses?"

"But—"

Her hand reached for him, falling on his forearm. The guards grumbled, shifting on their feet.

"There is no enemy. There is only us. Let us go to the gardens, where we walk at night. There is nothing there that can hurt us."

"You promise?"

Seanna nodded, her eyes filled with tears. "I promise. You're safe with me."

More gasps as the sky lit again, forcing Pietra to back up and scramble against a wall. His legs gave way, sliding down to land heavily. Seanna lowered herself down, her hand reaching for his. Anne's view was blocked by the guards inching forwards.

Hartwinn was hot on her heels. He grabbed her wrist, turning her. "If you go to—"

"I'm the only one who can calm Henry down. You cannot ask me not to go. That is cruel, Hartwinn. You cannot ask me to stand around when I know he is panicking somewhere. You see how Pietra is. Henry is *worse*. I know we have much to talk about, but not right now. You must let me go to him."

"You have an hour. Not a minute more. Then, we shall talk."

Anne winced—not at his tone, but at the hot throb of pain in her wrist. He had gripped her with such force her nearly mended bones ached. His eyes dropped to where they connected, his lips parting, and he let go as if she was coated in poison. Anne didn't give him the opportunity to apologise as she turned on her heel and launched into the crowd, leaving her past behind and running towards her future, her fate, her heart's match.

Chapter Thirty-Four

Anne sprinted through the castle, her breath coming hard and fast. He wasn't in his rooms, nor was he in hers. He wasn't lost in Hartwinn's office, nor was he under the table in his war room. Everywhere she looked, he wasn't there. And she was running out of time.

Anne leant against a wall, breathing through a sharp stitch, racking her mind to think of where he could have gone. Then, a bright spark of a thought.

He is not in Valliss.

Anne pushed off the wall, kicking her slippers off as she ran with all she had. Her skirts yanked high as she bounded down stairs and across the chilled courtyard, right to where they both felt the safest.

The stables.

Anne's eyes rose once to the night cloaked carvings as if she was sending a quick prayer to Oryah—a goddess she'd never thought much about. Now, she'd kneel at her altar, praising her for bringing Henry into her life.

Anne rushed through the door, finding not a soul. All of the servants would be celebrating, drinking until the early morning.

"Henry?" she called out, turning and looking. "Henry, are you here?"

A whinny came from somewhere deep in the soft glow of the moon-light lit stables.

Carrots.

She was beckoning her.

Anne strode through the stable, her bare feet slapping on the stone. What she found made her pause, as an exhale left her. Henry was tucked in the corner of Carrots' stall, with the mare's head pressed against his. His shaking hands were slowly stroking the velvet patch under her chin.

His glassy eyes rose to hers as his brows twitched together. "Fate."

Anne slipped into the stable, hay digging to her feet. She slowly lowered down, her skirts poofing around her. She reached over to Henry, and with her thumb, smeared the wetness across his cheek.

"*Mo chridhe,*" Anne said, her tongue fumbling over the unfamiliar syllables. "You are safe. Nothing can harm you here, for you have Carrots and me to fight off any ghosts or ghouls that haunt you from your past."

Henry searched her face, breath coming in heaves. "You would do that for me?"

Anne softly nodded before whispering, "More than that, I promise, Henry."

He turned his face, pressing his lips to her palm. "Then I promise I will battle this overwhelming panic so I can be the husband you deserve—"

Anne leant in and stole his words with a soft kiss. "You're already the man I need, Henry Ashmore. Ghosts and all. I wouldn't have you any other way."

"You do not mean that—"

"You are *not* broken, Henry, nor something I need to *fix*."

Henry pressed his forehead against hers. "I may never be able to—"

"Fully love me?"

"No, each part of my broken heart calls for you, Anne. Love is not the worry here," he said quickly, in a rush to get out his words. "These nightmares follow me, and they will until we are placed in the soft earth. Maybe they'll be the thing that puts me in that grave."

"Then they shall take me too. But I will go down swinging, fighting with all I have. I will not let those dark days swallow you whole, nor will I let your hand tremble alone. I will be there for you."

"You are giving up—"

"*Nothing* because there is nothing sacrificed, Henry," Anne said, tears of joy, of that overwhelming emotion, sliding down her cheeks. "A life with you is an honour, even if some nights your nightmares may shake you awake. As long as you can hold me when mine do."

Anne took a steadying breath, then leant down and pressed a kiss to his forehead. Then, to his temple, skimming over the wet part of his cheek. Finally, she found his lips. Their embrace wasn't that desire-filled clash of tongues and mouths. It was slow, tentative and, best of all, building. The intensity rose with each turn of heads, press of lips. Without losing rhythm, Anne slid onto his lap. His fingers dragged over the knot of her bodice, pulling at the ribbon.

Anne broke the kiss, her chest heaving. She rested her forehead on his and lowered her gaze. She could feel his eyes burning into her as he searched her face.

"We should go back," Anne breathed.

"Do you truly wish to go back?"

I wish to never go back, Anne replied silently. Her eyes rose to his, and she allowed that aching, demanding desire to pool in her eyes. That was her answer.

His fingers trailed down her spine, only to spread out on her lower back. "Then what do you wish for me to do?"

She reached for his free hand and pressed her lips to each of his fingertips, then brought them to her cheek. Anne allowed a soft, serene smile to stretch on her face—one she wore while they were dancing.

"*Everything.*"

Henry leant in and allowed his lips to brush hers, and without wasting another moment, Anne dived into the drowning ocean of wanting, desire, lust and need. Henry's eyes widened for a moment as she dragged him under. Her tongue slid into his mouth, allowing him to taste it. Each nerve in her was vibrating with a fiery promise of pleasure, sending her core molten.

Soon, clothing was stripped from bodies, discarded in hurried throws. Henry brushed her hair over her shoulder to press his lips down her throat, over the swell of her breast. His manhood pressed against her rear, hard and eager, making her entrance clench.

"Good goddess, you are perfect."

A blush covered her cheeks. "Stop it—"

"*Never*," he replied as his teeth dragged over her prickling skin. "I will never stop telling you how beautiful, how perfect you are."

"You're—"

His hands drifted closer to her slick core. Anne whimpered a nearly silent, impatient sound. She rocked herself forward, demanding he relieve her of the tormenting throb between her legs.

"What am I, Fate?"

"A torturous, wicked man."

Henry smirked as he drew a line right through her centre. "Wrong."

Her gaze flashed to him, brows meeting. A mixture of blinking confusion and heady desire rose in her.

Henry leant closer, peppering kisses over her jaw as his forefinger slowly circled her swollen nub, sending the waves of pleasure around her. Her nails dug into his shoulder as her hips rocked against his fingers.

"I am yours."

And in a soft voice, she replied, "As I'm yours."

Her hand slid down over his scars and body hair to grip the thick length of him, making his hands dart to her waist. Holding her. Angling her hips, she dragged the head of his manhood through her slick, only to tease him around her warm, wet entrance.

"*Fuck*," Henry breathed, pressing his forehead to her shoulder.

With one lip-biting moan, she speared herself onto his manhood, filling herself completely with him. Henry groaned, face clenching as Anne's hips undulated lazily.

"Good Deus," Anne murmured, her eyes fluttering closed. She paused with him fully seated inside of her. "Your cock feels like it was made for me."

His hands gripped her hips, skin dimpling with the tension. "You need to move, Fate, for this will end—"

"Needy, are we?"

"Shut—"

His words were cut off with the sharp hiss of a curse as soon as she began slowly rocking her hips back and forth. He captured her hardened nipple in his mouth, sucking and nipping. Anne moaned, his tender caresses of her breasts only adding to the distracting, intense throbbing at that swollen bundle of nerves. His hand slid between them, circling her slick folds.

She was going to release on his manhood, and he would soon follow her.

Yet, Anne as she threw her head back, a pair of unimpressed, judging eyes fell on her.

Carrots.

Anne had totally forgotten about the mare, who stood as far away from them as the stall had allowed, pressing her large body against the wall.

"Henry, wait … Maybe, we should go somewhere more *private* …"

He laughed into her shoulder, sweat dripping from his brow. "Where?"

Anne rose, scooping up her underwear, shimmying them on. She helped him up with a heave, only to have him spin her and press her against the cool, stone wall. He pressed his lips between her shoulder blades, right up the sensitive spot where her neck met her jaw, teeth scraping, teasing her for what would come.

"We will not make it there if you keep kissing me like that—"

His hands slid over her hips, yanking her right back against him. "Then lead the way, Anne," Henry said, his voice a low growl. "It's taking all I have in me not to take you again."

The stable master's office was small, but warm, quiet and, most of all, *private*. Anne, only in her lacy undergarments, led an equally naked Henry into the sparse room. Her soft giggles filled the air as she picked her way to the cluttered desk. Heavy ledgers and books holding all the horses' information were scattered across the desk. She glanced over her shoulder, to Henry. His eyes had darkened, as he bit down on his lip. That wild wolf inside of him was pushing against his skin, readying to devour her. And yet, not a lick of fear or that buzzing worry filled her—only thudding, thrilling arousal, mixed with that fluttered around her heart.

Henry would never hurt her, but he would make her squirm, beg and demand for release. He stepped forward, forcing the small of her back to hit the table. Henry caged her in with his muscular, tensed arms. An almost feral grin spread across his face, sending his eyes glimmering. He leant down, dragging his nose over her collarbone, and right up her neck. Breathing her in, only to swirl a deep exhale of his nickname for her, "*Fate.*"

Shudders cascaded down her spine, prickling her skin.

Anne's hand snaked up, gripping him by the nape of his neck, drawing his lips close to heres. "Break me, Henry. Ruin me. Take me to the edge of pleasure and drown me in it. I'm not afraid."

"I am not going to break you. I am going to make you whole. I am going to bond with you."

"How?"

"I have to bite you ..." he said with a nip to her earlobe.

"Where?" Anne crooned, her hand trailing over the roundness of her breast. "Here?"

"No."

Her hand slid down over her stomach, right to her drenched centre. "Here?"

"No."

The table cut into Anne's stomach as Henry whirled her around. Pressing his hand firmly between her shoulder blades, forcing her over the table, he peppered kisses along that taunt muscle up her spine, right to her nape.

"Here. This is where I will mark you as mine. So all can see that you are my heart's match. Would you like that, Fate?"

Anne nodded, lost for words in her need for him.

Henry's free hand slid up the backs of her thigh, gripping onto her lacy undergarments—if one could call it that. It was barely a strip of lace, just covering her round rear.

"What in Oryah's name are you wearing?" he groaned, sliding a hand over the curve of her body. The shifting of the fabric created a devilish friction between her thighs.

"Something I thought you'd like ..." Anne groaned into the wood.

"It stays on. Good goddess, it says on," Henry ordered, voice rougher, deeper.

His searching eyes never rose from her round rear, nor did his hand cease the soft caress. It was as if he wished to always remember the feeling of her soft skin, edged with even softer lace under his palm.

"Gods, you are ..."

"What?"

"Just so *fucking* perfect. I cannot believe you are *mine*."

His words sent her blood singing, and that fluttering in her chest slamming against her rib cage. His foot kicked her leg out, spreading her wider for him. Fingers slid under the damp lace to find her wet, warm and willing.

"You got this soaked just for *me*?" Henry crooned, his fingers circling around the throbbing bundle of nerves slowly, round and round. Tormenting her.

Anne moaned into the wood, hands scurrying over the table, knocking books to the ground with heavy thuds. Her fingers snapped to the edge of the table, the sharp edge cutting into her palm. Something to latch onto before Henry drove her from this plane of existence.

Her release would come fast and hard. Yet, she didn't expect for him to pull his hand away as the sweet relief was mere moments away.

"*Please,*" she begged breathlessly, her core pulsing around nothing. "Please, *mo chridhe.*"

"Not yet, Fate, not yet."

Before Anne could even whisper another pleading beg, his thick manhood slid through her slick. And then, in one solid thrust, Henry was inside of her. She cried out, not from the sudden intrusion, but at the delicious, aching stretch of him. Even her body was made for him. Fitting together perfectly.

Henry started slowly as if he wished to make this last. Even so, each thrust was brutal and deep. Hitting her in a spot no one had reached before, making her clench, forcing muttered, groaning curses to leave Henry. His hand slid over hers, slipping between her fingers. His pace quickened, his hips slammed against her rear. Anne couldn't do anything but moan, pant and pray her legs wouldn't give out on her.

Henry leant over, pressing kisses up her spine—the same trail he had laid before. Without warning, he bit down on the sensitive skin of the nape of her neck. A sudden shot of pleasure blasted from her core, catapulting her over the edge. Her release slammed into her, driving a loud, almost sobbing cry to leave her, as her body arched underneath him.

The bite joined them, bounding them together. In life and death.

Waves of pleasure flooded her every nerve, every vein and inch of her body. Right to her thundering heart. She was lost in the swirling depths Henry had cast her to. It was only his pounding heartbeat which brought her back. A sound she sprinted too as her own rapid heart sang, harmonised with his. Until a divine, ethereal melody emerged in her ears, filling each silent space in her.

"Can you hear it, Anne?" Henry asked softly, pressing kisses around the bite.

A sob left her, her hands tightening around his. "I can hear it. My gods, it's beautiful."

"That is the song of our hearts," Henry whispered, his voice a fraction wobbly. "I've been hearing it ever since you rode Carrots into the forest, it's what drew me to you. Not a pack of wolves, but you."

"You've been hearing this the *whole* time?"

"I've heard it for as long as I can remember, Anne. A song I cannot get out of my head, worming its way in. That's how I know you were my match. Our melodies sung to each other."

Anne pressed up, turning her head to capture his mouth, tasting the mix of heat of whisky and the copper taste of her blood. "You've made me whole, now ruin me for any other, Henry Ashmore."

"There will be no other, Fate, for either of us," he said, his voice deep, gravelly.

With a singular hard thrust right to the hilt, he claimed her.

"This sweet, tight cunt is *mine*."

"Fuck—"

His thrusts became harder, deeper, more fervent, ripping the curse from her mouth.

Henry tore the scrap of fabric from her body, then, his hand found the back of her knee. Lifting it to the table, spreading her even wider in an almost lewd way. Anne cared not. Her mind was wholly focused on how to remain on this plane of existence without falling into the abyss of pleasure. As she was sure she would never surface.

Blood dripped down her, pooling in the curve of her spine. But with each hurried, frantic touch, he smeared it across her back, over her shoulders, between her fingers, and on him.

No more filthy words left Henry's lips. Only chest-rumbling, deep groans as he dived into her. Yet his hand always returned to hers, gripping and holding it. His kisses were copper tasting, but soft and tender. And the bite marks he left on her body only sent those waves crashing into her.

When his fingers found her at last, it wasn't more than one or two strokes before they plummeted over the edge together. Henry let out a snarling growl, forcing himself deeper into her. Anne contorted under him, and a moan slipped through her teeth. Her pleasure edged into pain as another release wracked through her body, sending every one of her nerves sizzling. A hot rush spilt inside of her as Henry's hips shuddered and tensed.

Anne flopped down onto the table as Henry's trembling arms caged her. He let out a heaving sigh over the seeping bite mark. It slid over her skin, prickling it.

Neither spoke.

Words were beyond them now that their hearts had entwined.

Henry gave the tender skin another press of his lips as if he was worried their bond had not completely sealed. He pushed off the table, and with a squeak from Anne, he swept her up into his arms. She grinned up at him as he set her on her rear before righting his underclothing.

Anne pulled him to her by the lacings of his undergarments pressing a kiss to his bloody lips. She deepened it, swirling her tongue around his. She broke the embrace, breathless, but not from what they had just done—every time he would kiss her, it would snatch her breath away.

"Can we do that again?"

Henry grinned, eyes crinkling, beaming at her. If she thought his kiss stole her breath, that grin drew it from her lungs to never return it.

"Give me a moment, Fate, or two. I need to put something on our joining bite. Then, I will make love to you all night—"

"And for the rest of our lives?"

"And the res—"

The door to the stable master's office swung open, and a lone Hartwinn stood in the doorway, their discarded clothing in his fist. His glare skimmed over her, bruised and bloody, and then turned it to Henry.

Anne screamed, scrambling to cover her nakedness.

"You prick!" Hartwinn shouted before launching himself across the room.

He shoved Henry. *Hard.* Henry stumbled back into shelves. Trinkets and books crashing to the floor. He tossed her chemise at her without even sparring her a glance. "Get dressed. We're leaving."

Anne shimmied off the desk, a slick of wetness trailing in her wake.

Hartwinn's eyes lingered on it as his whole body tensed. His jaw shifted side to side, as his gaze turned on to Henry.

"You *fucked* her?" he hissed through his clenched teeth.

"Yes," was all Henry said, his eyes blazing with indignation.

Hartwinn swung, his fist clipping his jaw, forcing him to stumble back into the same shelf. Henry shot forward, slamming into him.

"Anne is mine, Henry! *Mine!*" Hartiwnn yelled as they wrestled. "You cannot have her."

"She is mine, Oryah blessed us!" Henry shouted back, gritting his teeth.

Both were evenly matched—it *was* Henry who taught him to fight. Their legs tangled. They shoved each other into walls, into pieces of bulky furniture. They threw harsh words and even harsher curses, fighting for dominance

"I don't care if Deus came down and told you that she is yours. I will have her."

"We are heart's matches—"

"That is bullshit, she is human! You would never give up immortal life for a *woman.*"

"She is not just any woman."

Anne, pulling her shift on, rushed over to the men. She gripped tensed, flexing arms, and demanded they stop. A stray elbow—she never knew who it came from—struck her in the stomach, forcing her back against the table. Anne cried out as her healing wrist took the brunt of her fall.

Both men stopped instantly.

"Anne—"

"Fate—"

The commotion from inside drew the men waiting outside for Hartwinn. Dayvis and Dilon appeared at the door, eyes wide. Without another moment, they rushed in, dragging the men from one another.

Dayvis wrestled Hartwinn across the room as he shouted, "A duel. I challenge you to a duel! The winner gets her."

Henry had simply allowed Dilon to stand in front of him. A steadying hand pressed to his chest. "I accept. You name the time and place. I shall be there."

"A duel?" Anne asked, her eyes flashing around the room. "Are you *mad*? You don't need to fight over—"

"Be quiet, Anne. I'm not speaking to you right now," Hartwinn snapped, sounding awfully like his father.

She stumbled back, his words piercing her.

"As per traditions of Zeroth, only to first blood. No killing," Dayvis announced. "No man will die under my watch from a foolish duel over a woman."

"She *is* my w—"

"Anne is not just *any*—"

Hartwinn and Henry yelled over the top of each other.

"Enough!" Dayvis yelled. "Dilon, escort Sir Ashmore back to his chambers and ensure he knows the rules of the duel, and that he has his man sharpen his blade. And I will walk Hartwinn back to the lord's wing, ensuring he has the same privilege."

"And me?" Anne asked in a small, pathetic voice.

Dayvis turned to her, his eyes meeting hers. A searing coolness sizzled against the wounds left by Hartwinn's harsh words. "You kneel at the feet of Deus,and pray he forgives you for the mess you made, girl. You knew what you had to do before it turned into *this*."

With that, both men were escorted from the room. Henry turned just before the door was slammed closed, his eyes full of hope and love.

Anne, now alone, cold and aching in places she once felt pleasure. She glanced down at the drops of her blood on the stone, then rose to the heavens. With her hands clenched by her sides, Anne didn't pray to a god who only knew love by submission, but to another, one who tore his own heart apart for the women he loved. Anne prayed with all that she had to Diabolus that Henry's sword would be the first to be bloodied.

Chapter Thirty-Five

A SHARP, SKIN-PRICKLING SLAP ECHOED AROUND ANNE'S bedroom as the last of her words floated through the air. Seanna stood with her hand still raised, shock written across her face. Her hand went to her mouth to muffle the gasp that left it.

"I don't know why I did that, Anne. I'm so sorry."

A tear rolled down Anne's face, falling on her cold feet. "I know why. It's because you *love* Hartwinn, Seanna, and I hurt—no, I just didn't hurt him, I *broke* him."

Seanna flinched back as if it were her who slapped her. "I do not. I would *never* do that to you."

Anne reached out, but her hand fell between them. "I'm not accusing you of ever acting on those feelings. You're a stronger woman than I. That is *obvious*. But you think I haven't watched you both dance around each other, tempted into a life you could have together. If only I wasn't here, ruining that ..."

Seanna breathed her name, shaking her head. "That isn't it. Not at all. You've got it all wrong."

"Isn't it?" Anne asked, the tips of her gnawed fingers skimming over the sticky damp material. "Then, explain to me why you haven't accepted any proposals—"

'I've told you—"

"Yes, to protect your *precious* heart," Anne cut in, with a scoff. "But that's a lie, isn't it? You were simply saving for someone who can never hold it. You were saving it for *him*."

"I-I ..." Seanna shook her head again. "I will not stand here and—"

"And what?" Anne cut in, blinking at her friend. "Face the truth, Seanna. He can be yours."

Seanna took a quick step forward, hurt lingering in her eyes. But the defiant tilt of her chin said otherwise. "Well, maybe I don't *want* him. Not now, not after—"

"It's Pietra, isn't it?"

Seanna recoiled from Anne's question. Her words were lost as her lips popped open and closed, only shocked puffs of air leaving her.

"I know you, Seanna, as well as I know myself. And you've loved Hartwinn as long as I have, and yet, you hesitate. He is the only reason."

"What do you want me to say, Anne?" Seanna asked, a distinct wobble to her voice—one Anne had never heard. She'd always been stoic, sharp. "That Pietra is nothing like I thought he would be? I'm plagued by thoughts of him. Stupid, silly thoughts. Like what is his home like? Is it warm and cosy, or cold and militant? What is his mother like? Is she loving, caring, or is she patient, kind? How does his mind work? Ticking like a clock, or scrambling like yours?"

Anne breathed her name, all the fight left her as she watched her friend crumble. Her face clenched as tears streamed down her face. Within two steps, Anne had her arms around Seanna. Yet, she pushed her away, scrubbing her face with the palm of her hand. "Now, all this does is make me *greedy*, Anne. Can you not see that? Clutching onto both will only leave me lonely, putting my heart at risk of breaking."

"Or you will find love, Seanna. Is that not worth the risk?"

"No, Anne. Not at all. Hartwinn would never forgive me, let alone *love* me if I betray him as you have. It would pulverise his heart."

Anne sucked in a breath and confessed, "I haven't wanted Hartwinn for weeks. I was lying to myself, to him. Worse, I've been a coward for not telling him when all I ache for, wish for, long for is Henry, Seanna. I *love* him."

"And yet, you never told Hartwinn. Anne, how could you? He is your oldest, closest friend. He would have come to understand—"

"No, he wouldn't," Anne cut in. "He would have never understood, for he cannot comprehend the plight of a woman in his court, let alone this world. I was his, by contract, by a handshake and by his misplaced feelings for me. He never would have let me go, not without a fight."

"Now, you may be shackled to him. Hartwinn may win—"

"Or lose," Anne said, her eyes flashing to her oldest friend. "He *must* lose. I cannot be without Henry."

"I get it, Anne," Seanna said with a sniff. "You're totally, sickeningly in love."

"No, there is more to it, Seanna." Anne turned, pulling her hair away from her bite mark. Now oozing and aching. "Henry is my heart's match. We bonded on that damned table. I cannot be without him, nor can he."

Seanna gasped, her eyes widening in shock. She reached out and pressed around the bruising flesh. "In Deus' name, what have you *done*?"

Anne let her hair go, falling in a tangled mess of blonde curls. "The first right thing I have ever done in my pathetic life. I *chose*. I didn't allow this world or its men to decide what I wanted. I did, and I chose Henry."

"You need to tell Hartwinn. Stop this madness before it—"

Anne shook her head, slumping on her bed. Her shift was spotted with blood, sweat and Henry. "He will not believe me. He will think it is a ploy, a trick. He is determined to fight for me."

Seanna chewed on her lip as she slid next to her. "Alderdeen hasn't seen a duel in years—"

"And over me? I'm not worth the bloodshed."

Seanna gave her a long sideways look. "You know, many women would be flattered that two men are fighting with live iron, especially the two most powerful men in court."

"I don't feel flattered, Seanna, I feel like I'm the most awful, horrible person to ever exist," Anne cried, another set of tears leaking down her cheeks. "And it makes my stomach churn with worry. Nothing remains inside of me, only coating the porcelain bowl of my lavatory. I cannot—"

"Anne, calm yourself. You aren't Diabolus, nor are you Heylla-bound. You're a fool in love, but a fool nonetheless."

Anne threw herself back, her eyes finding those carved names in the beams of her bed. Only adding to the sickening flipping of her stomach.

"Will you be there?"

"To witness you break his heart—"

"To pick up the pieces."

Seanna exhaled, lying next to Anne. There was a hesitancy and reluctance in Seanna that she rarely saw. "No, Anne, you cannot ask me to do that. Not while I wrestle with my own feelings. I'm not the one who—"

"Will heal his heart?"

"Not when I could end up breaking it by choosing another."

Anne curled onto her side. She tucked a hand under her cheek and smiled. "Tell me about Pietra, then. I don't have time to know him as you have."

"He's funny, in a quiet, takes-you-by-surprise way. Yet, I think I talk the most, but I don't believe he minds. He ..."

Anne let out a soft giggle, and urged her on with a wave of her hand

Seanna shook her head quickly as if rattling out a thought. "I'm not straying down this thorny path with you. I will marry a nobleman, and I will bear his children ..."

Anne's hand reached up and tucked a strand of dark hair behind Seanna's ear. "Do you truly wish for that?"

"I never thought I'd have a choice, Anne. Yes, I may stomp my foot and decline suitors, but I will marry sooner or later. And I will live the life my mother lives, and her mother before her. And I'm ... not *you*."

Anne's head popped up. "What do you mean?"

"You're courageous and brave—two things I admire most about you, and qualities I wish to have. Yet, even if I had those compelling me forward, I still would wonder about what people would think about me loving a fae."

Anne sighed. Those whispered thoughts and ingrained feelings about Henry and his kind were hard to break. Almost impossible.

"Love will make you do a lot of things, and fight this world is one."

"But is it love? I wish to know him, but I'm not so sure I can call it that yet."

Anne's smile dulled a fraction. "Do you want it to be love?"

"I don't know, Anne. In the end, he will never be truly mine, as I will never be truly his."

Anne reached out for her hand, slipping her fingers between hers. Her thumb circled over the ridges of her knuckles. "You're still hesitating, Seanna. Is Pietra that good of a kisser?"

Seanna blushed, turning a flushed, mottled pink, and spluttered, "I– I mean, he wasn't bad, nor was he ..." She paused, exhaling. "Actually, I think it was one of the best kisses I've ever had."

Anne's heart ached at the sadness that dredged her words. "Oh, *Seanna* ..."

"Not that it matters, Anne. Pietra says he is leaving, returning to Orynile now that the ball is over. He said he doesn't belong here, not like Henry or Wyn. I will never see him again."

"What do you wish for, Seanna?"

Her friend glanced at the ceiling, screwing up her lips. "If I was to have what I wished for, I would throw away all I have, and ... that *terrifies* me. Enough to allow it to be just a wish that never comes true."

Anne searched her friend's face. No words would be a comfort to Seanna's pain, inflicted by men who took from her, and left her with nothing but a cold bed, and a lingering sense of worthlessness. Anne drew Seanna's hand to her chest, clasping her. She leant in closer until their foreheads met.

Seanna's eyes fluttered closed. "I'm going to miss you terribly."

"And I will miss you more, sister."

Anne sent a silent prayer to Oryah, asking for one more favour, testing the limits on the goddess' good favour.

Oryah, let Seanna find more than a cold bed and a lonely marriage. Instead, may she find a love that wraps around her chipped at heart, proving to her that she deserves to be loved, not just possessed. She deserves to be loved and loved in return. More than anyone.

Anne pulled away as the sun shone through her stained glass windows, casting the pair in a rainbow of colours.

The morning had come without her even realising it.

A knock rattled the door.

"Anne, I'm not ready to say goodbye to you," Seanna said, tears wetting her cheeks.

"This isn't goodbye, Seanna. This is just the beginning, not the end."

Anne cast her eyes around her room for maybe the last time, seeing herself in each corner, on each surface even floating through the air. And for once, she didn't cling on, holding it with such force it would crack.

Instead, Anne exhaled and let *go*.

It was a room in a castle she had called home for so long, but now she had a different home, not one of brick and mortar but of safety and unwavering love. That was more important. Anne rose, and answered the door in her shift. Cidran and Wyn stood on the other side, pensive looks on their faces.

"It is time," Cidran said solemnly.

Anne met each of their gazes, nodding. "Then let me dress. I presume they will not start without the woman they are fighting over."

Wyn cursed, stepping forward. "Sundryl—"

"Will be impressed with his commitment to ally with the humans. Henry's heart's match is a human, after all."

Anne turned, yanking her hair up. The bite mark oozing, and sore, shone in the morning light. Both men exhaled, and only Cidran laughed, slapping Wyn on his chest.

"Of course, he gets all he wish—"

"Come now, Wyn. This isn't a moment to be sour, but a celebration. This is usually done with a bit more fanfare, then in a stall."

Anne cleared her throat, feeling her cheeks warm. "It was the stable master's office, thank you."

"Regardless, Anne is right," Cidran said with a soft, wondrous tone. "Henry has decided to remain here in Alderdeen, fostering a bond between the humans and our people. He is fighting for *peace*."

Anne glanced over her shoulder, a determined look on her face, "And he will *win*. He must. Not just for us, but your people. He will come out victorious."

Chapter Thirty-Six

The cold, morning air bit at Anne's exposed décolletage as her trembling hand curled around the tail end of a golden ribbon tied in her hair. Between each pull, she dragged over the embroidered A between her fingers.

Her lucky ribbon.

Trudging behind Cidran and Wyn across the dewy grass, Anne peeked around the men to find a crowd of people gathering under the sprawling oak tree that sat just under Valliss Castle. One day, that tree will grow right to the sky, towering over Valliss. But for the moment, it would stand witness to the shedding of blood.

Before Anne even called out, Henry's eyes found her, a small smile playing on his lips, forcing her own to twitch in response. He was dressed in a soft linen shirt, leather pants—not a single plate of armour, but on his hip was a sword. Sharp and ready to draw blood. There was a softness in his gaze, as he flicked his eyes to Hartwinn.

As if to say, *go to him, stop this before I do.*

Anne shook her head. *Not yet. I can;t go to him just yet.*

Davyis nodded to Wyn as he approached, motioning him to come whisper secrets by the tree. Freya shifted foot to foot, healer's bag in her arms, a pensive smile slashed across her face as Seanna approached her.

Pietra and Cidran stood, silently together, looking almost as if they could be brothers. The same shining red hair and freckles, even the tight coil of muscle was tense across their shoulders.

Her eyes found him last—Hartwinn, wearing the same clothing as Henry.

Her oldest friend, her first love and the man who could barely look at her.

Yet their eyes met, and that overwhelming hurt filled the ever-expanding space between them. Nothing would fix what broke in them when he found her with Henry. Only time could attempt to heal it.

Hartwinn's jaw shifted side to side, grinding his teeth as his eyes became glassy. He sniffed and said, "Can we get on with this? I have a castle full of nosey nobles wondering where we all have gone, and I don't wish to explain *this* to them."

"Shall we begin with an exchange of favours?" Dayvis called out. "As is both fae and human tradition, women would give the battling men gifts to ensure their luck."

"How is it done?" Anne asked.

"You simply give a flower—"

"Or a ribbon—"

"Or a kiss," Pietra shouted, a rare smile spreading on his face.

Anne reached up and, with one tug of her lucky ribbon, released her long, wavy locks to cascade around her face. She dragged the silk between her fingers. Freya, juggling her healer's bag, reached down and plucked a flower from the earth-splitting roots of the oak. She could guess what Seanna had for Hartwinn.

The two women, one by one, approached Hartwinn. Freya passed Hartwinn the flower, giving him that calm, reassuring smile. Seanna, daringly, pushed up onto her toes and pressed a kiss to his cheek. But she turned quickly away, only to share a fleeting look at Pietra whose jaw clenched.

They will shatter each other's hearts, Anne realised. *Seanna is not ready to turn her back on the world she knows, nor is Pietra ready to fight for her. He is scarred, battle worn, and Seanna is fresh air after that press of suffocation—it is a desperate kind of love. Yet, neither is ready for that first gasp. Both were holding their breath.*

Then it was Anne's turn, she stepped forward, the ribbon still dancing between her fingers. She glanced at Dayvis, who raised his brows. He mouthed the word, "*Decide.*"

Her arms dropped her to her side. "This is madness. Stop this—"

"Choose, Anne," Hartwinn said, drawing his sword with a squeal.

"But, I will break your heart, and destroy our friendship, because I will always choose *him*," Anne said, her voice wobbling.

Hartwinn's face screwed up. "You've already broken my heart a thousand ways, but me finding you in that stable, naked, bruised and bloody ... And worst of all, *used* as if you were some common whore."

He spat the word "*whore*" not in a way to shame her, but in a way that he cared for the delicateness she was being touched with, and Henry wasn't delicate at all.

That cracked at her resolve.

He cared so deeply for her even when she had hurt him so—yet, she knew deep down, it wasn't enough. She didn't need care, she needed *love*. And she needed that poured from a chipped, and cracked jug. She needed to be loved by Henry.

"And yet, Hartwinn, I would do it again. I would choose him over and over. There is nowhere in this world he could go that I would not follow. There is no law, vow or promise I would not break for him. There is no life that I would not search for him, ache for him, love him. If that makes me wicked, and destined for the pits, then I shall *burn*."

"Give your favour, Anne," Dayvis announced solemnly. "It is time for the men to fight."

Without a flicker of hesitancy, Anne turned and slowly, picked over patches of longer grass. Her skirt trailing behind her, right until she stood only a hairsbreadth distance from Henry—her heart's match, the man she would spend the rest of her days with.

His eyes found hers, concern creasing his forehead. "Anne—"

"I need to give you my favour, for *luck*." Her shaking hands rose as she asked through a sniff, "May I?"

Henry nodded, lips parting as she ran her fingers over the tight braid until she found the curled tail. Hushed murmurs came from the fae— but she never looked away. Not even once. She tied the ribbon in a tight knot at the end of the braid, with a furrowed concentration.

A tear splattered on her hand.

Henry leant down and pressed a soft kiss to her brow.

"It will be all right, Fate," he murmured against her skin. "It will be all right."

"One day," Anne whispered. Her hand smoothing on the soft curled end of his braid. "But today, it just hurts."

"Step aside, Anne," Hartwinn commanded, his voice hard, uncaring. "*Now.*"

Anne latched on to Henry's sleeve. "Please, don't do this—"

Two strong, calloused hands gripped her elbows as she was pulled from Henry, her tears spilling down her cheeks. Her fingers fought for purchase, but Cidran was stronger. Her cries for the men to stop filled the air as Henry's gaze hardened and rose to Hartwinn. Even Anne felt the deathly chill creep over her skin. He was the man who stared down enemies on a muddy, bloody battlefield. The beast Henry was trying to forget. It was the Wild Wolf.

Yet, Hartwinn simply raised his sword.

"This is your last and final warning to lower your blade, Novak."

Anne's tear-filled eyes flashed to Hartwinn, her arms wiggling against Cidran's grip.

"Let me go—"

"You cannot interfere," Cidran said. His voice had a worried edge to it. "Not with this. Let them battle out the hurt between them."

"I can't just watch—"

"You made this mess, Anne Davoy. You cannot turn your eyes away now," Dayvis whispered.

Anne nodded, stopped her futile fighting and did what Dayvis had commanded: watch the two men she loved fight.

Hartwinn yelled, launching forward, sword swinging. Henry ducked out of the way, pulling his own sword free. Metal screamed against metal as the men clashed. Arms straining. Jaws gritted. They weren't evenly matched. Henry was the far better swordsman, yet Hartwinn had heartache pumping through his muscles, forcing him forwards. Hartwinn dove as Henry slashed, swords meeting. The men pressed against each other as the metals' screams filled the tense air.

"You were the only man I ever truly respected, Henry. Heylla, I used to pray you could be my father over my own damn father." His flushed cheeks were wet. "I prayed so hard my head hurt."

"*What?*" Henry gritted between clenched teeth, yet his arms softened.

"You were a better father than I had. Instead of belittling me, you showed me what it meant to be a man. You shaped me more than that bastard," Hartwinn hissed, yet his voice wobbled. "And then, you *betrayed* me."

"For the pain, I am sorry, Hartwinn. I am so sorry ..." Henry's feet slid backwards as his face pinched as if Hartwinn had cut him. But there wasn't a single drop of blood to be seen. "But please, Hartwinn, I cannot stop myself from loving her. It is cruel to ask that of me."

Hartwinn pressed on, both with his new found power and his words. "And that is the problem, Henry, I cannot ask you that for that cruelness isn't inside of me. But my heart is broken, and I don't know how to stop hurting."

"I know time can heal the pain that has formed between us," Henry said. "But this is not it. Fighting me, demanding her as if you have some right to her. This is only going to create more hurt."

Anne's eyes widened in fear as Hartwinn's sword edged closer to Henry's face. He was going to win, and she was going to lose Henry. Forever.

She had to do something.

With the last of her strength, Anne yanked herself from Cidran's grip and sprinted across the short clearing. Her hair billowed behind her as she picked up pace, ignoring the sharp calls behind her.

Anne had to get to him.

Her body slammed into Henry. They collapsed to the ground in a tangle of limbs and iron. She glanced up to Hartwinn breathing her name as the sharp point of the blade lowered to her heaving chest, pressing against her skin.

Anne pushed forwards, not enough for the blade to puncture her skin. "If he bleeds, I do too. For we are one heart beating in sync. For we are a heart's match."

"*I knew ...*"

Hartwinn's words faded off as his eyes narrowed then widened. For the first time in weeks, she didn't see that pain simmering away, but a strange, confusing flare of something in his eyes. Anne exhaled as the breath was knocked from her, as if he had punched her square in the stomach.

She saw *hope.*

It lightened his gaze, shifting those rumbling dark clouds that had settled to a clear blue sky. For the first time since he slipped that ring on her finger, she recognised her oldest friend, the man she grew up beside. She saw the man who will change the world.

She saw Hartwinn.

A dull thump of metal hitting the plush grass filled the tense air. Hartwinn's sword was shining, gleaming in the grass, and not in his hand. He stood over it, shoulders back, chin raised, lordly and proud.

"I will not duel for someone who does not love me."

Anne scrambled to her feet, and took a step towards him. Exhaled gasps, and shared worried looks came from the crowd of people watching on.

"There is something growing here, much more powerful than a handshake agreement, or even the entanglement we found ourselves in, Anne. And I can see that now. It's *true* love."

She breathed his name. Her gaze flashing over her shoulder to Henry, who was now standing. He beamed a soft smile at Hartwinn— something akin to a father's delight making his eyes twinkle.

When she looked back at Hartwinn, he was twirling the flower in his fingers, brow furrowed, chest rising and falling. Then, he began, "This is my vision for Alderdeen. A world where those born on different sides of a battlefield can love *freely* without fear or shame." Hartwinn sniffed and glanced up to the still awakening orange sky. "Gods, this hurts so much more than if Henry simply kicked my arse and drew blood. But I will not shackle you to me, Anne. I will not be my father. I *will* be different. And, maybe one day, I can forgive *both* of you. "

"I am still willing to kick your arse, Hartwinn," Henry called out, humour lacing his tone.

A few chuckles came from the crowd before demands to be quiet drowned it out.

Hartwinn blew a puff of air out of his mouth, mist curling. With a deep-set furrow of his brow, he raised his glassy eyes to Anne, and within moments, his lips had lifted and formed a sad, bittersweet smile. "Both of you are the spark of change that this world needs, and I will not—nor can I—stand in its way. In *your* way. Not anymore. I must change with it seems, as well. See the world differently, be different."

Anne took a handful of rushed steps towards him. "Hartwinn—"

"You are free, Anne Davoy. You are *free*."

The world seemed to slow, as she turned to Henry, who grinned down at her. Elation worked its way through, bursting out of her like a spark of dragonfire. Her feet couldn't take her to him fast enough. She slammed into him, as he embraced her, lifting her off her feet. Her hands gripped his face, and their eyes met. He slowed, only to press his forehead against hers. A song of two hearts beats played in the edge of her hearing, a harmonised divine melody.

"You hear that, Fate? Mine. Forever."

"What do we do now?"

Henry pulled back, his eyes searching hers. And in those woodland irises was something she thought would be always tinged with sadness. It radiated at her. Something words couldn't explain, but a feeling settled in her chest, right around her heart.

Love. Unwavering love.

"Anything and *everything*," he replied.

CHAPTER THIRTY-SEVEN

THE WALK BACK TO VALLISS WAS THE OPPOSITE OF THE trudging death march it had been before the duel. The air was light, jovial almost. Even Hartwinn shared grins through the cloud of heartbreak he was obviously fighting. Seanna, linking arms with Freya, batted her eyelashes to a blushing Pietra. Dayvis and Wyn walked close, with the old knight's hand clapping him on his back, sharing secrets. Henry and Cidran laughed, shoving each other, their eyes twinkling.

But Anne hung back, drifting side by side with Hartwinn.

Neither spoke. They'd vomited enough—now, the chucky, acidic truth lingered.

Anne watched as all passed through the gate to Valliss, disappearing. She had paused, turning, to look down at the waking city, imagining what it will be like in the years to come. A bustling city, or a sprawling kingdom with King Novak ruling it from Alderdeen?

"Anne," Hartwinn said softly, settling next to her. "We will have to talk about your lands."

"Do we?" she asked, exhausted at the thought. "Right *now*?"

"I ..." He paused, swallowing. "I think you should gift them to Alderdeen ... to me."

Anne turned, narrowing her eyes. "I will not hand them to you so you can give Ewan permission to march across them."

Hartwinn shook his head, slipping his hands into his front pockets. "That is a vow I can make. I will not give Ewan a single foot of your land. I wish to protect them, care for them as we have since your parents died. You will not be able to stop him if he wishes to simply not ask for permission, Anne, but Alderdeen *can*. And as a ... test of good faith, I will bequeath them to my firstborn daughter. Ensuring that your lands will always be passed through a woman, never falling into the hands of that man."

"You would do that?"

"Yes, your title—"

"She can have it," Anne said quickly. "She will need it to rule."

"And for your riches?"

Anne kicked at the dirt, pursing her lips. "That, we will need to discuss more."

"Keep it. You will need coin for this new life you and Henry are building."

Anne turned and looked at him. Tired, worn but there was a lightness to him as he was invigorated for a future he wished to build. She reached out, and gripped his forearm. "You're a good man, Hartwinn. Not many could stomach, let alone tolerate this."

He shook his head, squinting at the sun. "I'm not, Anne. Not yet, at least. Give me time to lick my wounds, and maybe, one day, I will not look back at this time with such heartbreak."

Seanna's voice rang out. She stood at the gate, leaning on the stone. A soft smile and hopeful eyes beamed at them.

"Nevertheless, you still deserve love." Anne pulled the diamond from her finger, finally freeing herself of the weight of it. "And this is yours."

His eyes never left Seanna as she pushed off the stone, swirling her skirts. Something would bloom there—love or duty? Anne couldn't tell, not yet.

Hartwinn held his hand out as she pressed the warm gold into his palm. "You might be right. Where are you going to go?"

"To Vespera, first I think ... Cidran is marrying the witch queen, Maeve. But I believe we will return to Alderdeen before the seasons change. This is our home, and I will stand beside you and Henry as you both lay the bricks of its new era."

Prologue
Henry

Blood.

There was too much blood.

More than the *Slanaighers* warned Henry about. Crimson stained the linen beneath Anne, even soaking through her bright white night-gown. It coated his hands in that slick, gumminess that he'd never forgotten.

Henry lowered to a knee, right between the legs of his woman, his heart's match—and now the mother of his child. A slimy curl of hair peeked out from between her folds.

Their child was ready to meet the world.

"You need to push—"

"Do you think I'm not doing that, Henry Ashmore?" Anne snapped, her clenched face angling down at him.

With a grunt, a gush of deep maroon blood was pushed from her, then splashed over the stone and up his pants. His eyes widened as his breathing shallowed out.

He was almost lost to a memory he never witnessed; Kitra dying in their cold, empty marital bed.

Anne's hand darted out, gripping his cheeks so tightly his lips pursed. Her determined gaze caught his. Her eyes are not a normal blue, or even a plain blue, but the colour of the sky on a hot summer's day. The kind that made one feel the warmth of the sun on their face, and the spiced breeze of summer. Usually, they soothed him, but his panic had taken him by the throat and it was strangling him.

"I need you *here*, in this room, not lost to the past—"

A pained scream ripped from her as her back arched. Her hand snapped to the poster of their bed, gripping it so tight her nails gouged lines into it.

"Fate—"

Anne flopped forwards, resting her forehead on his shoulder. Exhausted.

She'd been labouring for hours, and the babe hadn't moved. Not even an inch.

Terrifying Henry.

"You battled through this world to find me, *mo chridhe*," Anne whispered, her hand pressing over his heart. "You can bring our daughter into this world."

That's when Henry knew he wasn't simply fighting for himself anymore. He wasn't even fighting for the woman who saw him, who smashed through those walls he built around his heart. He was fighting for his family, in a home built on their love.

The Rosda Manor

Henry had built it for her and their family to grow, love and live in. Yet he had tried his best not to be disappointed when their love didn't make a baby for what felt like years. The rush of potential life was dizzying. He had found Anne crying with bloody fingers more times than he could count, and watched as a soft, wallowing listless overcame her that would linger for days, weeks. He hadn't allowed that spark of excitement to ignite inside of him until her belly grew heavy and rounded, and she waddled around the manor barefoot, unable to put on slippers. Then, late at night, he'd whisper to that round, stretched belly that he would be a better husband, a better man and a better father than anyone had ever been.

And he had proved to be with every passing day.

He loved Anne with all his heart, his body and soul. Now, his family needed him. Desperately.

"She is stuck."

She raised her eyes to him, sweat and tears covered her face. "*Stuck?*"

"She has not moved not for hours. You are getting too tired to push."

Anne reached down between her thighs, fingers feeling. "Then you have to get her out."

"Out? *How?*"

Anne wet her cracked lips, her eyes filling with more tears. "You'll have to cut her out."

Henry scrambled back, shaking his head. "I cannot. Freya said she would do that. That all I was supposed do was birth—"

"You must, or I will *die*, dragging you with me, leaving baby Kali without parents."

Henry blinked up at his heart's match. "Kali?"

Anne nodded, her hand smoothing over the round protrusion of her belly. "That is her name. I have decided. After my mother. And I will not have any arguments about it."

Henry sniffed as tears threatened to spill. "What a beautiful name for our beautiful daughter."

"You have to get Kali out—and *now*, Henry."

Anne's maid, Abigail, burst through the door, towels and linen cloths in her arms. Worried look cutting across her face. "I've got these as you command—"

"And I'm here!" Seanna called out as the tall, dark-haired woman shoved past the panicked maid. She threw herself next to Anne and tenderly brushed a strand of sticky hair from her dripping brow before linking fingers with her. "Now, is she almost here? I'm impatient to meet her. I was labouring with Reagan for days before he decided to grace us with his presence ..."

The wretched look Henry shared with Anne silenced her.

"I need a clean knife," Henry said softly. "And something Anne can bite down on."

A flurry of chaos surrounded them as Seanna and Abigail flew around the room, but Anne held Henry's gaze. "You can do this."

"I know I can."

"Then, stop looking at me like I'm Carrots and you're a new stable-hand. It's not *helping*."

A dagger was held out to him, doused in stinging whisky. He simply stared at the shining blade. He had held iron his whole life, but it felt different.

It felt *wrong*.

Anne's hand snapped out and gripped the blade, pushing it into his chest. His hand enclosed over hers as their eyes met. Furious, passionate love poured from her and surrounded him. She was his match—and he would be praising Oryah for the rest of his days for bringing him such a strong woman.

"Bring our daughter into this world as you always wanted."

Yet, Henry's hand wouldn't stop trembling as he made his first cut to her sex, holding in a gag. But it was just enough for the babes head to slip through. Blood poured over his hands and down the front of his shirt. He discarded the bloodied blade, falling with a cluttering clang against the stone. He lifted and spread one of Anne's legs, allowing her hips to open.

"Push, Fate, push!"

Anne bared down with a grunting growl, her face a picture of sweaty determination. Her hand clasped in Seanna's. Within moments, a head was pushed from her body. Henry lowered her leg and slid his fingers inside of her, gripping the slimy shoulders of his babe, just as Freya had shown him in the late night lessons he had demanded. He was going to make sure *he* brought his precious daughter into their world. No one else.

"Good gods, Henry, at least buy me a drink—"

"Enough," Henry commanded, his head rising to meet her gaze. Resolution filled him to the brim. Nothing mattered more than this. Not the ghosts that haunted him, not the future of his city. He was holding his family in his hands, and he wouldn't let them go.

"One more push, and Kali is in this world."

Anne nodded, a flash of fear in her eyes. "I love you, *mo chridhe*."

"And I you. Now, I think it's about time I met our daughter, don't you think?"

Anne nodded, tears streaming down her cheeks, and with a final, grunting push, Kali was brought into the world, right into Henry's arms. He had no words to describe the way his heart stopped, only to restart at the sharp cry of their newly born infant.

Shouts and boots filled the air as Freya, followed by two other healers, stormed the room as if they were soldiers on a battlefield, cutting cords and assessing Anne with a keen focus. Yet, Henry couldn't look away from the scrunched brow, down to her tiny button nose, to those ten perfect fingers and ten toes. He bundled Kali into a cloth, rubbing the muck and blood from her face.

His now-complete world opened her eyes and blinked at him.

Henry felt a tug, a yanking in his chest—not one divinely made, but one of true love. He knew that their love had made her, but quietly, he wondered if the great goddess had a hand in creating such a wondrous life. A soft *"thank you"* left his lips as he drew his daughter to his forehead.

"Welcome to the world, Kali Ashmore. I want you to remember you are already so loved, wanted and needed. I cannot wait to show you the new world we have built for you."

The End.

CHAPTER ONE
MIA

THE COLD, WET MUCK REVERBERATED AROUND HER IN brown, muddy ripples as Mia's body trembled. Each splatter of rain fell on tired and battered skin, only to soak into her ruined clothing. Mortias, gazing down at her with those burning amber eyes, extended his hand towards her. She stared at it—it looked ordinary, calloused and worn. Not elegant, dancing fingers, but those of a man who was born to grip a sword and swing it. She wondered if his skin would be warm or if it would be frigid, like a snake.

She wasn't going to find out.

Spitting the mouthful of blood into the mud at her knees, Mia slapped his hand away. "Where have you taken me?"

Mortias stared at his hand, then nodded to his men. "Somewhere we wish not to linger, Sweet Creature."

Boots rushed towards her. Bodies dashed and cut over her vision of him. Mortias looked like Idris—but worse, he looked more like the man in her dreams before Kali's murder; the other side of the coin, the face just below the water.

She caught a flash of a looming dark tower against the night sky, but it was all too inky to truly see where they were.

Rough hands yanked Mia to her feet. Sharp pains shot down the back of her leg at just the light pressure of her foot. She had done some sort of damage, but more concerningly, a distracting ringing had begun. Mia ached to put her finger in her ear and wiggle it to dislodge the sound, but tight hands gripped her.

She forced herself to remember her captors, down to each line and freckle.

Behind her, a familiar voice softly cursed to himself. She hadn't fallen through the heavens alone.

"My king, you should really be—"

Mia snapped her head to the side, eyes rolling. She saw flashes of grey-flecked hair and those serious eyes. *James.* Rage, followed quietly by hurt, rose in her.

"You fucking traitorous bastard," Mia shouted, almost foaming at the mouth, rabid. Her arms twisted, feet kicking. "Wait until I get my hands on you. You're going to wish you went to the pyre with the rest of them."

She heard a scoff. Right in her ear, James whispered, "Your mother raised you better—"

"My *mother* taught me how to throw a punch, so let me go and I'll show you, prick."

"Please, Sweet Creature, be calm," Mortias urged, pinching the bridge of his nose. "You'll only injure yourself further."

"Like you care about my well-being."

Mortias' palm slid down his face. The direct, intense look he gave her over his fingers chilled her already icy skin, sending her stomach dropping to her boots. "You will *never* say that to me again. You understand?"

Mia nodded, not trusting her voice not to shake. Rage seeped from her right into the mud.

Mortias sighed. "This is not how I wished for our first meeting to go—"

"We've met before."

He reached towards her, but his hand dropped away. Regret briefly flickered across his features, then vanished. "I suppose, but that does not count."

"You were there when they burnt my father alive..."

Frowning, he absent-mindedly brushed the scar on his face. "I'm surprised you remember that."

"Hard to forget your father screaming in pain."

"Cidran was—"

"A lazy, smirking bastard, who thought himself better than the whore he was," James cut in, voice hard. "Maeve gave him more power than he was worth."

Mia's eyes found him, covered in the same muck as her, scowling into the distance.

"Tell your men to let me go," she demanded, fighting, but her muscles had no tone, no strength. She had used it all on killing Jesper. Now, she wished to use whatever she had left to throttle James—and make him take back all they had shared. He had shattered that fragile trust into a thousand pieces. None would ever fit back again. Those cracks would always remain.

Mortias glanced at her, then to the darkened night sky she had fallen out of. "You're in no position to make any demands, Ophelia."

"Mia. My name is Mia," she spat, glaring at him.

"Truthfully, you should care little about what I call you. Creature, Mia or Ophelia. You should really care about what I can offer you."

Mia scoffed, glancing away. She couldn't bear to see that silver light reflect over the sharp edge of his nose, down over that dip in his upper lip. He looked so much like Idris that it hurt. The painful slashing cut through the soft flesh of her broken heart. "What can you offer me? You have nothing I want."

That made Mortias turn to her, hand resting on the pommel of his sword. He considered her with that birdlike gaze, sharp and pointed. He was assessing her—or worse, leering at her. She was born to be his bride, after all. Not that she ever wanted to be bound to that monster. He leant in, making Mia force her body back against the males who held her. He edged close enough to see the fearful expression flash across her face in the reflections of his golden eyes.

"*The world*, Sweet Creature. I can give you the *world*."

Acknowledgments

Well, well, well...we made it to the end of another book, and these never get any easier!

Yet, here are my thanks and immortal gratitude:

To my beautiful, ever patient husband, *Nathan*. Your support has been incredible, and I cannot thank you enough for all the late night brainstorms, wiping my tears away, constant encouragement, snacks and letting me ramble about these fictional characters until we both know them inside and out. I love you forever.

To my wonderful, and ever positive, editor, *Brittany*. You have helped shape this story into what it is today. From your cheerleading, to trying to teach me where a comma goes, or if things should be capitalised. Yet you've made this process such a smooth, and incredible journey. Here's to more brooding men, and bad (bitch) witches!

Thank you to my found family—*Lauren, Mel, and Kaitlyn*. From countless messages brainstorming ideas, to arguing over the *town bike*, to lunches where I hide from the truth (I make things too complicated!!)

You girls have been my rock, my greatest support, and at times, my harshest critic (I *can* do better than that, Lauren!). This incredible world, wouldn't be the same without the love you've shared. It's been a true pleasure to have you in my life.

To my Beta Readers—*Tiegan, Courtney, Dahne & Ali*. Thank you! I appreciate the time and effort you put into making sure The Rose and Her Warrior shines! I literally couldn't have done it without you. From the kind, encouraging words, to those words which spurred me on to knuckle down and produce this fantastic novel. Thank you, I hope we can share this love for fictional worlds in the future!

And, lastly, you, *the Reader.* I could (or literally would not) be here without the love and support you have shown me. You have made my dreams come true, and I will be eternally grateful for it. I cannot wait to bring you more stories full of love, lust, and heartbreak.

Lots of love,

About the Author

I'm Demi Clorissa, a proud Wiradjuri woman, who writes heart breaking dark romantic fantasy. You will find body diverse FMCs, men who YEARN, and emotional damage (that will make you reach for the tissues) within the pages. I'm inspired by strong women, and those who they decide to love.

When I'm not writing you'll find me reading anything I can get my hands on (mostly fantasy), watching trashy TV shows, reading BL and spending my afternoons at the cinema. I love food (but I'm a self confessed awful cook!). I'm blessed to have a little dachshund, Della, who is often curled around my feet as I craft my next emotional scene.

ALSO BY DEMI CLORISSA

THE DIVINE BRIDE SERIES:

THESE SHADOWS BECOME HER

THE ROSE AND HER WARRIOR

THESE MEMORIES THAT BIND HER

THESE FATES THAT FORETOLD HER (COMING IN 2026)

THE DAUGHTER OF THE WOOD SERIES:

BLESSED BY THE MAIDEN (COMING SOON)